ALSO PUBLISHED by A.P. CRUICKSHANK

No Turning Back

From the Smallest of Beginnings

For further information please go to:

www.apcruickshank.co.uk

www.apcruickshank.com

The Betrayal Of Innocence is dedicated to

Barbie and Lew

Prologue

The animal was still in her, wanting more, but Ellen felt nothing except unutterable hatred. Then she saw it; a speck, on his neck and as the shirt slipped further, she saw colours marking his skin. As the brute shoved and thrust, grinding away, whilst he ripped her apart, Ellen focused on those insignificant blemishes. She became hypnotised by the images imprinted on his body and something deep down told her that those unremarkable imperfections would save her, would drive her on, would stop her giving in. As Ellen descended into nothingness, they became her one defiant reason to live.

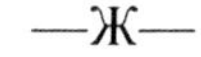

PART 1

The BIRTH of BETRAYAL

Chapter 1

1885

Like so many Jewish families who had chosen to settle in Western Europe in the first quarter of the 1900s, the Aizenbergs had a history of persecution and statelessness. Nevertheless, their resolve to put an end to centuries of hardship and deprivation proved decisive in their determination to find a safe haven in which to live, prosper and raise children.

Commonplace to many of these families was an inimitable patriarch, and in the Aizenberg case, it was Joseph. Born in 1854 to extremely hardworking but desperately poor parents in Yerevan, the capital of Armenia, unlike most of his friends, his childhood focused on education. Joseph proved to be a diligent student with an analytical mind, who enjoyed learning and as a result he understood that if he worked hard his future was secure. His parents were set on him becoming a doctor, however, the rabbi who taught him wanted him to serve in the synagogue and his senior tutor insisted he join the military and use his undoubted talents in the service of his country. Joseph on the other hand had greater ambitions. Shortly after his fifteenth birthday, he began work as an apprentice to an elderly, extremely influential local politician and it proved to be the start of an extraordinary journey.

*   *   *

Unusually for an Armenian, Joseph had married relatively late; he was thirty one. His new bride, Elizabeth was just twenty-one and apart from the ribbing he suffered at the hands of his closest friends about being far too old to satisfy one so young and beautiful, it had left Joseph with a genuine appreciation of life and an insatiable love for his new wife.

They first met in the hospital where Elizabeth worked as a nurse after Joseph, who was returning to Yerevan after one of his many trips away, was thrown by his horse. A local priest had found him lying unconscious beside the road and taken him to the local hospital where he was diagnosed with nothing more serious than some painful bruises. Elizabeth was the duty nurse and whilst she treated his cuts, Joseph discovered she had a love of walking, especially in the mountains. Before leaving the hospital, Joseph, quite out of character for someone so shy, asked Elizabeth if she would like to join him on a walk the following weekend and with little hesitation she accepted.

Within the year they were married and Elizabeth moved to Yerevan to join her new husband. Within five years they had produced four children: Emil, who was born in 1886, Howard a year later, Barbara two years after that and finally Golda, who was born in 1890. They set up home in the Kong district high in the western hills overlooking the city on one side and the river Hrazdan on the other. Life was just about as perfect as it could get for Joseph.

* * *

Although a Jew, and one proud of both his beliefs and heritage, through his commitment to hard work and an uncanny knack of getting the impossible done, Joseph rose to become a senior member of the predominantly Christian leadership of Armenia.

For hundreds of years Armenia had been under the rule of the Ottoman Empire and one of Joseph's key responsibilities was being part of the delegation that negotiated with representatives of Sultan ‘Abdul’-Hamid II on areas of mutual interest as well as concerns.

It was a duty that Joseph took seriously, but deep down he accepted that there would never be agreement between Armenians and the Sultan. He understood, as did most of his colleagues that the gulf between the strict Islamic code of conduct expected within the Ottoman Empire and the less rigid beliefs of the Christian majority within Armenia, was insurmountable.

As with many other ethnic minorities within the Empire, Armenians wanted equality; some even arguing for independence. This level of discontent was seriously undermining the Sultan’s determination to prevent his far-reaching realm from disintegrating.

In the end, it was only a matter of time before ‘Abdul’-Hamid II and his advisors grew tired of the widespread dissent and they decided to make a stand.

Beginning in 1894, the Hamidian Massacres engulfed Joseph’s homeland and over 200,000 of his countrymen were slaughtered in a clearly orchestrated Ottoman-sponsored genocide.

* * *

Fortunately for Joseph, after many years of working together, he had become extremely close to Ahmed Al Bashier, a senior legislator for the Ottoman Empire and it was this friendship that saved his life.

As the troops began their bloody work and at extraordinary risk to himself, Ahmed travelled through the chaos of the initial military crackdown to warn Joseph of the approaching slaughter. With little time for goodbyes, Joseph escaped with just minutes to spare.

It wasn't until many years later that he learned that Ahmed's protection had also saved his family. Without the intervention of his friend, they would have been slaughtered in reprisal for his escape. To his horror, he was also told that after years in prison, in 1902, Ahmed was beheaded. His execution had taken place in the presence of the Sultan and in front of his own family; the charge against him being treason and showing compassion towards foreign nationals, especially Jews.

As Joseph escaped west through Armenia, over the same mountains he had explored with Elizabeth, the villages he passed through were full of rumours of the slaughter of thousands in Yerevan. Many times he tried to turn back, questioning how he could desert his family at such a time, but he knew that as a member of the Armenian government, he was 'a wanted man' and as a Jew, he would have an exceptionally high price on his head. Reluctantly, he accepted that if he returned he would be arrested and executed.

* * *

In late summer of 1896, Joseph entered Turkey illegally and immediately faced the question of what he should do next. There were two options; remain in the local town of Igdir, find work and wait until he could return home or carry on travelling west, reach Europe and after finding work, send for Elizabeth and the children.

Days quickly turned into weeks in Igdir and Joseph found work as a book keeper, earning on a casual basis. It kept him busy, allowed him to keep his savings for the future and importantly helped him justify not making a definitive decision about what he should do in the longer term.

One Saturday three months after his arrival, on his way to his favourite cafe for his weekly treat, a coffee, the question of the future was taken out of his hands. As Joseph entered the town square he saw large numbers of soldiers questioning people and checking documents and knew that without official papers, if stopped, he would be arrested. Immediately returning to his lodgings, Joseph realised that if he was to avoid being caught and sent back to Armenia, he had to move on. Little did he realise how many years and how much despair there would be before he saw his wife and children again.

* * *

That night, with a mixture of sadness and uncertainty, Joseph left Igdir and headed west through Turkey. He found travelling without documents unnervingly slow and more often than not perilous; twice being attacked and injured. He avoided busy routes and wherever possible towns and villages, and finally, after he had completely lost track of time, even what year it was, Joseph arrived in the port of Izmir. Twice during the journey and once in Izmir he paid travellers heading towards Yeveran to deliver letters to his home but accepted that there was little chance they would find their way to Elizabeth.

After a few days searching the port for a ship bound for Europe, Joseph found a working passage on a fishing boat heading for the waters around the Island of Malta. In exchange for the little money he had saved, the Captain agreed to put him ashore on the Southern coast of Italy and on 1st January 1900, an uncertain but elated Joseph landed in Europe. After so many years escaping Armenia, he was not only safe but free.

However, within just a few minutes of saying goodbye to the skipper and crew of the Turkish fishing boat, the reality of arriving penniless in an unknown country, with no idea where he was or what he was going to do, began to eat away at any relief Joseph felt.

Head in hands, sat on cliffs overlooking the bluest of seas, Joseph felt completely out of his depth. In which direction should he travel? Where was the nearest town? Where could he find work? Where could he stay? The questions kept coming and Joseph began to wonder if he'd made the most catastrophic mistake of his life.

* * *

It took a further three and a half years, travelling the length and breadth of Italy, accepting any job, no matter how lowly paid or physically demanding, for Joseph Aizenberg to find regular work. During those months, although angry and bitter at the never ending separation from his family, Joseph practised Italian at every possible opportunity; he was determined not to sound like a foreigner.

In the summer of 1903, Joseph arrived in the northern city of Turin and after spending two nights sleeping rough and three days knocking on shop doors begging for work, he eventually found a bakery which offered him casual employment.

The work was hard and demanding but Joseph recognized how lucky he was. He was also told by the manager that if he worked diligently, a permanent position might be available and as a result Joseph worked all hours on offer.

Although friendly to everyone, Joseph never became close to his fellow workers. They resented not only his positive attitude to work but also his reluctance to spend money drinking with them at the end of a gruelling day. However, as a result, he quickly gained a reputation as an extremely reliable and trustworthy employee and was asked by the manager to take on some additional work. The tasks weren't difficult but Joseph still made sure he did everything precisely as ordered and within the deadline demanded. Additional responsibility quickly followed and within just eighteen months, Joseph had risen to the position of assistant manager.

Although he had no previous experience of working in a bakery, he proved to be extremely effective when dealing with supplier problems, customer complaints or any other 'issues' the manager preferred not to acknowledge, but needed resolving.

* * *

With an increased wage and money he'd saved, Joseph decided his next priority was to find a home for his family and after weeks of searching, discovered a dilapidated smallholding with twelve hectares of land. Although just about perfect for his family and meagre budget, he had to accept it was adjacent to one of the poorest of suburbs.

Once the farm was legally his, Joseph was thrilled; finally his family had a home.

* * *

In the summer of 1904, Joseph was invited to the local Jewish community annual picnic by Ricardo Levin, a local businessman he'd met through the bakery. Much to his surprise, he had a thoroughly enjoyable day, finding everyone he met friendly and welcoming. As the celebrations were coming to an end, Ricardo asked if Joseph would like to meet up with other Armenians who had settled in Turin and although shocked he readily accepted.

Ricardo arranged a lunch for the following week and when Joseph arrived he was introduced to Saul Tahter and Eric Manoukian and from the outset it was quite obvious the three Armenians would become close friends. Following the meal Ricardo left for another meeting and over far too many drinks and numerous stories from the past Joseph discovered both men had left families behind when they escaped the civil war; Eric in 1895 and Saul the following year. Also like him, they faced the same frustrations in not being able to contact family and friends, and it occurred to Joseph that if they pooled their finances, they could pay a courier to take letters back home. When he rather hesitantly suggested the idea both men were overjoyed and within a month, Joseph had found what he hoped was a trustworthy courier.

Five weeks after sending a letter and money, Joseph received his first ever reply from Elizabeth and sat with a tear in his eye as he read notes from each of his children.

In her letter, Elizabeth wrote that the children were conscientious students who studied hard and he smiled as she added that they were growing up far too quickly. She also described conditions in Yerevan as extremely difficult and explained she was working long hours to make ends meet. She added that the money he'd sent was a blessing. Her final comment however, stopped Joseph in his tracks. Elizabeth implored him not to return home, explaining that ex-government officials in hiding were still being hunted down and executed. Before signing off she again begged him not to return until it was safe.

* * *

Towards the end of his second year as assistant manager in a bakery that was becoming ever more successful, Joseph's future seemed assured. That was until he was approached by a stranger at the end of an early morning shift. The man introduced himself as Flavio Lotti and asked Joseph to join him and some friends for a drink.

Taken aback, Joseph's initial reaction was to thank him and refuse but there was something about the man that intrigued him. Together they walked across the Piazza della Consolata and an extremely self-conscious Joseph couldn't believe it when Flavio pushed open the door of the Al Bicerin, considered the most expensive café in the city.

Joseph was led to a table at the rear of the room where a man and woman sat waiting. As they approached, the man turned and Joseph saw he was young, probably in his twenties and well dressed. The woman was about the same age and Joseph's immediate thought was that she was astonishingly beautiful.

After he was offered a seat, Flavio introduced them as Antonio Compagni and his sister Gabriella and without any preamble Antonio said,

"What do you know about chocolate?" Joseph was irked by his offhanded manner.

"Nothing." He replied bluntly.

"Do you know how it's made?" This next question came as ingenuously as the first.

"Err, no, not at all."

Joseph saw Miss Compagni touch her brother's arm.

"Might it not be better to ask Mr. Aizenberg a little about himself before we get into details?" she asked and Antonio grunted.

“Although your Italian is excellent,” Flavio said, “you were obviously not raised here. How come you’re working in Torino?”

Joseph was bewildered and asked himself why he was being questioned and more importantly, why he should answer them?

“I’m sorry,” he eventually said, ‘but why am I here?”

“Because I wish to speak to you,” Antonio answered arrogantly. Joseph was exhausted after a fourteen hour early morning shift and had had enough, so he rose, doffed his hat to Gabriella whilst ignoring her brother and said,

“Thank you for the invitation,” and with that he left, leaving Antonio incredulous. No one of Joseph’s standing ever walked away from him. However, it was revealing that Gabriella Compagni had the merest hint of a smile as she watched Joseph thank the waiter and leave the cafe without even a glance back.

Flavio, apologising to Antonio, jumped up and followed.

“What the hell are you doing?” he shouted, running to catch up.

“It should be me asking that question,” Joseph replied clearly irritated.

“Look, I’m sorry. Antonio can be discourteous but he means no harm and there’s something important we really need to discuss with you.”

“I think not,” Joseph replied walking away.

After a few moments however, he turned back and said,

“What I will do is return tomorrow at the same time and meet you here. If Mr and Miss Compagni still wish to talk, I will join them.” And Joseph prayed he’d not thrown away a God sent opportunity.

* * *

"Mr. Aizenberg, please let me apologise for my brother. These are difficult times and, well, he is under a great deal of pressure. I know that doesn't excuse his rudeness but…."

"Please, it's really not necessary," Joseph interrupted.

Flavio called for a waiter and Joseph thought it odd when he ordered for the three of them.

"May I call you Joseph?" Gabriella asked and when he nodded she added, "Would you mind telling me about yourself. I know this might sound odd, but it will help me with what I want to discuss with you." Joseph felt completely at ease, such a contrast to the previous day, and so began telling Gabriella about Armenia, his family and his work for the Government. Drinks arrived and without thinking Joseph sipped the steaming liquid. He immediately stopped talking, drank again and saw both Flavio and Gabriella staring at him.

"What is this?" he asked, taking yet another mouthful.

"Later; please carry on," Gabriella answered, and Joseph told her about his escape from Yerevan, the journey across Turkey and landing in Italy. When he described his arrival in Turin and his work at the bakery, Gabriella began asking questions about his co-workers, his manager and the reasons for the company's recent success. Joseph wanted to answer but found it impossible without being critical of his colleagues or disloyal to his boss. When he explained this, he was once again pleasantly surprised when Gabriella apologised for placing him in such an uncomfortable position.

Again with no discussion, Flavio called to a waiter and ordered more drinks and Joseph was asked to continue. He went on to describe his family, the acquisition of the rundown farmhouse and his hopes of reuniting them as soon as possible.

When the second order arrived, Joseph noticed both Flavio and Gabriella again watching him; it was as if they were waiting for him to start, so he obliged, and although there was a difference from the previous cup, the flavour was if anything, more satisfying.

"Well? What do you think?" Flavio eventually asked.

"Delicious," Joseph answered, although his need to know why he was there was increasing.

"Both drinks are called Bicerin," Gabriella said after taking a sip from her cup. "It's been served in this café since 1763 and when Turin, or as we call it Torino, became the first capital of a combined Italy in 1861, chocolate had been made in the city for a hundred years."

"That's incredible! I've never heard of it," Joseph replied with a laugh.

"If you'll bear with me, I'd like to tell you about chocolate." Joseph nodded, puzzled as to what any of it had to do with him.

Gabriella began by explaining that Bicerin, along with other drinking and hard chocolate had created great wealth for a few Turin families and made the city famous. She described how the first chocolate arrived as cocoa beans with Christopher Columbus after he had visited the Isle of Guanaja in Honduras, and as Joseph listened he was fascinated that someone like Gabrielle could have such an obvious passion for a drink he'd never heard of.

She went on to explain that in 1678 a Madame Reale, who was Queen of the Savoy State, granted the first ever licence to sell, as well as process and produce chocolate to Gio Antonio Ari. As Joseph listened, he realised Gabriella's enthusiasm was rubbing off on him; he was genuinely intrigued by her story.

With obvious pride Gabriella said that a few years after the first licence was approved, her great, great, great grandfather, Giovanni Scalfaro, was granted one. She described him as a visionary man, one whose company specialised in developing unique tastes for drinking chocolate, and in order to sell his creations he opened three cafés in the heart of Turin.

"For over a hundred and fifty years, Scalfaro's as it became known was a name synonymous with unrivalled quality and as a result, our family prospered. However, twenty years ago when my father inherited the company, factories and cafés, he struggled. With an increase in local competitors and new chocolate companies starting up across Europe, Scalfaro's ran into difficulties."

Joseph only realised what trust Gabriella was placing in him when she explained that due to the ever-growing problems her father eventually took his own life.

"In simple terms, my father inherited a vicious circle; there were no profits, so there could be no reinvestment; with no reinvestment, there was no sustainability and as a result Scalfaro's stagnated, falling well behind its rivals. Its downfall was there for all to see."

As her father was an only child, on his death Antonio and herself became equal owners. She added, candidly, that neither of them had the necessary experience or knowledge and without Flavio's considerable assistance, the company would already have folded.

"If I'm honest, the easiest solution is to sell up which is what Antonio wants to do. Certainly two of the cafés are in prime locations; one's even on the banks of the Po River. But who would buy the third café or the factories? They're losing money and I will not let the workers down. Many have given years of loyal service and they don't deserve to be treated cruelly." Gabriella looked across at Flavio, "So, without telling Antonio, I asked Flavio to search the city for someone to take over, someone not known in the trade."

Joseph was fascinated; loyal, hard working workers, two prime locations, a hundred and fifty years of history, an owner who cares about the workers; all ingredients for success.

"We need a visionary leader, someone we trust who can plan for the future and see it through." Joseph still had no idea as to what it had to do with him and could wait no longer.

"Miss Compagni, the company has experienced an incredible journey over the last few years and I am sorry much of it has been painful, but what exactly do you want from me?" Both Gabriella and Flavio stared at Joseph and laughed.

"It's you we want to take over the running of Scalfaro's!"

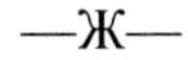

Chapter 2

September 1938

As the plane touched down on the water, Ellen couldn't believe they had arrived in Italy. However, from the moment they transferred from the plane to shore, she saw soldiers everywhere checking and re-checking documents and generally harassing new arrivals.

It took nearly two hours for the family to pass through immigration, followed by more frustration as they couldn't find a taxi to take them to Rome's Termini railway station.

Eventually, they made it onto their train only to find they were subjected to a long and extremely uncomfortable journey. For Ellen though, none of it mattered; she was in Italy, the place she had always dreamed of visiting. She spent the entire journey staring out of the window mesmerised by everything she saw; from the people, who she decided were no different, to the buildings which were very different, to the scenery, which was beautiful and strange in equal measure.

* * *

"But it will be such an adventure!" Ellen had said excitedly to Noah, her rather anxious younger brother, when they first heard they were to attend the funeral of her Uncle Emil.

"Of course it's sad; all funerals are, and as it's Uncle Emil's, well that makes it even sadder, but Italy is my favourite country."

Ellen had loved her uncle Emil and because he had no daughters of his own, he spoilt her unashamedly. Unfortunately though, she saw him only a few times a year when he travelled to London to see her father Howard, and she couldn't remember the last time she had seen his family; Aunt Marguerita and cousins Simon and Leon.

When Tova, Ellen's mother, had spoken to her and Noah about the funeral she explained that her father had very much loved his older brother and had been devastated at the news of his death. Apparently, the brothers had been inseparable until Joseph, their grandfather had kept Emil in Italy to run the family business and sent her father to London to work.

* * *

Most evenings the family ate supper together and on the day they learnt of Uncle Emil's death, as Ellen was clearing the table, their father told them that they should be ready to leave for Italy as soon as he could book their passage. He explained that they would have to travel from their home in London to Southampton and then on to Rome on an Imperial Airways flying boat. From there they would take a train to Turin. For Ellen things only got better; not only were they going to Italy but for the first time ever she would get to fly.

As her father spoke, Ellen noticed her mother was unusually quiet and it was only later in the evening, when she heard her parents disagreeing that she knew something was wrong. Of course her parents argued, but it was usually quickly forgotten, however, from the moment her father had announced that they would all travel to the funeral, Ellen sensed there were problems.

Two days later, on the eve of their departure, Ellen went downstairs from doing her homework to tell her father that she'd got 87% in her latest history exam and that in the Swimming Gala, against all the local schools, she had won three races including the longest and most difficult. However, as she was about to join her parents in the lounge, she once again heard them quarrelling. Although she knew she shouldn't Ellen sat on the stairs to listen.

"But why the children?" her mother asked.

"You know why. With Emil gone I'm now the head of the family," her father replied firmly, before adding gently, "I know it's a worry but we must be there for Marguerita and the boys. Nobody could have predicted what's happened, Emil being so young. It must be heartbreaking, especially for the boys." Ellen spied her father take her mother's hand, "The whole family is now my responsibility...," he kissed his wife's fingers, "so, I'm sorry but we must all go."

"But Mussolini's a close friend of Hitler and look what that madman is doing. I'm really worried, I mean what happens if…."

"Nothing will happen." Howard put his arm around his wife as she became tearful. "Italy's not as trouble-free for Jews as it was, but it's still safe. I remember Emil telling me that Turin's like London; Jews are integrated, mostly well-educated, middle-class professionals. Their families speak Italian, attend public schools and universities and, apart from going to the Moorish-style synagogue on major holidays and family occasions, are barely observant." He looked into his wife's eyes before saying, "Everything will be fine, I promise you."

"But, I don't understand," Tova repeated, pulling her hand away in clear frustration. "Why the children? Of course I'll go but Ellen and Noah, they can stay with Barb and Yossi?"

Ellen was incensed. Not to be travelling was bad enough but having to stay with her mother's friend and her husband, neither of whom she found very pleasant, was just too much. Ellen decided she had to act so she marched in to the lounge.

"I'm sorry, but we have to go and I really don't want to stay with Barb and Yossi, I really don't!" Surprised at the interruption, her parents turned towards their daughter and her mother asked,

"Were you listening?"

"Yes, but, please, oh, I'm sorry, but you can't leave us behind. Noah feels the same as I do; we really want to go." Ellen knew that mentioning Noah was a lie but she felt the seriousness of the situation definitely warranted it.

"Come and sit here," her mother said pointing to a space on the large couch between her and her husband. "Have you been following what's going on in Europe?" The question surprised Ellen; she knew precisely what was happening. However, it was news that was rarely mentioned at home. Her parents, who had always talked freely about almost anything, had repeatedly steered away from the subject whenever either Noah or she had mentioned it.

"If you mean the problems in Germany, then yes I have. In fact, at school we talk about it most of the time," Ellen answered just a little too precociously and her father put his hand on her arm to show his disapproval. Ellen knew she had spoken rudely.

"Oh, I'm sorry, but I really don't want to miss the chance to visit Italy." Her mother took Ellen's hands and said,

"The situation throughout Europe is getting worse."

"But the problems don't involve Italy," Ellen answered. "Okay, Mussolini's a friend of Hitler and the Germans are doing terrible things in Austria and Czechoslovakia, but Italy isn't part of that. And if there is war, our teacher says Italy won't be involved."

Howard looked at his wife and then towards Ellen and said calmly,

"That may be true, but your mother's right, we must be careful. Now off to bed."

Ellen repeated her apology for eavesdropping, kissed her parents and went upstairs.

* * *

At Turin's Porta Nuova Station, they were met by Mr. Umberto, Auntie Marguerita's gardener come driver. After about half an hour of moving slowly through the city centre, Ellen was fascinated as they drove through a magnificent set of gates with a small gatehouse and down a long drive lined with tall trees.

As they approached an enormous mansion, Ellen saw her Aunt waiting on the front steps with two boys. Ellen's mother told them that the boys were Leon and Simon their cousins and she smiled at Mr Umberto as she pointed to a woman who was standing in the background and explained she was Mr Umberto's wife, Mrs Carla, the housekeeper.

* * *

The next day family members began to arrive and they included her father's two sisters; Barbara from Canada who was with her husband Aldo and their daughter Rita, and Golda from America with her husband Joshua and their three children; Nathan, Israel and Pino. Ellen couldn't remember meeting any of them before and was amazed at how close they appeared to be.

Although Emil's funeral was incredibly sad, Ellen loved being around her extended family and found it intriguing that they all spoke perfect English. When she asked Leon why, he told her that it originated with their grandfather Joseph who had insisted English was the only language spoken in the house.

Immediately following the funeral, as the family sat in the garden, Ellen noticed a palpable disbelief and anger at her uncle's unexpected death. She heard many references to the doctor's explanation that he had died from a heart attack brought on by pressure of work but no one agreed. She listened intrigued as her Aunt Golda even suggested the police may have been involved, but her father quickly told her to be quiet, adding that the hospital report had clearly stated the cause of death.

* * *

The following day, apart from Ellen's family, everyone left for home. There were many tears and promises to stay in touch but Ellen was mystified as to why no one had stayed with Aunt Marguerita and the boys for at least a few days. When she asked Simon why they'd left in such a hurry, he told her that people feared Hitler was driving Europe towards a continental war, so everyone wanted to leave.

That night, unable to sleep, Ellen decided she needed to know more about what was going on and as she didn't read or speak Italian would need Leon's assistance.

The following morning after discussing what she wanted and finding her younger cousin eager to help, the two of them searched the house collecting all the newspapers they could lay their hands on. Then, sat under the large tree in the garden, Ellen placed the papers in chronological order and Leon began to translate.

The oldest papers, which were three months out of date, had little of interest, however, when Leon began to read a July copy, they were both stunned as the headline read: 'Manifesto on Race. Jews to be targeted.' The article stated that following Germany's Nuremberg Laws which had been implemented in 1935, ten respected members of the Italian scientific community had signed a new race manifesto. Leon told Ellen that from what he could understand many of the comments supported the new legislation but many also condemned it. As Ellen needed more information, Leon read one article which claimed that the clear aim of the manifesto was to turn Italian Aryans against their Jewish neighbours. It then added a footnote stating that it was something that should never be allowed to happen.

Leon moved on to a three day old newspaper and again translated the headline: 'Italy introduces new Racial Laws', and went on to read a list of who was affected.

"Jews will be barred from studying or teaching in schools of higher learning.

All Jewish teachers in public schools will be removed from their positions and all Jewish children will be barred from attending public schools.

The citizenship of all foreign Jews, obtained after 1919, will be revoked and they will be deported within six months.

Finally," he said wide eyed, "all foreign Jews will be arrested and held in camps until they can be deported."

* * *

Ellen's worries were confirmed the following day as she was in the garden with Noah and Leon. The three children were playing chase behind the large tree when Ellen overheard her mother and Aunt Marguerita talking. Although she knew she shouldn't, she moved closer to listen.

"But I don't understand why there were problems," her aunt was saying. "Surely, as American citizens, they should have gone straight through emigration."

"I don't like it," her mother replied, "especially these 'racial laws'. Do you know, I actually read that they have been implemented as an act of appeasement to Hitler, although the article did say Italians should ignore them." Tova took a sip of her juice before adding, "We will have to leave and as soon possible." She looked at her husband, who was sleeping. "Howard, did you hear me?" She prodded him. "Wake up! I said we must leave and that includes Marguerita and the boys."

"But Tova," her sister-in-law replied shocked, "I can't just leave; this is our home, built by Papa Joseph. We will not be pushed out. Anyway, my friends are saying that no one will take any notice of the new laws." She looked sadly into her drink before saying, "And what about Scalfaro's? Papa Joseph built it up from nothing and Emil worked so hard to ensure it is a strong business for Simon and Leon to take-over. No, we can't leave." Marguerita reached into her sleeve for a hankie before adding, "Oh, I don't know, everything's so confusing. If Emil was here he..."

"But that's just it," Howard said, clearly not asleep. "It's confusing because it's rumours." He smiled gently at his sister-in law but then heard the frustration in his wife's voice.

"It's not a rumour that Marguerita and the boys come under the new classification of Foreign Jews. Papa Joseph only received citizenship for the family in 1920. That means," she said turning to her sister-in-law sternly, "you are classified as Jews; those to be deported." Tova then spoke to her husband, clearly not finished.

"Mussolini is a German puppet and even if Italy's not at war now, it will be, and what happens to Marguerita and the boys then?"

"But where would we go?" Marguerita asked, tears flowing. "My boys are Italians."

"Dearest Marguerita, I'm so fearful for you," Tova said gently, to the surprise of her husband. "Hitler wants to destroy us. It's madness, but there is no way Mussolini will stop targeting Jews so you must leave with us."

Overcome with despair, Marguerita left her in-laws to their afternoon tea and returned to the house. As soon as she was out of earshot Tova said irritably,

"For God's sake, if we don't leave immediately we'll be stuck..."

"I agree. Things are worse than I'd anticipated and you're right. Marguerita and the boys should come with us. I need one day with Flavio Lotti to sort out Emil's affairs and Marguerita's finances." He took his wife's hand and kissed it before adding gently. "We'll leave first thing the day after tomorrow, okay?"

Ellen was heartbroken. One day; there'd be no time to visit the sights. However, overriding her frustration was her anger. What had being a Jew to do with anything? Weren't Jews just like anyone else?

Ellen being Ellen, she had to know more and found Simon in his room. She started by asking him about the problems at the port and he explained that Auntie Golda's family were held by emigration officials for ten hours simply for being Jews. Ellen then asked about Germany and Simon tried to explain but admitted he was just as confused as she was. He did say that his father had told him there was no logical reason for what Hitler was doing to Jews.

Ellen then explained about the conversation she'd overheard and it was obvious Simon didn't know. Without another word he left the room.

*   *   *

Next morning over breakfast, Marguerita explained that having discussed it with the boys the most sensible thing would be to leave Italy and travel to London and Howard added that they would all therefore be flying out early the next day.

Later that morning, as it was another beautiful day, Tova laid the garden table for lunch whilst Carla and Marguerita prepared the food. Just as they were about to sit down to eat however, the doorbell rang and Simon answered it.

"It's the police," he stuttered as two men in uniform strode assertively into the garden. As one of them spoke to Marguerita, Tova asked Carla to take the children into the house.

"They want our passports," Marguerita said turning to her sister-in-law, "and when I asked why, they just told me to get them." As Tova went inside to collect the documents she told Marguerita to find out what was going on.

A few minutes later she returned with six passports and handed them over as the more senior policeman spoke and Marguerita translated.

"He's asked if this is all of them," and for some reason Tova was suddenly fearful for her husband.

"Tell him these are the passports for all those who are here," she answered and when Marguerita looked to question her sister-in-law, Tova said bluntly, "It's the truth."

The policeman spoke again, this time with considerably more hostility in his voice.

"He repeats; he wants all the passports." Marguerita translated.

"Then repeat the answer," Tova answered tersely. "It's the truth. Howard's not here and has his passport with him." Marguerita eventually did as she was told.

The senior officer then thanked her, bowed to Tova and they left.

* * *

When Howard returned he was in good spirits. He poured himself a drink and told the family that he'd managed to complete his work so there would be no delay in leaving. However, his mood darkened when his wife told Simon to take the children upstairs and explained about the police. Although shocked, Howard was also mystified; why would they take the passports, especially the children's? It made no sense.

Quite unexpectedly the doorbell rang and Tova asked her sister-in-law if she was expecting anyone. She wasn't, and after answering the door Marguerita returned with three men. Although not in uniform, they were unmistakably security police.

One of the men approached Howard and in heavily accented but proficient English, asked for his name and why he was in Italy. Howard replied that he was the younger brother of Emil Aizenberg who had recently died, and was in Turin to attend the funeral.

"And why did you and your family not leave with the others?" the officer asked, in no way attempting to hide the fact that the police were quite obviously watching the house. Tova, seeing her husband was becoming agitated, replied for him.

"We want to make sure Emil's family are going to be…" Slowly, pointedly, the man raised his hand to silence her.

"Did I ask you?" Turning back to Howard he repeated the question.

"As my wife was trying to say," he answered curtly, "I want to make sure my sister-in-law and her children are well cared for."

"So are you now head of the family?" the man asked.

"Err, yes." Howard replied warily.

"Then it is you that has responsibility for the company?"

"I suppose so, yes."

"Your passport." The man stuck out his hand and waited whilst Howard handed over his lifeline out of Italy.

"Come with us," he then said as one of the other officers placed a hand on Howard's shoulder and began to manoeuvre him towards the door.

"Leave my husband alone!" Tova said brusquely. "You cannot arrest him. We are British citizens," but seeing the dismay on her husband's face she realised her mistake and said quietly, "Please, where are you taking him?"

The officer smiled disdainfully towards Tova, ignored her pleas and followed his colleagues and Howard to a waiting car.

Tova and Marguerita both stared utterly disbelieving as the car pulled away.

"Why have they taken Uncle Howard?" Simon asked as Ellen ran to her mother.

"Where have they taken Daddy?" she cried.

"I don't know sweetheart." Tova could no longer hold back the tears as she held her daughter.

As both families stood together, the room was filled with distress. The certainty that their lives had abruptly and irreversibly altered was all encompassing and the same question came to everyone's lips. Without Howard, who would look after them?

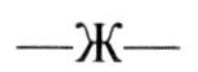

Chapter 3

1907 - 1909

It wasn't a difficult decision. Joseph accepted that opportunities at the bakery for further advancement were non-existent. The one position he could aspire to was Manager and it was clear that the more he succeeded in resolving the most destructive of problems, the more his boss positioned himself with the owners to take the credit. Joseph was neither angry nor bitter; quite simply, his immediate boss was greatly valued by the people who mattered.

Two further meetings with Flavio and Gabriella followed. Antonio was not present at either and Joseph agreed with a handshake to join Scalfaro's as General Manager.

When he handed in his resignation, the owner immediately asked for a meeting. He offered Joseph a substantial increase in his salary and a newly created title, which in effect would promote him above the existing Manager. The fact that he knew who Joseph was and that he had resigned was a pleasant surprise but Joseph understood the immense faith Gabriella had shown in offering him the leadership of Scalfaro's. He was also acutely aware that by including a profit incentive to bolster his rather low starting salary, unheard of in contracts in 1907, Gabriella was publicly announcing her commitment to him. In the end there really was no decision to make. She was not only offering the opportunity for Joseph to prove himself, but if he did, then significant financial rewards would follow. It was, quite simply, a once in a life-time offer.

Joseph immediately wrote to his family with the news and begged them to be a little more patient. He was desperate for them to join him but needed time to get things ready for their arrival. In truth, because of the uncertainty over his future, Joseph had done little to improve the derelict shell he'd purchased, but promised himself he would focus on the house as soon as he was established at Scalfaro's.

*   *   *

July 12th 1907 and Joseph stepped into Scalfaro's for the first time as General Manager with a mixture of excitement and trepidation.

Scalfaro's clearly had potential but significantly Joseph understood that the most effective way to achieve anything close to that potential was to re-ignite the confidence of the workforce. Employees were the key to success and without their support his aims would become considerably more difficult if not impossible. His first objective therefore, was to visit all parts of the company to meet with every employee and he gave himself just one week to complete the task.

Through these discussions, Joseph discovered that without exception, employees had great affection for Gabriella but he became aware that Antonio's name was rarely mentioned. Joseph also took serious note of the many who described the terrifying hardship that would befall their families if Scalfaro's was sold or closed and understood why Gabriella would not countenance closing the business.

At the start of his second week, Joseph asked Flavio Lotti if he would help him create a long term strategy for the company. He readily agreed and Joseph set him the task of visiting all profitable cafés in Turin and all local chocolate making factories. He then wanted him to travel to Switzerland to visit the new generation of chocolate makers including Henri Nestle, Philippe

Suchard, and one of the first producers of dark chocolate, Rudolphe Lindt. Joseph asked Flavio to record everything he saw, meetings he attended and details of the machines used, especially in Swiss factories. Although his first reaction was to be slightly irritated by Joseph's overly precise instructions, he quickly came to realise the new boss was a man who knew exactly what he wanted and would accept nothing less. Gabriella, of course, was delighted.

During the weeks Flavio was away, Joseph's fifteen hours a day in the office focused on understanding every component of the company alongside learning the 'art' of chocolate making. As a complete beginner in this field, Joseph was acutely aware of the pitfalls awaiting a novice. He acknowledged there would be employees who would try to undermine his position and was determined not to offer them any grounds for criticising his leadership. Joseph accepted he had to provide everyone with irrefutable evidence that he was a dedicated and trustworthy manager; only then could he hope to gain the respect essential if he was to transform Scalfaro's.

* * *

As his work progressed, Joseph felt he should keep Gabriella and Flavio abreast of his ideas and plans for the company and it was agreed they would meet weekly. During the first meeting, the question of Antonio's involvement arose and it was decided that when he was in Turin, he would attend. However, Flavio explained that for the foreseeable future, Antonio would be in the USA looking at business opportunities.

For the purposes of official documentation the meetings were titled Board Meetings and those present,

‘Directors’, and Joseph came to value the opportunity to discuss the company on a regular basis with his co-Directors. He also knew that with the continued absence of Antonio and support of Flavio and Gabriella, all essential developments at Scalfaro’s could be implemented with minimum dissention.

* * *

As mid-summer 1908 approached, Gabriella and Flavio invited Joseph to join them for dinner to celebrate his first year as Managing Director of the company, and celebrate they did. Afternoon tea at Scalfaro’s riverside teashop, followed by dinner at Turin’s finest restaurant and to finish, an evening attending the premiere of a new production in one of the city’s oldest theatres, the Teatro Carignano.

Joseph had not enjoyed a happier evening since leaving Armenia and as he sat in his office early next morning, he felt genuinely elated at the progress being made.

His policy of working with, and listening to the employees, so critical to his success, resulted in him being viewed as immensely demanding but also fair and understanding. Joseph treated everyone equally; he had no favourites, made no friendships and as a result he quickly gained the respect and loyalty of the workforce. The results were impressive; for 1908, productivity was up sixty-three percent and for the first time in years, Scalfaro’s broke even in the fourth quarter. However, even those statistics couldn’t match the elation throughout the entire company when in the second quarter of 1909 a small but decisive profit was registered. It was at that moment all connected with Scalfaro’s knew their future was assured.

* * *

Joseph was also feeling more hopeful about the arrival of his family. The latest letter from Elizabeth explained that the Sultan had been deposed by the Young Turks and with their new government came hope and optimism for the people of Armenia. He began to dream of returning home.

Joseph's social life had also improved. After declining a number of invitations due to pressure of work, he joined one of his oldest acquaintances in Turin, Riccardo Levi, for drinks and met other members of the Jewish community. It was a most enjoyable evening, especially when for the first time in years Joseph ate authentic Jewish food.

After years of insecurity Joseph finally felt at ease with his life. Turin was his home and after considerable badgering from both Gabriella and Flavio he applied for Italian papers. He also asked Elizabeth to find a tutor to teach the family Italian, enclosing as much money as he dared to cover the cost. Joseph understood that if his family were to avoid the problems he had faced on arrival in a strange land, they needed to speak and understand the language.

* * *

Although delighted with the progress made at Scalfaro's, Joseph understood that further growth was doubtful without significant financial investment to upgrade working practices and machinery. He was convinced that for the company to compete in the competitive business world of the early twentieth century, it would have to move with the times. Joseph recognised that seeking financial support with the company in such a perilous state was not realistic unless he could clearly define the long-term benefits. He therefore drew up an ambitious development plan, including strategies for its implementation and likely profits.

In November 1909, Antonio returned from the Americas and Joseph decided to present his plans for Scalfaro's at the next Board Meeting. He was aware however, that Gabriella, Flavio and especially Antonio would find the recommendations complex and would need time to digest the information so he suggested the meeting be held away from the distractions of Turin.

Arriving at the Hotel Trattoria just outside of Turin early the following Friday morning Joseph ensured everything was ready. He and Gabriella had discussed plans for the first evening and decided that dinner would be the perfect opportunity to update her brother on the progress Scalfaro's had made during his absence. They also felt it would be an ideal opportunity for Joseph and Antonio to get to know each other a little better. Unfortunately, the entire evening proved a huge disappointment, not only for Joseph, but also Flavio and Gabriella. It was quite obvious, either deliberately or otherwise, that Antonio had absolutely no intention of discussing Scalfaro's and spent the evening describing the business opportunities and people he'd encountered on his travels.

On the Saturday morning, the four directors met in a private function room and Joseph began to lay out his vision for the company. He opened up by offering an overview including a brief history, employment issues, the financial stability of each area, the infrastructure in terms of strengths and weaknesses and finally his painful but crucial evaluation of how Scalfaro's had come so close to bankruptcy. Joseph held nothing back, knowing his comments could have serious consequences.

At the end of the session Joseph excused himself from lunch, returning to his room for a sandwich. He wanted to give a somewhat chastened Gabriella, Flavio and Antonio time to digest the information he'd presented.

Following lunch, Joseph returned to the function room to find all three members of the Board deep in thought. He had expected a barrage of questions or arguments, especially from Antonio, but none materialised. Slightly thrown, he began the afternoon session by explaining the changes he had implemented since taking over as Managing Director. He highlighted both the positive and negative effects each had had on the operation of the company and the workforce. Following a mid-afternoon break for tea, Joseph moved on to his primary recommendations for the future. This was the crux of the weekend and he wanted to cover as much detail as possible before the end of the day, allowing time during the evening for questions and where necessary, a revisiting of areas discussed. He knew that if a consensus could be reached, then the following day could be given over to the Board signing off on a definitive plan for reinvestment.

Joseph began the post-tea session by emphasising that Scalfaro's was a company moving towards significant profit and argued, forcibly, that some of those profits should be ploughed back into upgrading weak areas of the business. It was at this point that Antonio began to question Joseph's strategy, stating unequivocally that profits were for the family and he made it crystal clear that Joseph's primary role was to work for the benefit of his employers. He then added, completely out of the blue, that as Italy faced a bleak future when war broke out he was considering moving to America. Joseph was incredulous and when

Gabriella said nothing, assumed she was already aware of her brother's plans.

Joseph would not be thrown and continued with his presentation knowing that his own future, alongside that of Scalfaro's, was suddenly under serious threat. Surprisingly, Antonio remained to hear him out.

"To ensure a successful future we need to introduce mechanised systems of chocolate production. Flavio witnessed the benefits on his journey through Switzerland and..."

"Rubbish!" Antonio interjected crudely. "If your plans are adopted the company will be finished within weeks."

With great difficulty, Joseph ignored the outburst, calmly stating that alongside upgrading the factories a percentage of the profits should go to the workforce. When Antonio laughed loudly Joseph argued that if the Board demonstrated its loyalty to the workers through a profit sharing scheme, the result would be far greater commitment from them. He argued this would drive up productivity and increase the quality of service being offered to customers. Joseph stressed that productivity alongside quality was the key to success.

Antonio was about to reply when for almost the first time that day Gabriella spoke up. She suggested they retire to their rooms to freshen up for dinner. She also proposed that after what had been a difficult day, they should reconvene the following morning to resolve the differences of opinions that had arisen. All agreed, however, Joseph offered his apologies for dinner and Gabriella and Flavio watched with unease as he picked up his papers and left.

Joseph was furious. How could he be expected to agree that profits from the hard work in Turin be thrown away on Antonio's half-baked ideas. The entire workforce, along with Gabriella and Flavio, had given so much to turn the company around and they deserved better, much better! As General Manager, Joseph accepted it was his responsibility to deliver stability and success; if he could not guarantee these, he would have to resign.

* * *

"May I come in?"

Joseph was surprised to see Gabriella, especially at 7.30pm and he offered her one of the two chairs but she remained standing.

"I know what you're thinking," she began awkwardly. "If Antonio goes ahead with his idea, you'll have to resign." Joseph turned away and began to pour them both a glass of wine. Of course she was right; he was just surprised Gabriella knew him so well. He passed her the glass and again offered her a seat which this time she accepted.

Gabriella slowly sipped her wine before continuing,

"I do understand, after all we have worked together for over two years."

"Is it really that long?" Joseph answered with a sigh, wondering where the time had gone, where the conversation was going and what Gabriella really wanted. As she took another sip of her wine, Joseph had to admit she was quite simply one of the most beautiful women he had ever met and one of the most perceptive.

"If you resign, it will all have been for nothing. Two years battling, for what? To let everything slip back to how it was, because you know that's what will happen."

"The last thing I want is to resign," Joseph answered bluntly. "And I agree. After everything we've gone through, walking away would be devastating." Joseph was becoming more animated but couldn't hold himself back. "You have to understand I cannot be party to something so divisive. Of course Antonio is entitled to do whatever he wishes. He made that perfectly clear." The bitter laugh at the injustice was extremely telling. "If he insists on undermining the principles I believe in, then I have to move on." Joseph's shoulders sagged, he closed his eyes and leant back in his chair; he hadn't realised how exhausted he was and when he felt a hand close around his fingers, he clung on tightly. Opening his eyes in surprise Joseph saw Gabriella kneeling on the floor next to his chair.

"You know," she said gently pulling him to his feet, "I think it's time someone looked after you." And Gabriella helped him out of his jacket before tenderly kissing him. It had been so long since Joseph had felt anything so intimate, so comforting, he pulled away. He was old enough to be her father. As he was about to speak Gabriella put her finger up to his lips.

"Ssh," she whispered and led him to the bed where she slowly undressed him whilst helping him to undress her. Even if he had wanted to, Joseph was powerless to stop. Gabriella was the most beautiful creature he'd ever seen and as she stood naked before him, he felt he had everything he'd ever needed. Slowly, gently they made love and afterwards as they lay contentedly in each other's arms, both knew their lives would never be the same again.

* * *

Joseph woke many hours later and reached out to the other side of the bed. It was empty and cold and he asked himself whether he'd been dreaming but Gabriella's scent touched every inch of the room. As he lay remembering, a far more relaxed Joseph knew he would have to deal with his guilt, but not then, not at that perfect moment.

Twenty minutes later Joseph entered the function room to find the other Directors sat at the conference table drinking coffee. He poured himself a cup, took his seat and looked at Gabriella. She was watching him and as their eyes met she smiled and Joseph understood that everything was fine.

Flavio began the meeting by suggesting each of them should express their thoughts as to where the company was and what they would like to see happen in the future. There was a general nod of approval with even Antonio appearing to agree.

Flavio suggested that as it was his idea, he should start.

"We're all aware of the serious problems the government is creating for the commercial sector so I partly agree with Antonio; Italy will face enormous problems over the next few years. However, I do not believe they will be insurmountable. The growth in union power, particularly in Turin because of the concentration of industry, is a worry. We have Fiat, Lancia, Olivetti to name a few and the power of the unions and their alliances with political parties, especially political extremists, will more than likely result in Turin becoming a political battleground."

"That's irrelevant. Even if I accept what you're saying, I don't see what it has to do with Scalfaro's." Joseph was intrigued as he witnessed Antonio contradicting his friend.

"Well, I'll answer in three parts," Flavio replied. "Firstly, as a citizen of Turin born and bred, what happens is of the utmost importance to me."

"Well, we don't all feel th..." Before Antonio could finish, Flavio interrupted him.

"May I finish?" Antonio's face reddened as he nodded his agreement.

"Thank you."

Joseph was stunned; he had never heard Flavio arguing with anyone, especially not his life-long friend.

"Secondly, it is imperative the workforce at Scalfaro's does not become influenced by union extremism. Many friends tell me their factories have already fallen under union control." Flavio continued by stressing that by giving pay bonuses to the workers from the profits they helped create, the Board were sending the most positive reassurances to employees.

"Unions establish themselves in factories where workers are dissatisfied, however if they feel appreciated and their work valued, unions find it difficult to gain a foothold.

"Thirdly, I fully concur with Joseph on his plans for reinvestment. I witnessed the new machines and they are seriously impressive. There is no question, by committing to these new processes, significant profits will follow. Finally, I want to stress that in my opinion it's not Joseph's plan that will bring the company to its knees but a rejection of it."

"Am I to take it that you feel the same way?" Antonio turned towards his sister.

"In principle yes," she answered emphatically.

"Well then, it seems I am the one out of step with the aspirations of this Board; a situation I need to consider very carefully." With that he rose, gathered his papers and left the room. The weekend that had begun with so much promise had come to a ruinous end.

* * *

The following morning, Joseph returned to his office feeling extremely dejected to find a letter waiting on his desk. It was from Antonio stating that he blamed Joseph for divisions within the Board and although he was in absolute support of policies that secured a successful future for Scalfaro's, he would never compromise on his opposition to mass-production of chocolate. He argued that traditional methods created and developed over two hundred and fifty years, could not be summarily dismissed. Finally, the letter stated that the impasse between himself and Joseph, in terms of the future philosophy of Scalfaro's, was of sufficient magnitude that Joseph's only recourse was to do the honourable thing and resign.

Chapter 4

October 1938

The morning after Howard's arrest Marguerita asked Clara to take the children into the city whilst she went to the bank and Tova tried to contact the British Embassy in Rome.

When the sister-in-laws met back at the house for lunch, a rather surprised Marguerita said she had been allowed to take out the bulk of their savings. This with the money Emil kept in the house should be sufficient for their immediate needs.

"It's as if they were being deliberately uncooperative," Tova then said as she explained about her frustrating morning. "I just don't understand how they could be so indifferent to British nationals who are in trouble. The only thing I can do now is go to the police."

Although initially against the idea, Marguerita reluctantly agreed to go with her to translate. As Umberto had left to meet up with Clara and the children, they decided to take a bus and it became obvious they were being followed by two men in a car who were making little effort to conceal themselves.

Half way to the city, Tova noticed a smartly dressed man board the bus and he sat behind them. After only one stop he asked the driver to drop him off and as he stood waiting, he dropped an envelope into Tova's lap which she concealed.

Once in the city, they found a cafe and as Marguerita was about to order coffee, the two men who had been following them earlier arrived and sat at the table next to theirs. Opening the envelope was no longer an option and in frustration, Tova told Marguerita to ask the waitress where the bathroom was.

When the girl pointed to a door, she picked up her handbag, found the bathroom and locked herself in. The letter contained nothing except some simple instructions which she memorized before tearing the paper into tiny shreds and flushing them down the toilet. On the way back to her table, as she walked down the dark corridor, Tova saw one of the men waiting.

"I am police. Give me bag!" he demanded in pigeon English as she moved to pass him. Tova handed him the bag and became increasingly annoyed as he rummaged through her belongings. When he discovered nothing, the man told her to raise her arms and began to search her. She knew she must not react regardless of the provocation; any dissent and she'd be arrested. As the man moved his hands from her breasts to her groin, Tova closed her eyes and tried to ignore the repulsive assault, however, when he began to lift her skirt, she had had enough. She slapped his hand away and pushed past him. Seeing her sister-in-law's anger, Marguerita quickly paid and they left followed by the men.

When they were out of earshot, Marguerita asked what had happened.

"Nothing!" Tova answered irritably and explained they were to go to Porta Nuova Station. Once there they should exit the building next to Platform 7 and listen for a taxi horn. Tova added that the note was unsigned. Marguerita was extremely troubled about following the instructions but Tova would have none of it.

"I have no choice. If I don't do this, how do I find Howard," she asked irritably.

As they passed the Porta Nuova platforms Marguerita said that the policemen were still with them so Tova quickened their pace. Immediately they exited the station, a taxi sounded its horn, pulled up alongside them and in excellent English, the driver told them to get in. As they pulled away, Tova smiled as she saw absolute panic on the faces of the two men trailing them.

Once away from the station the driver pulled off the main road, drove down a narrow street and then into an ever narrowing lane, continually checking in his rear view mirror. After another two minutes they slowed and passed through a set of large wooden gates which slammed to behind them. They stopped in a walled courtyard and the driver pointed at some large doors,

"Don't knock, just go in," he said.

With increasing apprehension they climbed the front steps where Marguerita hesitated.

"Don't worry," Tova said trying to hide her own fear, "if it was something bad they wouldn't have gone to all this trouble," and she took Marguerita's hand and pushed open the door that led into a large ornate entrance hall.

As Tova shut it behind them, they heard footsteps on marble stairs and saw two men descending; the younger one introduced himself in aristocratic English, as George McDonald-Grey; the other man said nothing, just moved to the front door and remained there. Tova immediately began questioning their host.

"How did you know we'd be on the bus?" Then, without giving him time to answer,

"And how the hell did the taxi driver know who we were? Explain please because right now we don't know who we can trust and we're extremely frightened."

Attempting to placate them, George clarified that he was a representative of the British Embassy based in Turin. He then offered them tea that was already laid out on a silver tray to one side of the room, before apologising for the clandestine methods used to get them there. He went on to explain his brief was to help

British nationals in difficulty and he worked with a team which included the taxi driver and owner of the house. George then admitted, with a mischievous smile, that it was far more by luck than judgement that the plan to pick them up worked, especially considering their police tails.

After pouring the tea, he offered a further apology for the lack of help when they contacted the Embassy. He explained that phone lines of all foreign government buildings were monitored by the security police and London had told its diplomats to avoid inadvertently giving details of British subjects to the Italian authorities. He stressed that as British citizens they were entitled to help and this was why he had been asked to meet with them as a matter of urgency.

Finally, he got to the crux of the matter and said that when the Embassy had become aware of Howard's arrest they had requested information from the Italian authorities. At the same time George was also asked to speak to contacts in Turin who may have been able to help.

"In payment for a few black market items," he said deliberately to Tova, "one of my police contacts explained that your husband has been detained for political activities against the state." Tova and Marguerita both stared at George in disbelief.

"What!" they said simultaneously before Tova added angrily,

"Political activities against the state. What the hell does that mean?"

George explained that apparently the Aizenberg family had a history of political subversion and it was claimed Joseph and Emil were senior members of a prohibited political organisation.

"When the secret police or OVRA, as they are known, became aware of my search for Howard, the

Embassy was informed, in no uncertain terms, to stay out of the matter. The Ambassador was told that any interference from a foreign government in the Italian judiciary would be seen as provocation and that your passports will be held by the security police until a full investigation has been concluded."

George excused himself to get more tea whilst Tova and Marguerita sat dumbfounded. 'Political activities against the State', was far more serious than either thought possible and images of Howard being tried as a spy and executed, plagued their emotions.

When George returned with a fresh pot and poured more tea, Marguerita asked why Howard had been arrested for the alleged actions of his brother and father. She stressed 'alleged' for she simply could not accept the accusations being made against Emil and Papa Joseph. As George was about to answer, Tova stated unequivocally that the whole thing was a set up; just an excuse to punish a successful family for being Jewish.

George, understanding the incredulity of the two women, explained that there had been a significant increase in anti-Jewish sentiment throughout Italy but emphasised this was primarily within Mussolini's government and not the general public.

"I'm sorry," he added patiently, "but it appears Howard's arrest was the result of becoming head of the Aizenberg family. The secret police want to establish his links to the illegal group attended by Joseph and Emil and say they will keep him locked up for as long as necessary."

Tova and Marguerita again sat in silence, each considering the implications of what had been said and both recognised that although Howard's position was extremely grave, they had to get the children out of Italy as soon as possible.

"Is there any way, without passports, we can get our children out of Italy," Tova asked.

"No, it's just about impossible," George replied candidly.

"But if the Embassy can't help, who can we turn to?" Tova asked in frustration. All three sat quietly for a few moments until Marguerita said in desperation,

"Please. Even if it means breaking the law or bribing people, we must get the children out." Turning away from the man covering the door, George said conspiratorially,

"You must understand, as a representative of the British Government, I must be seen to respect the law. If it was known I advised you to do anything illegal, I would be in serious trouble and the Ambassador compromised.

"All I will say is that Mussolini will not stop at the new 'Racial Laws'. As Jews, I strongly advise you to leave. Go after dark and go north. If you make it to the border, you may be able to cross into Switzerland and head for the Embassy in Geneva. I'm aware of other Jewish families trying to get out that way. Oh, and one other thing, do not try to leave through the Frejus tunnel into France. Reports say the military are covering all routes into France and there is little chance of you reaching the embassy in Paris."

Both women thanked George, but before leaving Marguerita asked if he could contact their families in America and Canada. He wrote down the details and told them he would do everything he could to update them on what was happening.

*　　*　　*

That evening, once the children were in bed, the sister-in-laws talked late into the night and Tova explained that although the children must leave, she couldn't, not whilst Howard was being held. Both women knew the solution was staring them in the face but neither wanted to acknowledge it. Eventually Tova said,

"It's you who must take the children." Marguerita knew she was right but found it impossible to agree so the arguments dragged on until Tova said tiredly,

"Why don't we ask Carla and Umberto? There's no one else we can talk to so let's see what they think." Marguerita wasn't convinced, however, first thing the following morning she visited the cottage with Tova. She explained to Carla and Umberto all that had happened since the funeral and asked for their thoughts. Carla spoke first saying that after thirty years of service, first to Mr Joseph and then Mr Emil, they would do anything to help. When Marguerita said what they really needed was advice, Carla and Umberto sat awkwardly in a self-conscious silence.

"Forgive me," Umberto eventually said, "but I feel that you, Mrs Tova, should stay. Carla will look after you and make sure everything is in order until Mr Howard comes back. Madam Marguerita, I will drive you and the children to the Swiss border."

"Umberto, that is so kind but it could be dangerous and I can't ..." Marguerita began but Carla interrupted,

"Madam, we have felt helpless watching things go from bad to worse. You are family, our family; the children are like our children. We have watched them grow into wonderful young men. Madam, families stick together when times get hard. That's all there is to it." Marguerita was about to reply when Carla turned to her husband,

"When should Madam and the children leave?" Tova and Marguerita knew they had lost control of the decision making but both accepted it was exactly what they needed.

"Tonight," he answered. "I will get the car ready and we'll leave after dark."

"Madam," Carla said to Marguerita, "After you have all gone, Umberto and I will look after the house for as long as needs be. This is also our home and we love it. We will make sure it's ready for your return."

As they rose to leave, a tearful Marguerita gave Carla and Umberto a hug.

*   *   *

Over breakfast the children were told they would be leaving that night. Noah decided it would be another great adventure but Ellen was beside herself; how could she leave without her parents.

"Will it be safe for you and Daddy?" she asked tearfully and Tova found it so difficult to answer; she wanted to be optimistic but would not lie to her daughter.

"Well, the situation is serious. Your father has been arrested for something he didn't do and I need to help convince the police he is innocent." She hugged her daughter gently. "Ellen, please understand it's not just Italy; Europe is on the brink of a terrible war and I need to know that you and Noah are safe."

"But it gives us no time with you..." The tears flowed and Ellen hugged her mother tightly.

*   *   *

The rest of that day was spent trying to prepare for the journey. The mood throughout the house was sombre and no matter how cheerful Marguerita and Tova tried to be, nothing could conceal their own unease as to what lay ahead.

Finally, after tearful goodbyes, Marguerita and the four children climbed into the car in the dark of the garage. All five, apart from Umberto, lay on the floor to ensure the police would think the gardener was taking the car out on his own.

As Clara held Tova and they watched the family disappear down the long drive, both wondered whether they would ever be reunited again.

Chapter 5

1910 - 1911

Late into the night, sat alone in his office, Joseph reread Antonio's letter. Of course he was angry but also puzzled; he simply couldn't understand Antonio's animosity towards him. Did he believe Joseph should be more subservient? Did he consider Joseph a mere employee rather than the man entrusted to save Scalfaro's? Was he jealous of Joseph's success? However, most damaging of all was Antonio ignoring, or worse, deliberately belittling the irrefutable progress made by all parts of the company.

Slowly sipping his wine, Joseph frowned as he knew a significant part of his frustration also stemmed from his inability to grasp Gabriella's reluctance to stand up to her brother. At least Flavio had argued his case with Antonio even if no progress had been achieved.

In the simplest of terms, the weekend had been an unmitigated failure and as a result, Joseph's future at Scalfaro's was threatened with serious repercussions for his family. How could he possibly move them to Italy when he didn't even know if he still had a job?

Joseph's mind was a myriad of uncertainty but overriding all his doubts was the issue of how to tell his family to delay their travel plans. He accepted that spending the night with Gabriella had been inexcusable but in a perverse way, it had confirmed that more than anything, he wanted his family together again. He did wonder irrationally whether the problems he faced were fair reprisal for being unfaithful to his wife and the letter he wrote that night to Elizabeth confirmed these thoughts. As he reread his words, Joseph prayed for forgiveness and then penned one further letter; his resignation.

*   *   *

Joseph didn't want to call an extraordinary Board meeting as that would require Antonio to be present. Therefore first thing the next morning he contacted Gabriella and Flavio and asked them to join him for coffee.

They arrived within the hour, obviously troubled by the invitation and Gabriella immediately explained that Antonio had left Turin that morning for America.

Although encouraged by his departure, Joseph knew that in the long run it made very little difference. At some stage, he would return and have the final say on anything and everything to do with Scalfaro's.

Over coffee, Joseph showed his two co-directors Antonio's letter. The reaction from both was predictable; they were concerned, even embarrassed, but would not openly criticise Antonio.

As Joseph listened to their excuses he felt abandoned.

"As a member of the Board Antonio is entitled to have opinions on the company and the way it is run. However, I believe this letter oversteps his authority." Joseph waited for comments but it was obvious none were forthcoming so, clearly irritated, he said unequivocally,

"Antonio's hostility towards me is based on imprecise information. He states, for example, that I want to replace all existing processes with mass-production. That's erroneous to the point of dishonest." Gabriella and Flavio looked at each other. "Yes, I want to modernise our machinery but not at the expense of traditional Scalfaro processes. If he had been a little more willing to listen, I would have explained that I want a cheap, mass-produced product alongside traditional chocolate. It's because we only have the latter, that we're in trouble; on its own it's simply not sustainable."

It was quickly obvious that Flavio and Gabriella were disappointed as well as surprised they had not been made aware of this plan and when Joseph realised their feelings, he apologised.

"I didn't speak to you prior to the meeting," he explained, "because I'd been working on the proposal right up to Saturday morning. Look, I'm sorry, but I'd spent weeks working on it knowing that if I wanted an agreement on significant reinvestment for the company I had to present clear, precise, easy-to-understand options. Then last Thursday, just for a change, Mussolini decided to introduce yet another batch of financial regulations which meant I had to redraft the entire proposal. I realise not warning you was a mistake and I'm sorry."

After a few moments thought Gabriella suggested he gave them both a copy of his plan to read; Flavio agreed and Joseph realised that the key issue of Antonio's letter had been deliberately or otherwise circumvented. Reluctantly, he left his office to speak to his secretary about the copies and was surprised when he returned to find Gabriella alone. She told him Flavio had offered his apologies but had another commitment.

Joseph and Gabriella stood in the middle of his office waiting awkwardly for the other to say something. Eventually they began to speak, then both stopped, both smiled and finally, both laughed.

Joseph was relieved when Gabriella took the lead and sat down.

"I think we should set out our relative positions," she said, just a little too formally. "I imagine the envelope on your desk is the letter neither Flavio nor I want to see; your resignation. Am I right?" Joseph nodded, smiled awkwardly and again marvelled at the woman sat with him. "Well, you can keep it because there is no way I will let you resign."

"But …,"

"No buts Joseph; you leaving the company would be a disaster, so no, I will not let you go." Joseph twisted uncomfortably in his seat. He had never heard Gabriella speak with such candour and try as they might to reach an understanding, each found the other's point of view seriously flawed. Finally, in desperation, Gabriella suggested they go away that weekend to sort things out. Joseph knew he should refuse but was powerless to do so, and if truth be known, he didn't want to; he longed to be alone with Gabriella again.

*   *   *

The following Friday they left Turin separately, finally meeting at the Hotel La Giocca in Pella on the shores of Lake Orta and it was one of the most beautiful places Joseph had ever visited. For the rest of the day, Gabriella and Joseph remained in their room, ordering room service and they made love, slept and talked. It was the first time they had truly had time to themselves and the differences over Antonio were quickly forgotten as they realised how incredibly at ease they felt in each other's company.

At one point Gabriella asked Joseph to tell her about his family and initially he felt awkward describing his 'other' life but she was so understanding that any discomfort quickly vanished. She then explained about her childhood and all the privileges that came with wealth and Joseph shared in her sorrow as she described the heartache as she had watched her father's life fade away.

Out of the blue Gabriella then mentioned she'd been married. This admission certainly answered one of Joseph's more pressing concerns; the effect on Gabriella's life if their affair became public knowledge.

"I was seventeen and it was a marriage of convenience for both families," she explained. "I was marrying into money; he was in his forties and marrying to produce an heir. Simply put, I was to provide a son whilst his money would help keep Scalfaro's afloat.

"Unfortunately," Gabriella then said thoughtfully, "no son arrived; in fact no pregnancy followed and within two years my husband claimed I was barren. Then, by paying a huge sum of money, as a donation to the Vatican of course, my husband gained permission from the Pope to annul the union and remarry. I was left with nothing. However, the day I was forced out of my home, my father-in-law presented me with a large sum of money."

Gabriella went on to explain that knowing the problems her father faced, she couldn't keep the gift and gave it all to him. She said that he tried to refuse but in the end took it, insisting on it being a short-term loan.

"And it certainly helped keep Scalfaro's going." Gabriella then rested her head on Joseph's shoulder as she said sadly, "You know, it was when he knew the money would never be repaid that he gave up." Joseph held Gabriella closely as she added crossly, "I told him so many times that it didn't matter but he wouldn't listen and in the end he killed himself."

Later that night, with Gabriella asleep in his arms, Joseph felt an extraordinary conflict overpowering his emotions; must he really choose between his family and Gabriella?

*　　*　　*

The three Directors met at a restaurant two days later to discuss the proposal. As the outcome of the meeting would ultimately decide his and the company's future, Joseph had already begun to plan ahead in case things went against him. Once seated and having ordered, Flavio began plainly,

"What's been achieved at Scalfaro's is quite extraordinary and completely down to you so, you're not resigning." Joseph was more than a little relieved.

"However," Flavio continued and Joseph's heart sank, "we must accept there are significant problems ahead because of Antonio." He touched Joseph on the arm. "Believe me when I say Gabriella and I are completely mystified by his behaviour towards you." Joseph looked towards Gabriella who was staring at him. She nodded her agreement with a gentle, reassuring smile. "But problems there are and they must be resolved because the alternative is unthinkable." Flavio took a sip of wine before saying,

"I admit I was surprised that prior to the weekend we had no idea of your plans, but readily accept your reasons. To me, your proposal is sound, achievable and exactly what is needed." Joseph was pleasantly surprised especially when Gabriella added,

"And I'm in complete agreement."

"Therefore," Flavio said, "you have our total support." And all three raised their glasses.

*　　*　　*

At their next lunch date, Joseph described the meeting to his old friend Riccardo Levin and as always, found his opinion direct and rational.

"Clearly in defiance of the absent Antonio, if both Directors have given you their support, you have the perfect opportunity to prove the man wrong. The alternative, well, you refuse the challenge and run away which is what you'd be doing by resigning. And don't forget, that's exactly what Antonio wants because he gets his way and leaves you with nothing."

Before the meal came to an end Riccardo asked Joseph if he would join him for drinks that Friday and he readily agreed. Although they had become close friends they saw little of each other outside their weekly lunch. Riccardo was married and had a well-established set of friends and Joseph continued to turn down most invitations due to pressure of work.

The evening again proved most enjoyable and Joseph met a number of interesting and influential members of the Turin business community. As he was putting his coat on to leave, he noticed he was not the only one calling it a night and walked out into the chilly air with Axel Steinman, a financier he'd met earlier. When he offered him a lift, Joseph readily accepted knowing he was likely to have a long wait for a taxi.

During the journey, Joseph was surprised when out of the blue Axel congratulated him on his work at Scalfaro's and although pleased with the compliment, he was intrigued that a stranger would know of it. As the car was drawing up to his office where Joseph was again sleeping on his favourite couch, Axel asked if he would like to join him and some friends for lunch the following week. He explained it was a working get-together and useful contacts often resulted. Joseph said he would be delighted to accept.

* * *

Joseph arrived at the restaurant early hoping to see Axel before the meeting began and immediately recognised Riccardo talking to two men. Surprised and delighted, he joined them.

When they sat down to eat, Joseph counted eighteen men around a large oval table and once coffee had been served, watched as the doors to their private function room were closed. Joseph recognised a number of highly successful and respected people and was extremely surprised when Riccardo told him that everyone present was Jewish.

Axel began by introducing him to the group and asked if he would like to say a few words. Taken aback, especially as neither Riccardo nor his host had mentioned anything about speaking, Joseph rose, accepting the challenge.

"Gentlemen, thank you for such a warm welcome," and Joseph simply said what he felt.

"What an incredible collection of talent around one table. I have only met a few of you before today but can assure you that your reputations precede you and can only hope that one day I am able to match such success." He smiled and looked around the room. "What do you get when you bring a group of highly successful and driven people together?" He smiled again; "Answer, a belief that anything is feasible and the potential for achievement infinite. Turin is remarkably fortunate. Thank you." As he sat down the room was silent and he wondered if his comments had been inappropriate but then the room erupted with applause.

* * *

Joseph received the hoped for invitation to attend the next business lunch and was delighted to accept. Following the meal, the meeting turned its attention to the issues facing companies not only in Turin but internationally and Joseph spent the entire time listening, quickly realising the value of having access to such a knowledgeable group.

Following that second meeting, at their weekly lunch Riccardo told Joseph that members of the business group would like him to join them on a permanent basis. He then explained that if Joseph accepted there were a number of conditions.

"We are highly selective in those we invite to join and as a result are unknown to the outside world. Because the preservation of that anonymity is so central to our success, members are not expected to discuss any aspect of the group's activities." Riccardo said that as all members held senior positions in their respective companies and most carried considerable commercial, industrial and financial influence, if it became known to government agencies that they were meeting 'clandestinely', the likely reaction didn't bear thinking about."

*   *   *

Historically, the production of chocolate at Scalfaro's had always been inefficient and pricing ineffective due in no small part to it being spread across three factories in two locations, four miles apart. Joseph began by restructuring the company into two decentralised strands, each working independently of the other.

One strand comprised the most experienced workers who would produce traditional chocolate of the highest quality at high prices and by necessity, was labour intensive.

The second strand would focus on the mass-production of chocolate. Using new machinery in the two factories on the same site, the process required minimal labour and would target the cheaper, high volume end of the market.

There was one further component of Scalfaro's new direction which was central to Joseph's thinking. He knew that if the company was to take on and then overtake competitors they would have to create a new and unique element to their product.

Joseph had discovered that unlike in Italy where chocolate was sold in blocks, the Swiss were making easily manageable bars and he wanted to take the idea one step further by moulding chocolate into shapes. The word Torino means bull so he wanted chocolate bulls for the local market and as the city was the centre of Italy's automobile production, he wanted chocolate cars. However, far more controversially, Joseph wanted to use Italy's catholic birthright to promote chocolate religious symbols.

As the restructuring gained pace, workforce gossip reached fever pitch when Joseph, Gabriella and Flavio called a meeting for all employees. As he stood before the whole company, for the first time Joseph was able to detail the changes and there was an immediate realisation that if the enormous potential of the new products was realised, there would be job security for all. With Gabriella looking on smiling, he then spelt out the cost in terms of workforce redundancies but even this was delivered with thoughtfulness and consideration as he explained that all job losses would only occur through natural wastage.

* * *

Once the specifics of his proposal had been completed and the company was operating within the new structure, Joseph's thoughts returned to his family. Begrudgingly, he knew that what he really wanted in his life was selfish beyond belief. Simply put, he wanted his family with him in Turin and his love affair with Gabriella to flourish but that was never going to happen. Joseph knew that delaying the arrival of his family whilst he continued to enjoy a relationship with her would be unpardonable and slightly reluctantly he pledged to complete the renovation of the house as soon as practical.

With this newfound resolve, Joseph immediately advertised for a husband and wife team to be his eyes and ears whilst builders restored the farmhouse. If all went well, the wife would go on to become his housekeeper; the husband his driver and gardener. Over two weekends Joseph interviewed twelve couples eventually choosing, Carla and Umberto Felini and he offered them a four month trial starting immediately.

Watching as the house and land were quickly transformed into a real home, Joseph came to realise that Carla and Umberto were exactly what he needed in the longer term and not only offered them permanent positions but also a small piece of his land, away from the main house, to build their own cottage. The Fellinis couldn't believe their good fortune and it was only a matter of time before they became an irreplaceable part of the Aizenberg family.

It was early 1911 and Joseph's life was as near to perfect as he could have wished.

—Ж—

Chapter 6

October 1938

When the three youngest children had finally fallen asleep, Marguerita asked Umberto if they were making good progress.

"Well, madam, the car is reliable and fast," and then to Simon who was still awake, he said, "Your father loved cars, especially this one, the 1931 Fiat 525S Coupe. Although a little elderly, he made sure it was kept in perfect condition." Then more thoughtfully he said to Marguerita,

"Madam, if we're stopped, without papers you'll be arrested so you'll have to leave the car and walk around any checkpoint, whilst I drive through. We'll meet on the other side." Marguerita finished his words for him,

"And if we don't find each other, you must promise to return to Carla." Swiftly changing the subject Umberto said to Simon,

"I'm not taking the most direct route to the border because I want to stay away from main roads and towns." He passed him a hand drawn map. "We're heading north to the town of Ivrea, which means we can avoid Milan. From there we stay on country roads to Biella and Borgomanero and then have to by-pass Varese before heading for Cantello and Rodero. Our destination is a village called Confine. From there we'll have to walk."

* * *

Over the next week, Tova and Carla visited the main police station almost every day but repeatedly faced rude or disinterested officials. It was quite clear that anyone in authority didn't know or care what was happening to Howard.

Each evening, after Carla had returned to her cottage, Tova sat alone feeling utterly lost. Sleep eluded her at night, which left her exhausted during the day and to compound her misery, there was no respite from her vivid thoughts of what might be happening to Howard.

The third evening following the family's departure, as Carla and Tova were about to call it a day, there was a tapping on the window of the lounge. Carla cautiously peeked through the smallest of gaps in the curtains.

"Good God!" she said as she rushed out of the room. Tova followed and she found Carla at the kitchen door with two men. She offered them chairs at the table and they removed their hats and coats whilst Carla closed the curtains.

"Madam," she said with a smile, "this is Riccardo Levin and Eric Manoukian, two old family friends." Tova shook their hands and suggested Carla open some wine.

"If you've come to see my sister-in-law," Tova informed them, "I'm sorry but she's left with the children." Riccardo replied in heavily accented English,

"We did want to see Marguerita; to give her this. It's from Emil." Tova and Carla looked at each other as the other man placed an envelope on the table and said,

"He asked us to deliver it if anything should happen to him."

"We've been friends of the Aizenberg family for longer than either of us care to remember," Riccardo said thoughtfully, "and we want you to know that Joseph and Emil were wholly innocent of the accusations made against them. What's happened is a travesty."

The men then related the most extraordinary story, before Riccardo looked sadly at Tova.

"I have little evidence to support what I am about to say, but say it I must. Joseph's death was no accident, as claimed by the police." Riccardo sipped his wine giving Tova time to consider the gravity of his accusation. "So after his funeral, along with Emil, we decided to find out what had really happened. However, immediately we started asking questions, all three of us were stopped by OVRA, the secret police and told to back-off or our families would be detained. Although incensed, we accepted the threat left us no choice but to stop our search." He looked across at Eric. "What we didn't realise, because Emil kept it to himself, was that he carried on looking for evidence that his father's death had been an 'official' killing. You see, we are all convinced Joseph's death was part of a conspiracy, not only against your family but other Jews in the community. Anyway, we're aware that Emil was warned a second time and again ignored it." Eric then interrupted and said definitively,

"In our opinion, both Emil's and Joseph's deaths were sanctioned by the state."

* * *

When Ellen woke the following morning she was astonished to see an enormous lake on her left and mountains rising behind the sparkling water. It was entrancing; the blues of the lake and sky against the blacks, greys and white of the snow-topped mountains. It was something she had only ever seen in books. Umberto, noticing her reaction in the mirror, pointed.

"Switzerland." He said.

"It looks close enough to touch," Ellen answered, staring in disbelief.

"Unfortunately, it's still a very long way."

As Ellen stared in awe at their destination, the pain at leaving her parents suddenly returned to devour any pleasure. Knowing the others were still asleep, she asked Umberto if when he saw them again, he would give them a message. He, of course, readily agreed.

"Please tell them goodbye, that I love them and thank them for all they have done for Noah and me, and that I cannot wait until we're all together again." Umberto looked out of his side window, holding back the tears as he realised Ellen was a most extraordinary young lady.

As the others began to wake, Umberto told them that the lake was called Lake Maggiore and they were approaching the town of Varese which they would have to by-pass.

Over the next few hours, they stopped twice for toilet breaks and passed the towns of Cantello and Rodero. Once through Rodero, they began to climb towards Confine and the road conditions became ever more difficult and treacherous. Winding, narrow, unmade tracks with sheer drops to the side became the norm and Marguerita, sensing Umberto's concern, suggested they take a break. After finding a safe place for the children to stretch their legs, he pulled the car over and out of hearing of the rest of the family, Marguerita asked,

"Is it still far?"

"Madam, it's not that," Umberto replied, looking at the mountains. "To get into Switzerland you must go over those." Before Marguerita could answer, Umberto added awkwardly, "I should have realised. I'm sorry. I thought the worse bit would be getting to the border not crossing it. I have never been this far north and, well…" Marguerita touched him on the arm.

"You've already done far more than I could have asked of you. Without you we'd still be in Turin." They stood silently for a moment, both amazed at the majesty of the mountains.

"What do you think we should do?" Marguerita eventually asked.

"Well, we can't continue on this track," Umberto answered quietly. "We need to go back down and find an easier way to cross."

"Okay, if we must, we must. We certainly can't walk over that," Marguerita said pointing to the jagged peaks surrounding them and began rounding the children up.

On the way back down, Umberto suggested instead of going back to Rodero they took the road northwest. They could then find a village and eat, whilst he spoke to some of the locals.

Later that afternoon, they drove into the village of Filand and Umberto left Marguerita and the children in the only café and headed for the bar. When they met up three-quarters of an hour later, he said a couple of local men suggested they head for Bizzarone as it was only a few miles from the border.

One look at the town of Bizzarone and it was obvious where they would sleep; in the car. After parking on the outskirts, Umberto again left them as Marguerita got the children ready for another uncomfortable night. He returned later to find only Marguerita and Simon still awake and told them that he'd met a member of the border guard in one of the bars and for a price the man would guarantee them safe passage into Switzerland. She was overjoyed and readily agreed to the cost. Umberto returned to the bar to give the man half the fee, with the rest to be paid only after they had crossed into Switzerland the following morning. When he returned a second time, Umberto explained that he had been told they had to be at the checkpoint no later than ten and that there would be hundreds of other people trying to cross the border, so they should arrive as early as possible.

*   *   *

At breakfast the next day, as Tova pushed Emil's still unopened letter across the table to Carla and asked her to keep it safe, there was a knock on the back door. When she answered it, Carla found a young boy standing on the step who passed a note to her before running away though the rear of the garden.

The note was addressed to Mrs T Aizenberg and Tova tore at the seal before reading the contents to Carla.

"Dear Mrs Aizenberg, I hope this note finds you and your family as well as can be expected. After further enquiries I have been able to locate your husband."

Tova's heart leapt and Carla crossed herself.

"Following his arrest he was taken to the police headquarters in Milan by the secret police. He was interrogated at length and I am sorry to say, it appears he suffered terribly at the hands of his accusers.

I'm told he is likely to be moved to one of the new internment camps until he is deported.

I am sorry I cannot be of more help but assure you I will keep looking.

Regards

GMG"

"It's from George McDonald-Grey, the diplomat I met with Marguerita," Tova said, before sitting silently deep in thought. The news was encouraging; Howard was alive and he was to be deported, not imprisoned indefinitely. The problem however, was she was none the wiser in terms of knowing where Howard was actually being held.

As Carla was clearing away the dishes, there was a rap on the front door and she returned to the kitchen trailed by the two policemen who had originally arrested Howard. With no preamble the senior of the two looked towards Tova.

"Come with me." Tova's heart sank, while Carla again crossed herself.

"Am I allowed to know where you're taking me?" she asked, far more respectfully than on the previous occasion.

"Get your coat," came the reply, the officer making no attempt to answer her question.

"Please, where am I going?" Tova repeated, becoming more agitated.

"Get your coat!" was the blunt, aggressive response.

"But I have rights. I am a British subje…" Before she could finish the officer slapped her viciously across the face and as blood poured from her nose, Tova burst into tears. As Carla rushed towards her, the other policemen grabbed her by the hair and pulled her back.

"Your rights disappeared the day members of your family joined a banned group of assassins."

* * *

Although six in the morning, the queue at the border was significant and Marguerita and the children joined all the others desperate to escape Italy. When Umberto found them after parking the car, he said, "Madam, I will go to the front and see if I can find the guard from last night," as he showed Marguerita the envelope of cash she'd given him.

Three hours later, with no sign of Umberto and the family moving towards the front of the queue, she began to panic. Without documents and the friendly guard they would be in serious trouble.

Finally, with only one couple ahead of them, Umberto reappeared with a smile.

“I am so sorry Madam. The man I spoke to only arrived a few minutes ago and says everything is fine for you to cross.” Marguerita couldn’t believe they were actually going to leave and with immense relief she thanked Umberto.

When the couple before them in the queue moved on, a guard called to Umberto, indicating the family should go to him. Marguerita and the children said a sad farewell to their faithful driver and as tears flowed, he watched them enter one of the buildings.

Umberto saw the silhouettes of the family through opaque glass in the windows and noticed beyond the cluster of buildings a large barrier; it was their road to Switzerland and freedom. Finally, after what seemed like a lifetime, he saw the ‘friendly’ guard leave the hut being followed by the family and they all walked towards the check point. Umberto prayed for God to keep them safe and watched the barrier rise. Madam and the children then turned to wave their goodbyes.

“Stay where you are!” Marguerita and the children suddenly stopped and turned to see three men dressed in long, black leather coats approaching them, two with pistols drawn. Umberto stared in disbelief as the men began questioning Marguerita. To his horror he then saw his friendly guard being led away in handcuffs.

Unable to understand what could have gone wrong, Umberto moved quickly past the front of the queue, his pace quickening as two of the men blocked the family’s path to the barrier.

As he ran, Umberto called out to the men to let the family go and couldn't understand why as he got closer one of the men was raising his gun.

Marguerita screamed for him to stop, to stand still, but he didn't listen, he had to reach them; his family, the people he truly loved. He had to protect them.

Suddenly there was a deafening snap of gunfire and Umberto felt excruciating pain. Looking down, he saw bright red oozing through his shirt but he wouldn't stop, he had to get to the children, to Madam, to keep them safe. He had promised Clara he would protect them.

Without warning, there was a second volley of gunfire and Umberto fell. He hit the floor with a heart-stopping thud, scraping his hands and face on the rock-hard ground. As the children screamed, Marguerita ran to her devoted friend and held Umberto tightly, trying desperately to stem the flow of blood.

"Madam, I am so sorr…"

"Shush, Umberto, shush," she whispered gently as her tears erupted, but before she could tell him how much they all loved him, Umberto's lifeless body slumped in her arms.

Ellen stared transfixed. Umberto dead, why? He was completely innocent, a friend helping friends. They were the guilty ones, not the amazing Mr Umberto. They were the ones running away and it should have been them that were punished not him.

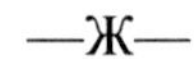

Chapter 7

1911 - 1912

For the next year Joseph's life was manic; the company, the house, meetings with the business group, his family and Gabriella all conspired to leave Joseph little time to dwell on the serious political turmoil enveloping Europe.

Whilst all involved in Scalfaro's adjusted to their new roles within the restructured company, production of both strands of the chocolate business began in earnest and the impact was immediate. Countless friends, many with justifiable envy, complained to Joseph that wherever they went in Turin the name of Scalfaro's was on everyone's lips.

Gabriella and Flavio were delighted with the speed and efficiency of the restructuring and the positive impact this had had on the company finances. Joseph understood that any success in terms of increased profits would negate Antonio's criticism of his work.

Looking back, Joseph also realised that it was during the period of enormous disruption at Scalfaro's that his friendship with Flavio changed. Although Flavio had always been one of Joseph's most ardent supporters, their relationship had been rather reserved, revolving around the company and work. However, from the moment Antonio demanded Joseph's resignation, Flavio's attitude towards him softened. He began to ask Joseph to join him for an after work drink or meal and during one very long evening where both men had drunk far too much wine, Flavio explained that he was in fact a trained lawyer. He then admitted rather hastily that he hated the profession and had only qualified to appease his father.

*   *   *

Work on the house continued at an impressive speed and Joseph was delighted with how Carla and Umberto were dealing with the builders. They in turn realised what a special employer Joseph was and worked all hours to ensure he was pleased with their efforts.

The final stages of converting the derelict farmhouse into a splendid seven-bedroom house with three hectares of landscaped gardens was completed in the last months of 1911. He moved into Hayastan for Christmas, naming his home after the historical title of Armenia. Carla and Umberto's little cottage was also finished a few weeks later.

Once settled Joseph made the decision to move his family to Italy the following summer and also that he would at long last return to Armenia to bring his family out. However, he knew he would need documentation proving he was not an Armenian and therefore followed up his application for Italian citizenship. It had been many months since Joseph had first applied and when he mentioned the delay to Ahab Levy, an influential member of the business group, he received his new papers within just a few days. He couldn't believe that after twelve years in his adopted country he was a legalised Italian citizen.

*   *   *

Joseph continued to thoroughly enjoy the monthly business group meetings; discussions were always lively and often contentious and he loved the cut and thrust of the debates. Issues of the day, both within Italy and internationally, were nearly always the starting point for the post-lunch meeting but Joseph was still stunned, when in the spring of 1911, the rotating chairman Nathan Zolli began by saying,

"Gentleman, in my opinion and those of many of my colleagues, Europe is heading for war." Joseph was aware of the deteriorating relationship between Germany and some of its neighbours, but not to the extent that it would lead to a European conflict.

A lengthy debate followed and Joseph noticed there was an evident split in opinions; those in agreement who wanted to discuss the effect a war would have on their businesses and those who dismissed such talk as inflammatory scaremongering.

As Joseph listened he was shaken by the mounting animosity between the two groups. Relationships within the membership were always affable and he put the occasional disagreement down to successful men and their egos. However, what he was witnessing was altogether more serious and had the potential to cause lasting damage.

*   *   *

Joseph and Riccardo met the following Tuesday for lunch and as soon as they had taken their seats Joseph began asking about the likelihood of war. He explained that when he left Armenia, he had promised himself he would stay away from politics and had therefore deliberately ignored the deteriorating situation across Europe.

Riccardo, knowing of Joseph's background, empathised with his friend's decision and told him that even if he wasn't aware of it, as recently as 1904, war across Europe had only just been avoided. When Joseph awkwardly replied that at that time he was destitute and travelling through Southern Italy looking for work, Riccardo smiled sympathetically before saying,

"Okay, in 1904 Morocco was owned by Britain and they agreed to give it to France. However, the Moroccan people wanted independence not the rule of another European power and to make matters worse, a year later Germany announced its support for the Moroccan Independence Movement."

"Why would Germany want to cause problems?" Joseph asked.

"Well, for the last fifty years Europe has seen a number of .., I'll call them skirmishes. This was just another example of the bickering that was prevalent."

"So how was the Moroccan problem resolved?"

"With diplomacy, but at a price." They ordered lunch before Riccardo continued.

"It was agreed that if France got Morocco, she had to give part of the French Congo to Germany. You see, Germany lagged behind Britain and France in the colonisation of the world. By 1900, for example, Britain's Empire stretched over five continents and France had large swathes of Africa, but Germany had only modest colonies by comparison and demanded more."

Lunch arrived and whilst they ate, Riccardo admitted his love of history, which explained to Joseph his friend's extensive knowledge of Europe.

"There are many reasons why Europe is in trouble today and most are the result of decades of worsening political relationships. I'm afraid it's too late to restore any of the goodwill that might have existed."

"What! Even if it means war!" Joseph asked. Having survived the horrors of civil war in Armenia, he could see absolutely no justification for it.

“Bear with me whilst I offer you an overview of Europe today,” Riccardo answered as they ordered coffee and Joseph sensed his friend was in his element.

“Alliances,” Riccardo said. “Over the last forty years alliances between European countries have led to two camps emerging. Let me give you a few examples. In 1881, Serbia agreed a pact with Austria-Hungary to prevent Russia gaining control of their country. In 1882, Germany and Austria-Hungary allied themselves with Italy to stop Italy backing Russia in any future dispute.” Riccardo laughed. “In 1894, Russia concerned over the German, Austria-Hungary alliance, agreed their own with France. In 1904, France and Britain signed the Entente Cordiale, an agreement rather than an alliance but still powerful, and finally in 1907, two alliances were signed as a result of German threats; the Anglo-Russian Entente between Britain and Russia and the Triple Entente between Russia, France and Britain. The upshot of this unqualified mess is a maze of obligations and if one European country goes to war, the entire continent is likely to implode.”

“What an appalling thought,” Joseph said more to himself than Riccardo.

“Secondly,” Riccardo continued, “nationalism across Europe is on the increase. The power base of the continent is there for the taking and the arms race has been gaining momentum for decades. Oh ...do you know by the way that the armies of France and Germany have nearly doubled in size since 1870, and then the others are expanding their war machinery at an alarming rate. Alongside all that, you have fierce rivalry between Britain and Germany as to who is master of the seas.” Riccardo took a sip of his coffee before saying with considerable candour, “Finally, add imperial and colonial competition for wealth, power and prestige, not to mention economic and military rivalry for control of industry and trade, and you end up quite literally with a recipe for Armageddon. I don't say this lightly but I genuinely believe we are on the brink of something cataclysmic. It might take a year, maybe three, but believe me, it is only a matter of time before we all witness something so appalling that Europe may never recover from."

As the third coffees and liqueurs arrived, Riccardo mentioned in passing that a number of his friends had begun to diversify their businesses, either moving branches of their existing companies abroad or starting completely new enterprises in other countries. He explained that as Europe deteriorated, many were looking towards Britain and the USA.

*   *   *

As Joseph sat considering Riccardo's grim prediction, he begrudgingly realised that part of Antonio's thinking was logical and accepted it was time he also considered the future. He had been unstintingly committed to Scalfaro's and it had left him, and indirectly his wife and children, completely reliant on its success.

After some hours, a bottle of the finest red and pages of scribbled notes, Joseph accepted if he created businesses separate from any commitment he had towards Scalfaro's, he would have safeguards for his family's future. Furthermore, if he based these companies in the USA and Britain, there would always be the option of a future away from Italy.

Last thing that night Joseph wrote to Elizabeth telling her firstly to ensure that the family had all the necessary documentation to travel abroad and secondly, to arrange for the governess to teach the entire family English in addition to the Italian they had been learning. Elizabeth had told him the children were taking their Italian lessons seriously and he was concerned about putting further demands on them, but the more he thought about it the more he realised the ability to speak English was crucial to their futures.

Next day Joseph asked Carla and Umberto if they would be prepared to learn English. When he explained he'd decided it would be the only language spoken at Hayastan they were delighted, realising that if they spoke English there would be a much greater chance of long-term employment with the Aizenberg family. Arrangements were therefore made for Carla and Umberto to learn English from the same teacher as Joseph.

*   *   *

Joseph appreciated he had so much in his life, however, unease over problems between Gabriella and his family began to rule his waking hours. Repeatedly he convinced himself that carefully managed, there would be no conflict but as the day of his family's arrival drew nearer, so his anxiety grew. At night, when he remembered life with Elizabeth and the children, Gabriella's beauty would always steal the scene. She was always there to love him and share his life. It was a perfect relationship and one he simply couldn't lose.

*   *   *

Following his lunch with Riccardo, Joseph spent the weekend at a hotel on the shores of Lake Maggiore with Gabriella. They met up on the Friday evening and after dinner retired to their room.

After making love, as Gabriella lay in his arms, she asked Joseph whether he was happy.

"With you; of course," he replied after a moment's hesitation.

"But...," she said knowingly.

"Where you're concerned there are no buts. Any 'buts' are with the rest of my life."

"Is it your family? Are you worried about bringing them here after Antonio's outburst?"

"His attitude does concern me, but it's not only that. In her last few letters Elizabeth has stopped telling me the news from home and it's all rather worrying."

"When did you last hear from her?"

"It's been a while." Joseph then told Gabriella about his lunch with Riccardo and his concerns and as they held each other, both accepted that the following few months would define their future together or apart.

The next day, over breakfast, a subdued Gabriella said,

"There's something I need to tell you." For some reason Joseph's heart sank. He didn't know why but whatever it was he was sure he didn't want to hear it.

"I've received a telegram from Antonio." This confirmed Joseph's concern. "He says that Europe is heading for war and he wants me to travel to the States to see the business potential. I really don't want to go but..."

"Then don't!" Joseph interrupted belligerently. Realising his rudeness he apologised, acknowledging that when it came to Antonio he struggled to be objective. However, he was also angry because he knew Antonio's plans were sensible and should be considered.

Gabriella took his hands across the table.

"It's not that simple," she said gently and explained that her brother had genuine fears about what lay ahead for Italy and was convinced the USA was where their futures lay. "I know you're concerned about Scalfaro's but Antonio cannot sell or move company assets abroad without my agreement. Please understand I have to give him every opportunity to show me what he wants and then I'll be able to make the right decision for everyone. I will travel to America and then return and talk to you and Flavio about the future." Gabriella was of course, absolutely correct; Joseph had to accept that as a senior partner she had a duty to look at all possible options for the company.

* * *

During the build up to Christmas 1911, Gabriella and Joseph rarely mentioned her forthcoming trip; both accepted it was going to happen but neither wanted to consider the months of separation that lay ahead. Antonio returned mid-December as planned and apart from two short meetings, Joseph had little contact with him.

Joseph loved his new home and the solitude it offered but he readily accepted an invitation from Carla and Umberto to spend Christmas Day lunch with them. As they sat down to eat, Umberto suggested they spoke only English which was agreed and there was much laughter as well as satisfaction in their endeavour.

A peaceful Christmas was followed by an altogether different New Year. After lunching with Flavio, Joseph moved on to a party being given by members of the business group and their wives and although he had a terrific time, it left him wondering how Elizabeth would adapt to the social demands of Turin.

Early in the New Year, Antonio left for Geneva informing Gabriella he would return in early March and they would leave for France one week later. He explained their itinerary would include ten days in Paris before they travelled to London. They would stay with friends in Berkley Square then sailing to New York on April the twenty-first.

Throughout February, Joseph and Gabriella saw as much of each other as possible and Joseph was surprised and relieved that their closeness was not commented on by friends.

* * *

Scalfaro's Board meetings continued and Gabriella, aware of her imminent trip to America, regularly attempted to introduce the question of the company's future. To her frustration Flavio always answered that there could be little meaningful discussion on the subject until all the facts were known and that would only be after her return.

However, when on their own, Flavio and Joseph did discuss the possible outcome of Antonio's plans and both had to recognise the merit of his ideas. Over one of their lunches Flavio surprised Joseph when he mentioned that Antonio had discovered a branch of his family in America but had still to tell Gabriella, wanting to surprise her on her arrival in New York.

"Apparently," he added, "this relative is opening a number of very influential doors and Antonio is determined not to miss out on any opportunity."

The day finally arrived when Gabriella and Joseph had to say goodbye. They spent their last night together, the first time ever in Turin, but neither slept. Both understood that the next day there could be no emotional goodbyes. She promised to write often and Joseph said he would look after Scalfaro's until her return.

* * *

And Gabriella was as good as her word, sending telegrams to Joseph whenever she found a telegraph office, keeping him abreast of their journey. Joseph on the other hand divided his time between Scalfaro's and researching future possibilities. He spoke to Flavio about Riccardo's warning.

"The talk of Turin is not about if but when war arrives. I know that many of my friends are also looking at alternatives to fall back on. When Joseph asked Flavio what he was planning his reply was surprising.

"Me, well I can't envisage living anywhere else. This has been my home forever and when I do travel I rarely enjoy the experience, so I will take my chances here in Turin."

*   *   *

Gabriella arrived in London from Paris on March 25th 1912 and wrote to Joseph saying that she loved the city and could have stayed forever, if only he had been with her. However, rather unexpectedly she also said she was anxious about the journey to America.

Once she reached London Joseph received telegrams every day and was therefore puzzled when he heard nothing after April 7th, two weeks before they were due to sail.

By the 14th, an increasingly fretful Joseph spoke to Flavio understanding that it was a delicate issue to raise with a life-long friend of Antonio. Flavio listened as Joseph stuttered through his pre-planned reasons for wanting to know about Gabriella. He then stopped as he saw Flavio smiling and could never remember a more uncomfortable moment, especially when his friend began to laugh.

"Joseph, I know," Flavio said gently. Touching his arm he added, "Do you really think after a life-time of knowing and loving Gabriella like a sister she could hide something like love from me?" Joseph sat stunned; one part of him was relieved, the other part terrified Antonio might find out.

"They're fine," Flavio continued. "I heard from them three days ago and all is well.

"But that's my point," Joseph said uneasily, "I was hearing from Gabriella every day." Flavio raised an eyebrow and again laughed. Ignoring his friend's reaction Joseph added, "But there's been nothing for a week."

"Stop worrying. Antonio contacted me saying that he'd managed to change their travel arrangements. Apparently he's found a once in a lifetime trip, whatever that might mean, so stop worrying."

* * *

Eventually, on the 13th April a special delivery letter, not a telegram, arrived from Gabriella.

'My Dearest Joseph,

I decided to write as I need pages to tell you all the amazing things that have happened....'

And Joseph laughed as he read Gabriella's news; visits to the theatre, shops, restaurants, attending parties, even a boat trip down the Thames and walk around London Zoo. As he came to the last page, he sadly realised that he wouldn't hear from Gabriella for the next few weeks whilst she crossed the Atlantic.

'And finally my love, I am so very excited. Antonio has managed, even at this late stage, to get us passage, not the best of berths of course, on the maiden voyage of the most modern and safest, ship ever built. Apparently it has all the luxury one could want. We

travelled down to a town by the sea called Southampton and went straight to see the boat. Joseph, it is enormous, spectacular, it's absolutely overwhelming! It's called the Titanic........

—Ж—

Chapter 8

November 1938

Ellen missed her parents desperately and her misery was compounded by being constantly moved from one place to another. At night they were locked up in small, cold rooms and during the day were forced to travel in unbearably uncomfortable lorries. Aunt Marguerita had told the children not to talk to anyone and so they kept to themselves by playing games or just talking and Ellen quickly realised how much she liked her cousins.

Late one afternoon, after they had been given the usual meagre meal of bread and soup, they were ordered into the back of yet another lorry and the canvas sides were tied down to prevent them seeing where they were.

After a sleepless night they finally came to a stop and were ordered out. Ellen climbed down and had to shield her eyes from bright sunlight, but then, as she looked around, to her astonishment she saw they were on the front steps of Hayastan.

The family were bundled into the front hall of the house and a man in an officer's uniform took Aunt Marguerita away. When she returned, she told the children that they were under house arrest which meant they were not allowed outside at any time.

"I'm sorry," she then said to Noah and Ellen, "but your mother has been taken away and I'm afraid there's still no news of your father."

Ellen held Noah tightly and they cried together. She'd been certain her mother would be there to welcome them home but now, just like her father, she was gone.

That night in bed Ellen was inconsolable. She couldn't get the picture of Umberto's bloodied, lifeless body out of her head and was terrified at what might have happened to her parents. As she lay in the dark, Ellen asked God where he was. She had always been taught he would be there when their needs were greatest, so where was he? She reminded Him that she'd prayed every day, so where was he, where was the great man? And why the hell wasn't he listening!

* * *

Tova had no idea where she was or what they wanted and she was terrified. Food was pushed through a small hatch in the door so by counting the number of times she'd eaten she guessed she'd been locked-up for three days. Her cell contained a hard bed and thin blanket, a slop bucket that was almost full; she dreaded the moment it would hold no more, and a very high window with no glass. She spent her days praying Howard was alive and that Ellen and Noah had made it to Switzerland and repeatedly told herself to stay positive.

* * *

The telephone and radio had been crudely ripped out of their sockets and many other 'luxury' items were missing but they mattered little. Most importantly the family was back home.

Their first morning, as they sat having breakfast, Ellen heard a key turning in the back door and called her aunt. The family couldn't believe it as Carla walked in.

Marguerita's heart sank. Of course she was overjoyed to see her housekeeper but loathed the thought of the agony Carla would feel on learning of Umberto's death.

Trying to avoid the children saying anything prematurely, she asked them to go upstairs. Once they had gone, with tears threatening she described what had happened. Carla sat shaking; her hands covering her face in between crossing herself.

"Please no!" she cried as Marguerita moved to her and held her tightly. For the next few, impossible minutes she told Carla everything, emphasising time and again how without Umberto's extraordinary bravery, they'd all be dead.

Wiping away her tears, Carla asked if she could go back to her cottage but later she joined Marguerita in the lounge carrying a tray of coffee. Seeing only one cup Marguerita went to the kitchen for another and asked Carla to sit with her.

"I'm so …" she began, but Carla interrupted her.

"Madam, please, what is done is done. Life must go on." But her tears came again and Marguerita once more hugged her.

"Carla, the cottage is yours," she said gently, "for as long as you want. You are part of our family and I cannot think of Hayastan without you."

She then described the rest of their journey and Carla recalled the dreadful day Madam Tova had been taken away.

As she was clearing up the cups, she said,

"Madam, I have something for you." She left the room, returning with the letter from Emil.

*   *   *

Tova had lost all concept of time when the guards eventually unlocked her cell and told her to follow them. She was frog-marched along a dark, cold corridor until she reached a room which contained only a desk and two chairs, one of which was occupied by an overweight, unshaven, grim-faced man.

"Sit down," he said in passable English and with no preamble began the questioning.

"How often did your husband visit Turin? What relationship did your husband have with his father and brother? Has your husband ever attended any meeting of a political nature in England?" Question after question followed until Tova was utterly confused but she continued to answer everything as honestly as she could.

That night, back in her cell, as she thought through the 'interview', Tova realised the security police or whoever they were, must be struggling to find evidence against Howard, or why arrest her? The only conclusion she could reach was that they required her to provide the necessary proof. In part she was grateful if it meant Howard was alive, but that was tempered by the thought that if she made any mistakes, it might be her that inadvertently gave them what they needed.

*   *   *

A week later, Marguerita was informed by the senior officer that Hayastan was being requisitioned by the military and they would all live in the cottage. When she asked why, she was told bluntly,

"You will remain in the cottage under house arrest until we have finished with the Aizenbergs." Before leaving he informed her that the family had until five o'clock that day to move, after that no one was permitted to enter the main house.

The move proved relatively simple but the living arrangements were more problematic. Carla offered to give up the main bedroom but was refused and it was finally agreed that Marguerita, Simon and Leon would share one bedroom with Ellen and Noah in the other.

A week later it was Ellen's 12th birthday, November 26th, and it was a day she would remember for all the wrong reasons. Aunt Marguerita, Carla and the boys made every effort to make it a special day, but there was no hiding Ellen's misery. For the very first time in her short life, her parents were not there to celebrate with her.

And things went from bad to worse a week later when Carla returned from shopping to tell Marguerita that new anti-Semitic laws had been passed. She said she'd heard that the government had banned marriages between Jews and Aryans, barred Jews from taking military or civil administrative posts and finally, prohibited Jews from employing Christians.

That evening when Carla overheard the children discussing the new laws she thought it best to mention it to Marguerita. Over supper it was obvious that not only were all four children extremely troubled but they were far more aware of what was going on than she'd ever imagined.

At the end of the meal, as the plates were being cleared, Marguerita told the family that in future suppertime would be for discussing anything worrying them.

The following day, when she had had time to read about the new laws she realised their ownership of Scalfaro's was under threat and immediately wrote to Flavio. Marguerita knew him as an irreplaceable and loyal member of the Board and a true friend of Emil who would always be there to help and at that moment, she was desperate for his counsel.

With the incentive of a large bribe, Flavio was allowed to visit the cottage and as he spoke with Carla and Marguerita it became clear he was unaware of the problems they'd faced since his meeting with Howard just a week earlier. The more Marguerita told him about Howard's and Tova's arrests, the trip to the border and execution of Umberto, the angrier he became and told them he would do everything he could to help. Before leaving, he also promised that Scalfaro's would remain a viable company until Simon and Leon were old enough to take over.

* * *

The interviews continued, sometimes twice a day and Tova took great solace from the fact that they obviously still needed information to condemn Howard.

As the guards arrived yet again and Tova prepared herself for another round of questioning, she acknowledged how fortunate she was to be British. She was sure that under the same circumstances, Italian citizens would not have been treated so leniently.

When the door opened she noticed it wasn't her usual guard.

"Come, now," the new guard said in poor English and threw a bundle of clothes at her.

"Bring those." he said and Tova did as she was ordered.

However, as she walked behind the guard along the familiar corridor, something was different and Tova became anxious. Had she said something, given them what they wanted; had she condemned her beloved Howard?

Shaking with fear, Tova was pushed aggressively though a large iron door and entered what appeared to be a reception area. In reasonable English another guard told her to sit at a table in the middle of the room and if she signed the form in front of her, she was free to leave. Tova began scanning the documents but it was in Italian; she understood nothing. Asking the guard what the document said, he replied dismissively,

"Sign it and go back to your family or refuse and stay here. It makes no difference to me."

Tova realised if she signed and the document contained damming evidence against Howard she would never see him again.

"I cannot sign if you do not tell me what it says," Tova answered cautiously.

The guard nodded and left the room and she waited to be taken back to her cell. However, many hours later, having been offered no food or drink and only one visit to the bathroom, the man returned, told her she could leave and two policemen escorted her to a waiting car.

* * *

During the second week of December, Ellen was sat on her favourite seat by the bedroom window when she saw four vehicles arriving at the back of the main house. She shouted down to the others as about thirty people, all shabbily dressed, jumped down from the back of the lorries before the guards searched them. They were then pushed through the kitchen door of the main house and within a few minutes Ellen saw their sombre, frightened faces staring out of the windows of Simon's old bedroom.

During supper that evening there was a lengthy discussion about the new arrivals. Leon thought the house was being used as a hotel but Simon argued that with so many guards and the harassment they had witnessed, it was more likely being used as a prison. The next day, Carla solved the debate telling Marguerita that as she'd returned from a shopping trip she'd spoken to a guard who said Hayastan was being used as a holding centre. When Carla added that he seemed interested in getting to know her better, Marguerita was horrified. However, Carla assured her that it was an opportunity to get information they couldn't afford to miss but promised she would be careful. Reluctantly, Marguerita agreed, acknowledging how vital a 'friendly' guard could be and told Carla to use some of the shopping money to buy him small gifts.

Hardly surprisingly, Carla had changed since the death of Umberto, sometimes appearing to have little desire to go on living without her husband and Marguerita remained extremely anxious that she might do something reckless.

* * *

As they passed the gatehouse Tova was overjoyed but as they drove along the drive she sensed something was wrong and this feeling was reinforced when they passed the front door of the main house without stopping.

* * *

Ellen was again in her favourite spot, reading by what little daylight was left when she spotted a police car moving towards the cottage. When it finally stopped outside, Ellen couldn't believe her eyes as she saw a woman get out. Running downstairs as fast as her legs would carry her, she screamed excitedly,

"Mummy's back! Quickly everyone; Mummy's here!"

Chapter 9

1912

Joseph looked up from his work and smiled as Flavio entered the office. Since Gabriella had left the two had become much closer, meeting two or three times a week for an evening meal or drink and both realised how much they enjoyed each other's company.

However, when he saw his friend's face, Joseph's smile disappeared; there were tears, something was dreadfully wrong.

"What is it?" he asked gently. Without a word, Flavio passed him a newspaper and left.

'TITANIC SUNK - THOUSANDS FEARED DEAD!'

Joseph stared in disbelief.

"What in God's name." he said out loud. With shaking hands he read the article but found the details so vague he telephoned Uri Gideon, a friend from the business meetings and owner of one of the smaller but more reliable local newspapers. When he explained he knew someone travelling on the Titanic, Uri told him that it seemed pretty definite the great ship had been lost at sea but stressed that facts were in short supply and it would be at least twenty four hours before any reliable information began to emerge.

Later that morning, sat in his office with Flavio, the two friends tried to unravel what could have happened. When Joseph asked his secretary for coffee she passed him a letter that had just been delivered. His heart leapt as he recognised Gabriella's handwriting.

Flavio looked at the postmark and said quietly,

"Don't get your hopes up. It was posted on April 11th before they'd set off across the Atlantic." As

Joseph began tearing at the envelope, Flavio rose to leave but Joseph said,

"Stay, Gabriella was just as important to you as to me…, please."

'My dearest,' he began, reading uneasily as Flavio returned to his seat.

'This will be very short as I have found someone to take the letter ashore. Joseph, it is so exciting! Yesterday, we boarded the Titanic and were shown to our cabin which is so comfortable considering how late we booked. We then set sail across the English Channel to Cherbourg in France. Last night we sailed to Queenstown in Ireland, arriving this morning and it's where I am sending this letter from.

I must tell you darling, we've met so many lovely people. Would you believe we had afternoon tea with the actress Dorothy Gibson. She was so sweet and then last night, drinks with the Broadway producers, Henry and Rene Harris, author Helen Churchill Candee and the US aide Archibald Butt. They were so charming and I just know we are going to have a wonderful time travelling to New York.

My love, this will be the last time I write until we arrive in America but you will be in my thoughts every minute of every day. Being apart has made me love you so much more. I cannot wait to be home.

My heart will be yours always. Please take care. I cannot wait to be in your arms once again. Warmest love, Gabriella.'

Hands shaking but determined to hold back the tears, Joseph handed the letter to Flavio.

"Are you sure?" his friend asked and Joseph nodded.

When he'd finished reading, Flavio placed the letter on the table between them and the two men sat in silence. Neither knew what to say but both accepted that until they knew whether Antonio and Gabriella were safe, there was nothing more to be done.

Early the following morning, Uri Gideon phoned Joseph and confirmed the Titanic had been struck by an iceberg and there had been considerable loss of life. He said there were survivors but the exact numbers and names were being held until after relatives had been informed.

Once the call had ended, Joseph left his office and bought copies of the latest edition of the papers and found a seat in a local café. With a coffee and large brandy he read the articles.

Only four days into its maiden voyage, at exactly 02.20 on the 15th April 1912, the greatest ship ever built, was lost at sea. It is believed that minutes before midnight on the 14th April, the Titanic struck an iceberg ... ...

Although the crew fought valiantly to save her, it only took two hours and forty minutes for the ship to sink ... ...

The Titanic carried a complement of 3547 crew and passengers and although figures vary, it is thought that up to1500 people or half of all on board may have perished ... ...

As he expected, Joseph found the information in the papers maddening. There were numerous articles about the ship, names of those on board and lists of those responsible for her. This included the owners, captain and investors, maps of the route, in fact anything and everything except what he really needed; a definitive list of survivors.

As he sat drinking his brandy, the agony of waiting for information was as painful as anything he'd ever suffered. No matter whom he phoned or spoke to, no one was able to help and it was during that agonising wait Joseph truly understood the depth of his feelings for Gabriella. He loved her in a way that could not be put into words; it was a love so momentous he really did not know if he wanted to go on if she was not with him.

*   *   *

That night, Joseph woke with a start; he'd been dreaming but remembered nothing. Once awake he could not get back to sleep and as he began worrying about Gabriella he suddenly felt like his body was burning up. The room began to spin violently and he found it impossible to get comfortable.

As he lay on the bed trying to get cool, his thoughts turned to his soon-to-arrive family and the fact that if Gabriella and Antonio had perished the company would be sold. The more he considered the situation the more agitated Joseph became and the more irrational were his feelings. What if Antonio had survived and Gabriella had not. Antonio would never countenance Joseph's continued leadership of Scalfaro's? What if Antonio and Gabriella had both perished; even from the grave Antonio would have made arrangements for him to be removed. What if... and Joseph's body began to shake ferociously. He was saturated in sweat and as he tried to sit up he felt an excruciating tightness across his chest causing him to gulp for air. The last thing Joseph remembered was a vivid picture of Gabriella gasping for air as she slowly sank under an ocean of water.

*   *   *

When he awoke, Joseph was disorientated. The smells surrounding him were alien and his bed hard and uncomfortable. As he opened his eyes, the pain from bright lights was excruciating and he heard someone telling him to lie back. He had no idea why but the voice calmed him and Joseph relaxed into yet another deep, undisturbed sleep.

Awake again, Joseph slowly opened his eyes and tentatively pushed himself into a sitting position. He saw a small, antiseptic, very white room and as he contemplated getting out of bed, a nurse came through the open door.

"Where am I?" he asked puzzled.

'Hospital," the nurse replied, "You have been very sick." She felt Joseph's wrist and also took his temperature and then left the room without another word.

He was given a small bowl of soup for lunch and he then slipped into another deep sleep. When he woke the nurse was by his bed with a doctor who proceeded to examine just about every part of Joseph's body and when he'd finished, he said bluntly,

"You appear to have contracted a minor fever, probably a seasonal virus, but because of your general poor health, your body was unable to cope. This led to pneumonia. Mr Aizenberg, you have been gravely ill and, I should add, extremely lucky. Many have died, even in this hospital, from similar complications."

"How long have I been here?" Joseph asked weakly.

"Four days," came the reply and the doctor and nurse departed leaving Joseph feeling extremely relieved he was on the mend. As he closed his eyes to rest however, Gabriella came into his thoughts and he realised he'd been unconscious for four days. Joseph quickly sat up and tried to swing his legs off the bed. He had to speak to Flavio. It was imperative to find out news of the Titanic but as he tried to stand, his head spun violently and he fell back onto the bed.

The next time he woke the nurse informed him he had a visitor and Flavio appeared around the door. As he pulled a chair close to the bed he said wretchedly,

"She's gone. I'm so sorry my friend but we've lost them both."

"I prayed for a different ending but deep down, I knew," Joseph answered emotionally.

The two friends hugged and when Joseph asked how he'd ended up in hospital, Flavio said,

"Well, when you didn't turn up for work for the first time ever, I drove to the house and Carla said she'd found you unconscious in bed and called the doctor who immediately had you transferred to hospital."

Flavio explained that two days later, a telegram had arrived from America informing him that both Gabriella and Antonio had perished in the freezing water of the Atlantic. He added grimly that their bodies had been recovered confirming their deaths.

"Next week if you are well enough, we have been asked to meet with their solicitors." Flavio looked wretched as he spoke, adding, "We must both face the real possibility that our association with Scalfaro's is at an end." He touched Joseph's arm. "After all you have done, the wonderful service you've given the company, I'm truly sorry but who could have predicted such a tragedy." Flavio sat thoughtfully before adding,

"As you know, Antonio had debts. To what extent I can't say, but I fear the situation is grim."

"Don't worry," Joseph answered, sounding more confident than he felt, "life has a way of putting us well and truly in our place." He then asked why they were meeting another lawyer when he was a lawyer himself.

"In the early days, Antonio and Gabriella tried to persuade me to become not only the Scalfaro's lawyer but also their family lawyer, but I felt it would be wrong. It could have led to a conflict of interest and might have jeopardised my friendship with them. If I'm honest it wasn't that hard a decision and I've never had cause to regret it."

The following Monday, Joseph was discharged from hospital but only if he agreed not to return to his office until the doctors gave him the all-clear. He agreed and decided his free time could be best used trying to resolve the thorny issue of what to do with his and his family's future without Scalfaro's in his life.

* * *

When Joseph and Flavio entered an impressive if rather ostentatious office and were asked to take a seat, Joseph saw twelve other people sat around an impressive oak desk. Behind it was a man who began by introducing himself as Giorgio Lanza before thanking everyone for arriving so promptly.

"As a result of the heartbreaking loss of Gabriella and Antonio Compagni, it is my sad duty, as the Compagni family representative, to execute their final instructions. I would like to add that Miss Gabriella was apprehensive about the journey and, just prior to their departure from Turin, persuaded her brother to record their instructions in the event of anything untoward happening. On March 5th therefore, they met here with my partner, Tommasco Rossi, and myself. During the meeting, which was documented and witnessed by Tommasco, Antonio became extremely exasperated with the formalities of our rather laborious legal system and stayed only at the insistence of his sister." There were smiles from those listening. "However, after half an hour he left, stating clearly and definitively in the presence of both myself and Tommasco, that as far as he was concerned the whole thing was a complete waste of time and that Gabriella could do whatever she liked with the assets of the company and family." Giorgio took a sip of his coffee before continuing. "I will now read through the instructions as I received them from Gabriella Compagni." Joseph listened as monies were donated to loyal workers and domestic staff whilst family items including paintings, jewellery, silverware, and cars were given to close friends, however, there was no mention of Joseph or Flavio. After an hour Giorgio said,

"That, ladies and gentlemen, completes the first part of the instructions. Thank you for your patience. Are there any questions?" Whist those gathered remained silent clearly overawed by Gabriella's generosity Joseph was mystified; why had Flavio and himself been called to attend when there had been no mention of either of them.

"No, then may I wish you all a very good day. Mr. Lotti and Mr. Aizenberg could I ask you to wait?"

"Gentlemen," Giorgio Lanza said after the others had departed, "I have asked you to stay as there are a number of additional clauses in Miss Gabriella's instructions." Joseph turned to Flavio who was looking at him with just the slightest of smiles.

"Mr. Lotti, Gabriella has left you the Compagni family home and all family assets apart from those included in the earlier instructions. She added one proviso; if you find any validity in Antonio's claim of a distant relative in the Americas, you should use your judgment on the rightful ownership of the family home. However, she was adamant that whatever the outcome in terms of ownership of the house, all possessions, financial, family and personal, should be passed to you." Flavio was clearly stunned.

"Miss Gabriella spent considerable time in wording the next instruction to make clear her conditions for the future of Scalfaro's." Joseph held his breath. "She felt certain Antonio would have told many friends of his displeasure with the way the company was being run and the future direction being planned. She therefore asked me to insert a clause in the instructions with reference to ownership of Scalfaro's which could not be legally challenged. Mr. Aizenberg; you will receive eighty percent of the full ownership of Scalfaro's and Mr. Lotti, twenty percent." Flavio turned and grabbed Joseph's hand and shook it. Joseph was shocked; of course Gabriella loved him, but to leave him control of the company and its future was far more than he could ever have dreamed of.

"There is a final instruction," Mr. Lanza added. "Miss Gabriella was insistent that all significant decisions should be made by both of you. She was clearly convinced that if you worked together, Scalfaro's would go from strength to strength. She also asked me to join you as an ex-officio advisor on the Board of Directors. Oh, and within this instruction she made the necessary financial arrangement. I hope you find this acceptable." Giorgio Lanza then rose to shake their hands.

"Gentlemen, these instructions may seem overly exact for someone as young as Gabriella but she was determined that if anything happened to her, you two should be protected. As it has turned out, her single-mindedness was sadly prophetic. Now, any questions?"

"Mr Lanza," Flavio said, "I was close to Antonio virtually from birth; we were like brothers. I hope you don't think this an imposition, but, well, he told me of considerable debts."

"Let me stop you," Giorgio interrupted. Quite deliberately, he then said, "You're right. Antonio was involved in a number of ventures which were not always as sound as he thought and at one time he had considerable debts. However, one enterprise involved the acquisition of real estate in the city of New York. This was a shrewd move. Apparently, because of concerns over the possibility of war, Europeans are looking to relocate to America, particularly New York, and property prices have risen substantially. In January this year, Antonio sold his property portfolio across the city at a considerable profit. This cleared all his debts and left sufficient capital to finance a number of new ventures."

*   *   *

The death of Gabriella was the most appalling loss Joseph had ever faced but he accepted that he needed to focus on whatever future awaited him. However, in his office he could feel her presence; when he walked the factory floors she still dominated his thoughts; every night when he went to bed he could smell her scent, could feel her touch.

The pain was constant yet Joseph accepted that in a matter of months he would welcome his family to their new lives and they had to come first. The thought of them arriving however, began overwhelming him to such an extent that he decided to talk to Flavio. Over lunch Flavio listened sympathetically and after some thought said,

"You should get away, go abroad, give yourself time to move on from Gabriella. You've been looking at businesses away from Italy so why not travel? What better way of taking your mind off the tragic events of the last few months than a new challenge.

Joseph agreed and relished the chance to lose himself in a new project. His family were not expected until August which would give him plenty of time to look at business opportunities.

*   *   *

On the 10th May 1912, Joseph left Turin, first travelling to Paris, then on to London, New York, Washington, Toronto and Quebec. In each city he searched for businesses with potential and opened banking facilities, transferring significant amounts of money from Italy.

He meticulously logged every transaction, every business opportunity as well as meetings he attended. He was invited to a variety of social functions and initially found these extremely difficult but accepted he had to make an effort. Every new acquaintance increased Joseph's contacts for the future; however, at night he lay awake thinking of Gabriella.

It was only during his time in Washington that the pain began to ease and the notion of welcoming his family to Turin was reignited. He realised he was actually excited at the prospect of seeing Elizabeth and his children again and he started making lists of things needed to ensure everything would be perfect on their arrival. Then, out of the blue, he made the decision to return to Yerevan to accompany them for the move to Turin.

*   *   *

After eighteen years, as he waited to cross into Armenia, Italian documents at the ready, Joseph felt exposed. Even accepting that the chances of being recognised were miniscule, there was still that nagging, immovable thought in his head that screamed beware!

When a border guard entered the carriage, Joseph's heart was thumping, however when the man asked the purpose of his visit to Yerevan and Joseph answered ‘business’, his documents were stamped with a friendly smile.

For five days he had travelled across Europe and the Middle East. The route was deliberately convoluted; the trains slow, dirty and uncomfortable, but he’d arrived and as the train moved out of the station Joseph watched enthralled as they entered the land of his birth.

* * *

Sat in the back of a dilapidated taxi, Joseph watched the city pass by and recognised very little. He felt like a stranger and had to admit he was.

In his last letter to Elizabeth which he had sent from Turin Joseph still didn’t mention that he was travelling to meet them. He wanted it to be a surprise. He merely told the family he’d made all the necessary arrangements and they should to be packed and ready to leave on August 14th.

As the taxi climbed towards the Kong district, Joseph saw the sprawling city on one side and the River Hrazdan on the other. He had forgotten how stunning the views were. Then excitedly, he saw the house and told the taxi driver to wait. He stared up at the building as he walked slowly along the short path to the front door. Deciding not to knock, he flicked the catch and pushed but the door was stuck. Confused, Joseph walked around to the back to find no signs of life.

The house was deserted and he had absolutely no idea where his family could be. His only option was to visit Elizabeth’s family who lived in Echmiadzin but as he was about to return to the taxi, Joseph saw an old man walking towards him. There was something familiar about his gait and as he got nearer Joseph recognised Tomas his neighbour.

"How are you?" Joseph asked smiling and suddenly an enormous grin appeared on Tomas's face as he recognised his old friend. He hugged Joseph before insisting he join him and his wife Tatiana for a drink. Sat by the fire, catching up with each other's lives, Tomas's face dropped,

"You don't know," he said quietly.

'Don't know what?" Joseph answered, suddenly concerned.

"I thought that's why you were here."

"Thomas, what is it?"

Tatiana told Joseph that early in May Elizabeth had been taken ill.

"She was the perfect mother, caring for her family but she never looked after herself," she said sadly. "By the time the doctor was called, it was too late."

"Joseph, she died the next day," Tomas said quietly as Tatiana cried and Joseph sat numb with shock. "Her funeral was three days later and over fifty people attended."

Joseph was overwhelmed. For eighteen years Elizabeth had waited, bringing up his children on her own and just when everything was coming together she…

When Tomas explained that his children were with Elizabeth's family in Echmiadzin, Joseph excused himself and left.

* * *

Joseph first visited Elizabeth's parents and found them both frail and angry. When they realised who he was, her father told Joseph ingenuously that with the recent death of his daughter he had little interest in either him or his plans. As Joseph tried to talk to them his mother-in-law said that the thought of losing the children was tearing them apart so he left knowing that to remain would have only caused greater heartache. He was close to tears as he walked the hundred metres to where Elizabeth's oldest brother lived.

After the initial shock at seeing his brother-in-law, Saul invited Joseph in and explained that the children were saying goodbye to people in the area.

"They're telling life-long friends they are being forced to leave, forced to go to Italy and will never return." Joseph was stunned with Saul's overt animosity and as he tried to explain quickly realised it was pointless. Saul made no effort to hide his resentment so in the end Joseph said,

"Why don't you just say what you feel." For the next fifteen minutes Joseph listened with sadness and growing annoyance as Saul lambasted him. He demanded to know why Joseph had deserted his family and made no effort to visit them, how Joseph was seen by everyone as a man who easily justified his own 'comfortable' lifestyle whilst his family lived on little and how sending money could never make up for his absence. He also accused him of taking the children away from everything and everyone they had ever known for his own selfish purposes. Then, most hurtful of all, how Joseph had left his sister to bring up their family on her own with no help from the one person she believed would always be there.

Joseph sat patiently and listened but inside he was becoming more and more incensed. Saul's rage was entirely unfair but how could he ever explain the pain and hardship he'd suffered over the years of travelling. The loneliness, fear, poverty and acute sadness he felt at being cut-off from his family. Joseph accepted the marked contrast between his lifestyle and that of Elizabeth but he'd worked hard seven days a week, year after year to achieve it and he would apologise to no one for that success. He refused to be embarrassed by his wealth and, under no circumstances, would he allow Saul's bigotry to affect his reunion with the children.

When he finally heard the family returning, Joseph said unequivocally,

"You are family and therefore I have listened but do not believe for one minute that I accept what you are saying. On the contrary, it makes me sad to think that Elizabeth may have felt the same way and I can only hope she understood me a good deal better than you do. I will be taking the children because unlike you, I have seen what the world has to offer the young. I can make a valid judgement about what is best for them and I know I can provide a life that is very different and in my opinion far more inspiring than anything they could possibly have here." Joseph stood and leaned across the table, placed a wad of local currency in front of his brother-in-law and added,

"Please visit us at any time. I will send the cost of your fare. Come and see us and then make the same criticisms you make of me now," but he knew he would never see Saul again.

* * *

Sitting with his children in the lounge at Hayastan, Joseph smiled. He'd always thought of them as children for the last time he had seen them they had been. Emil, the oldest was twenty-three and a head taller than Joseph, Howard was twenty-two, Barbara twenty and Golda, the baby, eighteen. All four had inherited the dark, brooding but striking looks from their mother's Azerbaijani heritage and were such a credit to her.

Sipping wine, listening to the sheer joy radiating from the siblings, Joseph remembered how fearful he had been when they had returned noisily to Saul's house. He had no idea what to expect and was taken aback and more than a little intimidated by how grown up they were. Of course, he quickly discovered those feelings were reciprocated. No one had told them their father would be there to take them away. Once the initial shock had faded and after he had offered his hand to his sons and arms to his daughters to hug, their reaction had been simply wonderful. It was at that moment Joseph knew whatever Saul might have said, Elizabeth had done right by him.

He laughed as he remembered the confusion over which language they should speak and then to Saul's obvious disappointment, they all started talking together in English or Italian asking their father question after question. Joseph looked at his children with such pride when he recalled the way they had been so accepting of him and since that moment the laughter and joy had hardly stopped apart from when they finally went to sleep.

Of course there had been poignant moments especially when they spoke of their mother and how much they all missed her but that never seemed to detract from the enthusiasm they had for the future that awaited them.

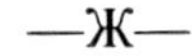

Chapter 10

1939-1943

As days moved into weeks and weeks into months, the excitement surrounding Tova's return faded to be replaced by increasing resentment as the family remained under house arrest. With so much time on their hands Ellen worked hard on her Italian using old newspapers and magazines to help but often had to ask her Auntie Marguerita, Simon or Carla to explain some detail. She also realised that if they were to be confined to the cottage her love of sport, especially swimming, would suffer. She had always been proud of her fitness; she could outrun, out-swim and out-jump not only all her friends but competitors in other schools. She was determined to stay fit and designed a daily schedule of at least one hour of exercise, even though it meant disturbing anyone who was in her way. She ran up and down the stairs, worked on her strength in the kitchen, her suppleness in the lounge and drove everyone to distraction.

Flavio often visited, bringing food and other small gifts he hoped would make their lives a little more bearable but was never able to give them any positive information about Howard or their own situation. On one occasion, he told Tova and Marguerita in frustration that whenever he spoke to anyone in authority, it was as if the Aizenbergs no longer existed. He added that he was invariably warned off asking questions.

In the end the two mothers became so worried about the children being cooped up they agreed that during the day the lounge would become a classroom. Yet again Marguerita asked Flavio for help. He spoke to a local teacher who found a variety of school books for Simon and Leon and an English teacher to see if she was able to provide books for Ellen and Noah. Tova also suggested that everyone spoke English and Italian on alternate days.

*   *   *

Throughout 1939, Carla would often return from trips into Turin with disturbing stories of Jewish persecution and harassment. It was quite clear that after twenty years as leader of the Fascists, Benito Mussolini was determined to fulfil his promise to rid Italy of Jews. For Ellen who had never been judged on her faith only her abilities, it was beyond belief that members of her religion should either be thought of as all the same or despised in equal measure and she began to read everything she could about the Italian leader. She was determined to find out what had caused Mussolini's hatred of Jews and on one of Flavio's visits, she asked if he could explain something to her. She went through a list of questions and although initially amused, Flavio realised Ellen was an extraordinary young lady. Not only was he impressed by her tenacity but also her intellect and quickness of thought. He found it difficult to believe she was so young.

Following her talk with Flavio, Ellen searched for information on Italian politics and her mother and aunt marvelled at her appetite for facts alongside her understanding of the European political landscape.

Whenever Flavio visited, Ellen did her best to monopolise him and he quickly realised there was a limit on how much he could help her. After some thought and a significant bribe, Flavio smuggled a radio into the cottage and much to the annoyance of the others, Ellen spent hours listening to anything to do with Italian politics and Benito Mussolini. She became obsessed with understanding how one man was able to manipulate and ultimately crush an entire nation.

* * *

Although he had been around the Italian political scene for many years, Mussolini's true rise to power began on October 22nd 1922 and the 'March on Rome' when his private army, known as the Blackshirts, threatened the King with civil war unless they were handed power. The Prime Minister, Luigi Facta, wanted to confront them but Mussolini gambled that under such extreme pressure the king would concede and he was proved correct. Even allowing for the fact that Senor Facta was the country's most powerful politician, King Victor Emmanuel III feared such a confrontation would lead to unprecedented violence on the streets and eventually withdrew his support for the Prime Minister. Facta had no option but to resign and the resulting power vacuum left the appointment of Mussolini as the nation's leader a formality.

"How was it that no one saw the danger of giving control to a man who won his power with threats?" Ellen asked Flavio and he had to admit he had no answer. As she continued to question the King's sanity he explained,

"As soon as Mussolini was named Italy's leader he declared himself Minister of Foreign Affairs and Minister of the Interior, giving him absolute control of police and local government. His power base became immediately indestructible."

"But why did the people allow it?" Ellen asked and for the first time Flavio witnessed a naivety in her thinking.

"Well, things changed at such a pace that by the time the general public knew what was happening it was too late. Even though the Fascists had a minority in the government, Mussolini or as he became, Il Duce, was still able to establish his absolute rule over the nation and he proceeded to drag Italians kicking and screaming into one the darkest periods of their history."

* * *

By 1939, rumours began to circulate that the Italian Government was setting up internment camps for both foreign and Italian Jews. Many saw this as inevitable following a meeting between Mussolini and the German leader, Adolf Hitler, when the two countries signed the Rome-Berlin Axis.

As Flavio continued to be the eyes and ears for the Aizenberg family, he told Tova and Marguerita that not only was war in Europe imminent but Italy would definitely side with the Germans. When Tova asked about the rumours of internment camps, he answered candidly.

"Well, I have heard that the Government are requisitioning empty buildings such as villas and movie houses with the intention of holding Jews. Apparently, Mussolini is planning to build at least twenty-five camps; the first is in the South and near completion. It's to be called Ferramonti di Tarsia and will hold three and a half thousand Jews." Tova looked shocked as she said thoughtfully,

"Simon was right; they're using Hayastan as a holding camp for Jewish families."

*   *   *

Life for the family changed little until June 11th 1940 when Mussolini declared war on the Allies. Tova was devastated by the declaration as all Allied diplomatic services in Italy were immediately suspended. She'd always clung to the hope that British diplomats would eventually come good, secure Howard's release and arrange for their safe return home. That dream ended with the Italian leader's belligerence.

Three weeks later on Simon's eighteenth birthday soldiers arrived unexpectedly at the cottage. The officer in charge seemed pleasant, even understanding, as he told them his orders were to arrest Simon. He explained that a Ministry of Interior directive stated that all German, Polish, Czechoslovakian and other stateless Jews between the ages of eighteen and sixty should be arrested. When Marguerita asked why that applied to Simon as an Italian national, the man replied,

"All Jews, including those with Italian citizenship, are no longer eligible for Military Service and as such, may prove a threat to the state. They must therefore be held in secure camps to guarantee the safety of the Italian people."

Before climbing into the back of the lorry, a terrified Simon kissed his mother and brother and promised to write every week. Ellen, with tears flowing, watched her cousin being taken away and wondered whether they would ever see each other again.

*   *   *

Little changed until November '42 which saw Ellen's sixteenth birthday. Although it was hardly a day for celebration as the family had been held prisoner for five years; five long years for being in the wrong place at the wrong time.

One week after Ellen's birthday, Flavio's finally brought them some welcome news.

"I've learnt that Simon is being held in the Montechiarugolo Internment Camp," he told them whilst producing three envelopes from inside his jacket and passing them to Marguerita. "These are from him." The family sat excitedly around the lounge fire whilst Marguerita read the letters out loud.

Simon said that considering the circumstances his life was reasonable, adding that the food was fine but nowhere nearly as delicious as Carla's. He was getting on well with the others in his hut and apart from missing everyone he felt he was lucky to be where he was. He'd heard rumours of Jews being treated terribly in other camps whilst others had been taken away never to be seen again.

* * *

As usual Ellen was sitting at her favourite window with a book when she noticed two adults and two children running across the back of the garden. Suddenly she heard shots and watched horrified as all four fell to the ground. She was inconsolable watching in disbelief as the children's tiny bodies twitched and bled, their eyes pleading, their mouths screaming in agony.

It was not until the next morning that the lifeless bodies were finally removed. As Ellen watched the soldiers at work, she saw frightened, wary faces peering out of the windows of the main house and asked herself whether they were just like her; innocent people unable to grasp the world around them as their families were torn apart.

*   *   *

Early one morning as the family members were eating what had become a very basic breakfast of bread, cheese and a little home grown fruit, Ellen heard a vehicle approaching. The family went to the window and watched as a lorry passed the back entrance of Hayastan and stopped outside their front door. The rear flap of the lorry was raised and an old, bedraggled man with a bundle of rags was pushed out. Ellen screamed; it was her father!

Sadly, what followed was not the joyous reunion they had all prayed for. Of course they were ecstatic however the man returned to them was not the Howard they knew but a mentally, emotionally and physically shattered imitation of their father and husband.

Without delay and much to the disappointment of Ellen and Noah, Tova and Marguerita immediately carried Howard up to the bedroom. Both were inconsolable as they stripped him and saw his emaciated, battered body, before gently laying him on the bed. Within seconds Howard was fast asleep. He'd not spoken or displayed any reactions; it was as if his past life had been stolen from him.

Over the following days, Carla, Tova and Marguerita sat with Howard in rotation making sure an adult was always with him. Ellen also sat in the bedroom just watching her father but there was never any change.

Immediately Flavio heard the news, he visited the cottage and was incredulous when he saw Howard's condition and left promising to speak to a doctor friend to see if he could help. Even a considerable bribe however, could not persuade the guards to let a doctor visit.

On the fourth day after his return Howard finally woke. He was completely disorientated, very shaken and weak, but after a bowl of soup and bread administered by Tova, he began to mumble a few words. He slowly regained his strength and became more coherent but it was evident he retained little or no memory of his imprisonment. Every evening, after Noah had gone to bed, Ellen spent hours with her father telling him all that had happened since he'd been taken away but could never persuade him to tell her of his own experiences.

Six weeks after his return, when the children were in bed, Howard asked Tova, Marguerita and Carla to sit with him and after thanking them for getting him back on his feet, he tentatively began to describe what had happened.

"My memory is a mess but from what I can remember, I was arrested because the secret police believe our family has been involved in an illegal anti-government movement." Marguerita was clearly devastated and Tova held her hand.

"I'm so sorry Marguerita but I think it's best if I'm completely honest." Howard understood her pain but knew it was the only way to come to terms with why they had been targeted.

"It became clear when I was being questioned that they believe Papa Joseph and Emil were not only members of the group but its leaders." As Marguerita wept, Howard went on to describe being tortured although he kept the details to a minimum. There was a limit to how much the three ladies could handle but he had to continue if he was to explain why the authorities had been so determined to establish what he knew.

"At one moment I remember being told that this group had tried unsuccessfully to assassinate Mussolini.

The man wasn't specific but he said it was in the mid 1930s. They gave me no further information except," Howard hesitated before adding determinedly, "and I remember his exact words; he said, all known members of the group have been removed from causing further problems." There was complete silence whilst the three women digested Howard's words before Tova very quietly asked,

"So you're saying Papa Joseph and Emil were murdered by the secret police."

Marguerita rose and returned with a letter. She passed it to Howard.

"When I returned from Switzerland this had been left for me," she said sadly as Howard began to read and the more he read the angrier he became.

*　　*　　*

Over the next few months and into the start of 1943, Howard and Flavio became extremely close. Flavio visited regularly, usually in the evening and always with a bottle of something. It was on one of these visits that Howard asked, more out of interest than anything else, why the family had been allowed to stay in the cottage rather than being taken away like so many other Jewish families. When Flavio hesitated, Howard asked again and Flavio explained that before the war he had been close to a senior officer in the Turin police.

"Once I realised that Mussolini was going to target Jews, for a monthly retainer I arranged with him that nothing would happen to your family." Howard, stunned, asked how much but Flavio refused to discuss it. He added obviously trying to pacify his friend that it was the same man he'd had asked to help when Howard had been arrested but he was unable to do anything without raising suspicions.

The two men also spent many evenings discussing the war. Battles were raging not only in Europe but also across Africa and Asia and for Italy, things could not have gone more disastrously wrong. Flavio explained that the Italian army was completely unprepared when Mussolini initially declared war and it meant the country was unable to protect its colonies. It was so serious, he said, that German soldiers ended up replacing the Italian army across North Africa and Greece causing serious problems for Il Duce.

"You see, almost from the onset of war, it was inevitable that Italy would face a humiliating defeat."

*   *   *

It was obvious during the early months of 1943 that the war was creating immense hardship across the whole country. Food rationing alongside the Allied bombing of Italy's industrial cities, especially Turin, was bringing the country to its knees and the people were becoming ever more confrontational. The anti-Fascist left were gaining support which manifested itself through a series of critically damaging strikes throughout the industrial north beginning in the Turin Fiat factories. In total over one hundred thousand workers took to the streets bringing Italy's war production to a standstill and rumours flooded the country that the people were ready to bring down the government.

However, Italians could not believe it when in July 1943 the Allies successfully invaded Sicily. They acknowledged that this would lead to a full-scale offensive on the Italian mainland and this came to fruition on the 3rd September.

King Victor Emmanuel III and senior members of the military recognised public disaffection was dangerously high and that Mussolini had lost control. Many even questioned his sanity and he was arrested. Secret negotiations with the Allies began whilst the government publicly proclaimed that alongside Germany, the war was still winnable.

In September 1943 an Armistice was finally signed between Italy and the Allies and Flavio visited the cottage with the news. For the first time in many years, Ellen dared to believe they might be able to return home.

* * *

Flavio's regular visits continued and he told Howard, with great optimism that heavy reinforcements for the Americans at Salerno and the British at Taranto were arriving daily. It was said that the Allies were pushing northwards. Towards the end of that month Flavio had further good news.

"You know, the more I hear the more certain I am that Italy will quickly fall. Apparently the Allies have landed a force of nearly 200,000 men and 30,000 vehicles which are moving towards the Germans."

However, Flavio's confidence proved premature. As September moved into October, information on the Allies' progress northwards became sketchy and on one of his visits he spoke to Howard out of earshot of the rest of the family.

"A policeman I know from Rome visited Turin yesterday and he told me that the news from the south is troubling." Howard sank into his seat.

"He's heard that the Germans have decided to face the Allies just north of Naples and have created a defensive barrier called the Gustav Line."

"But the Allies are on top," Howard said, distraught with the news, "and all those reinforcements." Unfortunately Flavio still had further ominous news.

"Yesterday, I saw a huge convoy of German troops arriving in the city centre and word is out that they have reinforced all cities in the north and intend to stay and fight."

After Flavio had left, Howard sat alone realising he would have to break the news to the rest of the family; he just didn't know how.

In the end however, the decision was taken from him as early the following morning, the family stood at the windows of the cottage watching lorry after lorry arrive at the main house.

Initially, families who were housed in Hayastan were loaded up and Ellen cried as she watched children being thrown onto the trucks. They were only a small part of Ellen's life but somehow, when she saw them each day they offered continuity and stability which helped her face the never ending nightmare they were living.

The activity at the main house went on for the next three days as hundreds of packing cases, furniture and office equipment arrived. The family debated and argued as to what was going on but in truth, they were extremely frightened by what they had witnessed.

* * *

Flavio visited next on the morning of October 30th. He arrived at the back door covered in mud, didn't knock and was extremely tense.

As he sat in the kitchen with the adults, the children were sent upstairs.

"I am sorry to barge in this way," he began, "it appears my police contact as well as myself have become persona non-grata with the secret police." He looked around the table and smiled gently at the shocked look on their faces. "You have all become my family and, dare I say, your affection has meant a great deal but even so, I must tell you what is happening." Tova held Howard's hand.

"Before I do however, I want to say that as far as Scalfaro's is concerned, whatever happens, the ownership of the company will return to your family. We all understand that it's in my name at present because of the anti-Jewish legislation but when things improve, and I am certain they will, Scalfaro's will once again be yours. In the meantime I have put a manager in place who will keep the factories ticking over. He is trustworthy and aware of the situation." Flavio stopped and asked for a glass of water which he drank thirstily.

"Now, what I have to say is dreadful but say it I must, so you have a choice. Last week rumours spread that the Germans were hunting down Jews throughout northern Italy. The majority of Italians never agreed with Mussolini's anti-Semitic propaganda and they are sheltering thousands of Jews. The Germans have made it clear that they will find them." The four adults held hands terrified by Flavio's words.

"And are they succeeding?" Howard asked quietly.

"Around Rome, yes, and that brings me to why I had to see you before I leave." The others around the table looked at each other when Flavio used the word 'leave'. "A few days ago the friend I told you about from the Rome police was asked to attend a meeting with his boss and senior German officers. He wanted me to know what was discussed and felt it was so important that he drove from his home late last night to see me." With shaking hands Flavio took another sip of water. "He said the Germans stated that all those being held in the Internment Camps were to be transported out of Italy and the first trainload of Jews; over a thousand men, woman and children had arrived at Auschwitz, one of their concentration camps in Poland. He knows of our friendship and wanted to warn you. He also needed to tell me that I am now on a high priority list of those to be arrested and I must leave immediately." Those around the table were devastated; not only was their situation desperate but their one true friend had to disappear.

Howard called the children to say goodbye to Flavio and gave him contact addresses of his sisters and their families in America and Canada.

As he walked away, Flavio promised to stay in touch, but all knew it was doubtful they'd be able to. Ellen watched through tears as Flavio walked out into the darkness; yet another wonderful friend was leaving her life.

* * *

The next day during lunch there was much talk about Flavio and his reasons for leaving but Ellen knew the children would never be told the whole truth. As they were clearing away the plates there was a knock at the front door and Carla went to answer it. When she returned she was with three German soldiers and with no preamble, one of the men said,

"This house is being requisitioned by the German military command. You will be collected in one hour. You must take nothing except a small bundle of clothes each." Before Howard could reply, the men walked out leaving him and the family shocked; it was the very last thing any of them wanted to hear.

He quickly realised their most prized possessions could not be taken and with Carla's agreement he placed two heavy metal boxes under the floorboards in the front room. Scalfaro's contracts, ownership documents for the houses and estate, jewellery, money, and after some considerable pleading, Ellen's copious notebooks were all stuffed into the hidey hole, alongside a hastily written note to Flavio Lotti. Finally Marguerita asked Howard to place Emil's letter with the other valuables.

Exactly one hour later, an army truck arrived and the family were bundled into the back escorted by four soldiers. As Carla moved to join them, she was pushed spitefully away and told she was Italian and would not be going.

There was no time for goodbyes, just tears and fear and as they drove away, Ellen looked back and saw Carla crying and waving. Five years of her life; all those magical moments of laughter, the love that had come from being cooped up all day every day, the friendship that had grown with her cousins and auntie, the joy on seeing her father and mother alive. As she watched the cottage disappear an overwhelming sense of melancholy flooded Ellen's emotions.

* * *

They had travelled for what seemed like an hour when the lorry came to a halt and they were ordered out. As Ellen landed on the ground, she looked around and noticed they were in a storage yard. They were told by their guards to follow and a few minutes later they joined a group of adults and children waiting by the side of a railway track. All were empty-handed apart from small bundles and no one spoke; no one was allowed to speak.

Ellen was shivering. It wasn't cold, she was just terrified and she held her father's hand tightly as a feeling of growing trepidation crept over her. She refused to let the tears come. She then heard a loud whistle and watched as a slow-moving train appeared. It came to a clanking stop next to them and a guard opened the doors of a cattle truck and told them to get in.

Ellen's family was at the back of the queue waiting to board and she watched as a child dropped his bundle whilst climbing up. His toys fell to the ground and as he tried to scramble back down to retrieve them, an officer drew his pistol and screamed at the mother to hold him. When the father, who still had to board tried to explain it was just a few toys, the officer struck him viciously across the face with the butt of the gun. The man collapsed on the ground, blood oozing from a deep gash on his cheek and three guards grabbed hold of him and threw him into the truck.

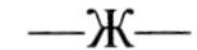

Chapter 11

1912-1915

From the moment they arrived at Hayastan, the four Aizenberg siblings appeared determined to live their lives with no regrets. On many occasions Joseph had heard them discussing their sadness at leaving the resting place of their mother and their village, but they also seemed genuinely appreciative of the wonderful opportunity being offered to them. As he studied his 'new' family, he noticed that every time one of his children felt sad or was missing home, the others would rally around, reminding them of how incredibly fortunate they were compared to the friends they'd left behind.

Although they had studied hard on their languages, all four struggled with colloquial Italian, however, even this appeared a minor concern and they laughed with each other over mistakes they made. There was also the small matter of Joseph's decision to use English at Hayastan and again the siblings simply took it in their stride, especially loving the hilarious moments that would arise when Carla and Umberto joined in.

Flavio Lotti, who simply found all four delightful company, was far more aware of the social scene in Turin than their father and introduced them to places and people that would help them adjust to the extraordinary changes going on in their lives.

* * *

A month after their arrival, Joseph felt it was time his family began working for their future. He talked through work experience he'd arranged and all four seemed genuinely excited, if a little daunted, by what lay ahead.

At the start of the following week Emil and Howard were based in the Scalfaro's factories, whilst Barbara and Golda worked in various positions at the offices and cafés. Wanting them to become knowledgeable in all areas of the company, Joseph arranged for them to start at the very bottom of the company ladder, learning the trade from experienced employees. For the following fifteen months up to the end of 1913, he set out to teach them as much as he could about the business.

* * *

In the years leading up to the arrival of his family, Joseph's entire life had been focused on the company and his relationship with Gabriella and it wasn't until Autumn 1913 that he grudgingly accepted he had been extremely naïve in not listening to the advice of friends. Relationships between European nations had continued to deteriorate at an alarming rate but it was only once his family arrived that the prospect of war became too real to ignore.

Even accepting the majority view of his friends that when war was declared, Italy would remain neutral, the last thing Joseph needed was his children to be somehow dragged into a conflict. As a result, early in December, he told them they were taking a holiday as a reward for the wonderful start they'd made in Turin.

They left Turin on December 7th for Paris and Joseph planned to retrace the journey he had taken prior to the children's arrival; he especially wanted to follow up on a number of business opportunities. After a few days in the French capital they moved on to London, then New York, Washington, Toronto, and finally

Quebec. In total, the family was away for ten weeks and once again Joseph marvelled at the ease with which his children faced all challenges. They appeared to love every moment of the journey even if they were somewhat overwhelmed by the complex, bustling world they faced.

In each city, Joseph met up with those who had been so welcoming on his previous trip and continued to explore businesses possibilities. He still preferred not to discuss his ideas with his children until he had finalised possible ventures, however he was acutely aware that with the rapidly deteriorating political climate across Europe, any final decision on when to speak to them was likely to be taken out of his hands.

*   *   *

The excuse the confrontational European leaders had been desperate for occurred on 28th July 1914 when a Serbian national shot and killed the heir apparent to the Austrian throne, Archduke Franz Ferdinand and his wife. In response, Austria immediately declared war on Serbia which was followed within days by Russia declaring war on Austria, Germany on Russia and France and Britain on Germany. At a speed no one could have anticipated, the European conflict snowballed out of control and much of the rest of the world was dragged into fighting within months.

The one consolation for Joseph was that as his friends had predicted, Italy declared its neutrality which gave him time to get his family out. With the help of contacts, three days after the onset of war, Joseph booked berths on a cargo ship bound for New York via Lisbon. Emil however, refused to leave. He'd decided to remain in Turin and carry on working at Scalfaro's and although this resulted in the first serious disagreement between father and eldest son, as Flavio was also staying, Joseph had little option but to agree. His initial concern was also eased after Carla and Umberto said they would remain to look after Emil.

Joseph loathed the thought of splitting his family again and was struggling to understand Emil's decision; that was until Flavio, who with just a touch of irony, explained that it might not have been just his loyalty to Scalfaro's that kept Emil in Turin. When Joseph looked utterly mystified, Flavio chuckled.

"Have you really failed to notice the growing fondness between your son and a certain young lady?" Joseph had to admit he'd failed to notice anything but then it suddenly came to him and he stuttered in confusion,

"You don't mean, David Bernstein's daughter, Marguerita?"

*   *   *

War led to a production boom in the industrial north of neutral Italy, especially in Turin with its car-manufacturing factories, resulting rather surprisingly, in a demand for luxury items including chocolate. As a consequence, Scalfaro's turnover and resulting profits rose rapidly.

It soon became clear that the decision to declare its neutrality created deep divisions within the Italian public. This was exacerbated by powerful voices in the government. They played on the pride of Italians by declaring that there would never be a better time to retake Trentino and Trieste, two relatively insignificant territories lost to Austria fifty years earlier. Following secret meetings with the Allies resulting in a pact giving Italy not only control over most of Trentino and Trieste but also a share in any break up of German colonies, it was unsurprising when Italy declared war on Austria on the 26th April 1915.

The most outspoken advocate of war with Austria, and therefore the person to gain most from the declaration, was a socialist agitator named Benito Mussolini. Being both shrewd and single-minded, he saw the public division over neutrality as a God-sent political opportunity and he used the moment to begin building an almost indestructible political reputation.

* * *

Following on from their arrival in New York it took over three weeks for Howard, Barbara and Golda to find work in Washington. Joseph had arranged somewhere for them to live and opened bank accounts for each of them. Once satisfied he'd done everything possible to get them started, with great sadness he left them and returned to Turin.

He arrived back in Italy on the 22nd September 1915 and as the hardship of war began to take its toll on Italian families, Joseph struggled to keep the company on a sound footing. Production slowed to a near standstill with just a skeleton workforce providing chocolate products for the wealthy and German military who seemed able to afford anything. The three cafés remained open but again with a skeleton staff, a few loyal customers and the military.

Early in 1916, eighteen months after the outbreak of war and six months after Italy had declared war on Austria, Joseph finally persuaded Emil to travel to America. Marguerita and her family left Turin to escape the conflict and as the company was continuing to struggle, Emil agreed to visit his siblings. Although ridiculously overpriced, Joseph managed to book berths on a ship out of Naples and father and son left Italy on the 7th February 1916.

Travelling via Lisbon and Rio de Janeiro, they arrived in Washington to the most wonderful reunion. On the first evening they were taken to a small, homely, Italian restaurant, one of the very first to be opened in Washington and throughout the meal Joseph had the feeling their table was being treated differently by the staff. It was only over coffee that Howard, with an enormous grin, told his father that the three siblings owned the restaurant. Emil couldn't believe it as Barbara explained,

"At the start whenever we wrote, we told you we were happy, but we weren't." She smiled guiltily, "So three months after you left we decided to do something about it."

"We moved out of our flat and into the one upstairs,' Golda said excitedly as she pointed at the ceiling. "It's pretty horrible but we agreed not to spend the money you gave us on ourselves but on this place." All three were laughing as both Emil and Joseph looked disbelievingly around the restaurant.

"But who cooks?" Emil asked incredulously. It was clearly obvious he'd decided that there was no way, especially without him, his brother and sisters could have organised anything.

"Well, we got the idea from an Italian friend called Joshua," Howard answered. "As he was struggling to find work we agreed to join forces. We had your money; he was a chef. Since we opened, Barbara and Golda have run the restaurant, whilst at the same time Joshua is teaching them to cook. I do the finances and administrative side of things. We're not making any profit but we're managing and we love what we're doing." Howard smiled at his sisters whilst Joseph sat absolutely flabbergasted. His children were remarkable and once again he wished Elizabeth could see her family so united and at ease with their lives.

*   *   *

Leaving Washington was once again heart-wrenching but Joseph faced problems at Scalfaro's he couldn't ignore. There were also two other factors crucial to his departure. Firstly, the Jewish community in Turin had always supported him asking nothing in return and as the months of war passed he'd witnessed many of these same families being stripped of their livelihoods and he wanted to help them.

Secondly, in all the years he'd been away, Armenia had never been far from his thoughts but it was only after he spoke to Eric Manoukian that he realised how appalling life had become for those he had left behind.

"What I'm hearing is pretty alarming," his friend told him over a meal one evening in June. "Even with the new Young Turks Government replacing the Sultan, life is no better."

Joseph asked why, remembering how optimistic Elizabeth had sounded in her letters but when he mentioned this to Eric, the answer was not unexpected.

"Oh come on Joseph, we have always been hated and despised across the whole region. Just think about the things you encountered when you worked for the government."

"But I assumed the Young Turks would at least make things more bearable for the people."

"The problem is that the Young Turks were Ottoman Officers in the Turkish Third Army and they were the ones who staged the coup to remove Sultan Abdul Hamid."

"But if they fought against the Sultan surely that's got to be good for Armenia."

"Well, it should have been but there was a countercoup by supporters of the Sultan and the Ottoman Army was sent in to remove them from power. However, the soldiers ignored the order and instead, slaughtered thirty thousand Armenians. The Young Turks survived and that was supposed to be an end to it." Eric took a long drink before continuing.

"Then, what should have been a period of calm was anything but. As a result of the 1912 Balkans conflict, which Armenia avoided, as many as three quarters of a million Muslim refugees were expelled from their homes and ended up living amongst Armenians. It was only a matter of time before problems started, especially as they clearly began to resent the relative home comforts of their Armenian neighbours."

"Where on earth did you get all this information from?" Joseph asked.

"Have you forgotten? I had a brother who until he was forced to retire, was high up in the Ottoman military.

Anyway, things really deteriorated when the European war began. The Young Turks claimed that Armenians were fighting alongside Russia and you know how much the Turks loathe the Russians. They even blamed Armenian volunteers for the humiliating defeat suffered in the Battle of Sarikamish and I was told because of it, thousands of Armenians in the Ottoman Army were executed to stop them collaborating with the Russians. In effect they were put to death by their friends on orders from their own officers.

"That's scandalous," Joseph said, struggling to come to terms with what he was hearing.

"Believe me, there have been endless acts of brutality against Armenians. The siege of Van for example, when the locals were accused of treason.

Initially they refused to give up their young men for execution and had to accept food from the Russians to survive. This resulted in the Ottomans declaring war on Armenians everywhere and one general stated that this legalized the persecution of all ethnic Armenians." Joseph could see Eric's anger mounting as he spoke.

"You want more proof? How about the witness who saw over five thousand Armenians being burnt alive at the hands of the Ottoman military, or last year when the Italian consul in Trabzon, Giacomo Gorrini witnessed thousands of women and children being loaded on boats and taken out into the Black Sea where they were deliberately drowned. How many more examples does the world need because I've got plenty? The villagers who were rounded up and burnt, children killed with morphine injections, toxic gas used to murder Armenians; oh, and even I can hardly credit this one; Armenians held in camps waiting for deportation being injected with the blood from typhoid fever patients. The list goes on as does the bloodshed." Eric took a deep breath and sat quietly drinking his wine waiting for Joseph to say something but he remained silent.

"It got so unacceptable last year," Eric eventually continued, "that the Ottomans were told by the international community that all Government ministers would be held personally responsible for crimes against humanity." Joseph shook his head in disbelief.

"How much worse can it get?" he said.

"Well, assuming my information is correct then a whole lot. In August last year in response to the so called Death Marches, when Armenians living in Ottoman territories were deported on foot, a New York Times article stated that, 'the roads and Euphrates are strewn with the corpses of exiles,' concluding with, 'the plan is to exterminate the entire Armenian people'.

Just a few weeks after that article, the Ottoman parliament passed the 'Temporary Law of Expropriation and Confiscation' stating that all property including land, livestock, and homes belonging to Armenians were to be confiscated and held by the authorities. Joseph, the Turks are hell-bent on destroying Armenia and eradicating Armenians from the face of the earth!

*   *   *

It took many days for Joseph to come to terms with the information Eric had given him. His moods swung from extreme guilt, especially for Elizabeth's family and the friends he had left behind, to anger at the brutal, inhumane treatment of Armenians, to utter hate for all those in positions of power. They simply used power to persecute, control and ultimately destroy those who got in their way and Joseph vowed to do everything he could to help the survivors of the ethnic cleansing of his homeland.

*   *   *

Over the following week, Joseph set out his priorities. First and foremost he would ensure all Scalfaro's employees who had been laid off due to the decline in demand for chocolate, were supported. Next, he would open a help centre for the poorest members of the Jewish community in the city and finally, he would set up an escape route out of Armenia for Jews.

As Joseph talked through his plans, Flavio marvelled at the compassion of his friend. With all his problems; his family far away in America, having to lay off workers and the fact that they were living the horrors of war on a daily basis, it appeared Joseph's only thoughts were for those less fortunate than himself.

Of course, Flavio fell into the trap set by Joseph lock, stock and barrel; he simply couldn't refuse to be part of his friend's ambitious plans.

Over the next few days, they transferred much of the company's assets into gold, jewellery and cash, both recognising that it was only a matter of time before the Italian government took control of the banking system. Once that happened, it was likely all significant deposits would be scrutinised by the authorities and become vulnerable.

Then, wanting to ensure that as soon as the war ended Scalfaro's was in a position to begin production immediately, Joseph and Flavio updated all documentation necessary to guarantee the ownership of Scalfaro's continued within the Aizenberg family. It was actually Flavio who insisted on this. He had no family of his own and if anything should happen to either of them, he wanted all the formalities completed to prevent any illegal takeovers whilst the chaos of war was still darkening their lives.

The two friends then called three of their most trusted managers together and explained that they wanted to help the families of workers laid-off. A list of names was drawn up and the families divided into three, one for each manager. Finally, it was agreed that on a weekly basis Joseph and Flavio would decide what should be donated to each family.

The reaction of the managers to the scheme was one of disbelief. For months they had watched as dozens of owners had closed factories and deserted the city, leaving behind starvation and poverty for their workforce and their families. Yet here were Joseph and Flavio dogged in their support of those they had caused to suffer.

*   *   *

Joseph's other two projects however, were far more challenging and he accepted he would need considerable help from his friends.

When he attended his first business group meeting after returning to Turin, he was not sure what to expect. Rumours of a mass exodus of business leaders alongside the wealthy were obviously exaggerated especially within the Jewish community, and he noticed only five regular members being absent. What was different however was an intense pessimism amongst his friends and he wondered whether this would affect support for his project.

Following lunch and the general discussion which focused on the increasing militancy of the workers throughout the industrial north, Joseph asked if he could speak.

"Gentlemen," he began, "I hope that I in no way offend you when I suggest that all of us sat around this table are extremely privileged." There was little reaction to his opening statement.

"If we think about the pain being caused by the war to so many families due to severe shortages of food and other essentials, as a group we are not overly affected. I accept that on occasion we have to do without some preferred item or change our menus to suit the daily food market, but overall, we have the money to circumvent the effects of these shortages." Joseph paused; he had the attention of all and noticed some embarrassed looks as his words hit home.

"Just look at our lunch today," he added with an imperceptible smile. "Please, this is in no way meant as a criticism. We have spent our lives working extremely hard to be able to keep our families safe and live a comfortable lifestyle. Also I do not forget some here have sons fighting for Italy and our prayers go with them." Joseph paused as he noticed heads nodding in agreement. "Gentlemen, we're all aware of families who have lost fathers and sons fighting for our freedom and even if we are far too old to join them, we can still take responsibility for members of our Jewish community who are facing starvation. I believe we should be supporting these families." As he sat down, Sonny Levin, the Chairman, rose and said thoughtfully,

"Well, I doubt any sat here would disagree with those sentiments. Once again Joseph has brought to our attention an issue we really should have been committed to months ago. Yes, the war has created complications for me but the reality is I have no excuse for my apparent indifference to the plight of others, especially those from our community."

"I agree," Joseph heard from across the table; it was Simon Klein. "Of course Joseph is right. He's not actually criticised us but should have. On the whole, the war has been good to us so we have no excuse for rejecting the idea."

After requesting other comments and getting no takers, the Chairman asked if all were in agreement. Receiving no dissenters, it was then proposed and approved that Joseph should lead the project. After accepting the role, he asked five members to join him and there followed a discussion and agreement on how the business group could best fund the project. His second pledge had become a reality.

* * *

Joseph was also determined to follow up on the terrible news from Armenia and asked Eric Manoukian and Saul Tahter to join him for lunch. During the meal, little was discussed except the frightening situation facing Armenians and the impact it was having on their homeland. Over coffee, with little preamble he said,

"We should set up an escape route out of Armenia and create a supply line to get essentials in." Both his friends sat in stunned silence, but Joseph persevered and the more he spoke the more animated he became and the more guilt he created within his two friends.

Finally Eric agreed to contact friends in Yerevan, who had remained behind specifically to help those in most trouble. They had formed a partisan group and were fighting the New Turks government.

* * *

Joseph was delighted with the way the three projects had been endorsed, however, things were not quite so straightforward in his private life; he felt like a prisoner in his own home. During his previous trip to Washington, he'd promised his family he would return regularly but it soon became obvious that travelling to North America would be impossible for a civilian. Joseph felt cut-off from his children and trapped. He had no choice but to accept he would not leave Turin for the duration of the war.

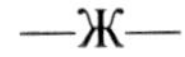

Chapter 12

October 1943

Ellen's family were the last to scramble on board and as all the other passengers were packed into the cramped space they huddled together in the swirling drafts by the door. There was straw on the floor but it offered little or no comfort from the hard wooden boards and Ellen sat on her cardigan in an attempt to make a softer seat for herself.

When the screech of the sliding door closing came to an end with a slam and darkness enveloped all on board, an eerie, frightened silence pervaded the carriage.

Ellen gripped her father's hand tightly feeling her heart pounding; she was determined not to let the tears come. She was nearly seventeen; no longer a child and understood that she had to be strong and brave regardless of what lay ahead.

As the train began to move, slowly at first, people began to whisper, asking questions and desperate for answers. An elderly man whose silhouette Ellen could just make out in the gloom, stood and said,

"Quiet please," and they all fell silent.

"Does anyone know what's happening?" he asked and people started calling out.

"Please, not all at once," he said loudly. When quiet had once again fallen he continued.

"My name is Josiah Burg and I am a rabbi from Milan. I was interned by the Germans at the Montechiarugolo camp." Ellen could feel the building panic in his voice as the man spoke.

"That's where Simon is," Leon whispered to his mother and then one by one all the families gave their names and explained where they had come from.

The last was Howard who gave his family's names and explained they'd travelled from Turin. When he'd finished Josiah Burg said,

"The only information I can offer is that I overheard one of the guards at the railway yard say we are going to Eastern Europe, probably Poland. Now we've all heard the rumours about the camps but..." A woman close to Ellen interrupted loudly,

"We have children with us and should not discuss such things." Ellen sensed agreement within the group and in a whisper asked her father,

"Why Poland?" It was her mother who answered impatiently,

"Ellen, please, not now. Let's just wait and see, alright."

Ellen, upset by her mother's offhandedness, turned and noticed a small crack in the wooden slats on the sidewall of the cattle truck. Looking through the gap she saw they were travelling slowly and as she stared at the passing countryside, she tried to come to terms with what was happening to them. She was frightened, understandably, after everything that had happened, but she was also confused. Why were they being taken north when there were internment camps in Italy, and if her family had been held for so long, weren't they just being deported as stated in the racial laws? She accepted there were no answers and curled up tightly wrapped in her father's arms.

* * *

After sleeping fitfully, Ellen woke and lay listening to the noises around her. Some slept soundly, others lightly. Some were constantly moving, others dead to the world. Some had gentle dreams, others terrifying visions. She sensed children in their parents' arms, husbands clinging to wives, sisters hugging brothers. The scene, which under other circumstances could have been joyous was bleak, dispiriting and heart-rending, all of which was compounded by her premonition that they were moving, irrevocably towards something indescribably evil.

She was no fool. During her years in Turin she had read and reread newspaper articles about the German camps, describing conditions so unbelievable, so inhumane, that she wondered why she was so inquisitive. If they were heading north which seemed likely, then they were evidently on the way to one of the Nazi camps. The question was why, and once there what would they find? Would they be required to work; slave labour for the German war machine, but then what about Noah? He was only thirteen.

Although never written about in the media due to censorship, Ellen knew about the Jews in Germany and the concentration camps which had been named 'death camps'. Although Flavio had never spoken directly to her about such things, on two occasions she had overheard him talking to her father.

"Whispers are everywhere," he had said sensitively on one occasion. "Forget what the politicians say or don't say; Jews from around Europe are being transported to the camps to die."

Sitting on the cold, hard wooden floor of the carriage, as the reality of death entered Ellen's mind, her tears flowed. Of course she was terrified, but she was also angry. She was still so young and had her life to live. She had marriage to look forward to, or a lover, and she smiled at the 'wicked' thought. Ellen then laughed quietly to herself when she realised that apart from her cousins, she'd been cut off from boys for longer than she cared to remember and her smile stayed with her as she remembered her fantasies, especially those involving Simon. She had always thought him terribly good looking and even though they were cousins, he gave her something pleasurable to dream about.

Without warning, there was a thump, the train stopped and the carriage suddenly came alive, everyone speaking at the same time.

For what seemed like an eternity, they remained stationary and it grew hotter, claustrophobic in the warming autumn day; the cramped conditions became unbearable. To make matters worse, Ellen was desperate to go to the toilet. She then heard the door slide open and had to cover her eyes as she was immediately blinded by the sun.

"We stop for short time," a guard shouted in poor Italian. "All out! Stay next to train."

Ellen and her family were the first off and it felt so good to stretch. Howard began talking to Josiah Burg about what appeared to be engine problems at the front of the train as Ellen watched a man and woman approach a guard and then move into some longer grass. She thanked God when she realised at last she could relieve herself.

Grabbing her father's hand Ellen explained what she needed and he moved with her to the longer grass. The guards watched but seemed unconcerned.

Whilst Ellen was squatting, she heard shouting that they should get back onto the train and one of the guards moved towards them.

As she quickly rose and walked with her father, a guard screamed as the young couple began sprinting towards some trees. Suddenly there was the crack of gunfire and everyone fell to the ground, Howard dragging his daughter with him. When she looked up, Ellen saw the couple lying motionless, splattered with blood and looked away in tears. They'd taken a chance, tried for freedom and failed, but they had to pay with their lives.

Ellen's family were last to board and were again seated next to the door. As the train pulled slowly away, Ellen looked out of the crack and saw the dead couple still holding hands. She couldn't believe the guards had just left them where they'd fallen and watched with loathing as large birds flew down and started tearing at their bloodied faces.

* * *

Ellen again slept fitfully, wrapped around her father and woke early to the repetitive motion of the noisy engine. She'd only been awake for a few minutes when they came to a halt. The grinding door slid open and she saw they were at a station named Como San Giovanni surrounded by the most wonderful mountains. She realised sadly that under different circumstances it would have been an almost perfect scene.

One by one the families were allowed to visit the station washrooms, always under guard and Ellen counted thirty people as they left the carriage. Having used the bathrooms last, her family returned to their area of the carriage allowing her to watch their progress through the crack and within minutes of departing, a rather large man stood and said quietly,

"I know this town. Como Dan Giovanni is close to the border. It looks as if we will be travelling through Switzerland." He sat down.

"That's impossible," came a voice from the darkness, "Switzerland's neutral. There's no way they would allow a German train, especially one with human cargo, to cross its borders." Joshua Berg then stood.

"Whilst we were at the station I spoke to one of the German guards. He told me we are travelling to Poland." Obviously trying to put a brave face on the news but failing, he added, "he also said we're taking this track because the usual route through the Alps, the Brenner Pass which connects Italy with Austria, is blocked with heavy snow." Joshua sat down and once again the truck fell silent; what was there to say? Everyone's worst nightmare had just been confirmed; they were heading for Poland.

*　　*　　*

As they travelled further north Ellen noticed that each night when the sun had set, the temperature fell dramatically and it became impossible to stay warm. She cuddled up closely to her father, trying to wrap herself in his coat, using his body for warmth, but nothing really helped, she was freezing and sleep was impossible.

Ellen had lost track of time even what day it was, but thought it was around mid-day when the train came to another halt. Slowly the door opened and again bright sunlight streamed in to the truck, dazzling everyone. She opened her eyes slowly and waited while they adjusted and then saw they had arrived at another station. When she looked for the station name, she saw it had been covered with dirty sheets. Mystified, Ellen asked herself why on earth the authorities would want to hide the name of the town.

She then put her head slowly around the side of the door and saw German soldiers guarding the train. The station was otherwise completely deserted.

Ellen was both surprised and elated when she saw a woman and young girl approach the carriage and begin to distribute mugs of steaming hot soup and crusts of bread. Because they were next to the door her family passed the food down the truck and as the intoxicating aroma of food passed her, Ellen realised how hungry she was.

As the young girl leant over to pass another cup of soup to Howard, Ellen asked,

"Where are we?" The girl's mother looked frightened and angrily told her daughter to stay silent but the young girl said in a whisper,

"Switzerland." As Ellen was about to reply, a guard moved quickly towards them shouting so she smiled at the girl and nodded her thanks. Again she was confused; how could they be travelling through a neutral country in a German train? The girl had clearly answered 'Switzerland' and why would she lie and why were all the station name signs covered up?

Ellen decided that when you added everything up including what the Rabbi had said about the only alternative route being blocked by snow, it was clear they were being betrayed by the Swiss.

Eventually, with everyone in the truck eating, it was Ellen's turn and she couldn't believe how such simple food could taste so good.

Whilst eating, Ellen noticed a man who had just left one of the offices opposite the platform, watching her. He was talking and laughing with the officer she'd seen when they first boarded the train and although she couldn't understand what they were saying, knew the language was German. They were both drinking something out of bottles and the man was wearing a white shirt and loose fitting trousers but no coat. Ellen guessed he must have been freezing. For some reason she was drawn to him as he had the purest blue eyes she'd ever seen; they were piercing, utterly penetrating.

Whilst Ellen was finishing her food, the man smiled at her and she watched indifferently as he spoke to the officer and again they laughed together; they were obviously well known to each other. She continued to watch as the young man nodded towards her and suddenly the officer shouted. Immediately the guards next to their carriage, boarded, caught hold of her arm and tried to pull her out onto the platform. What was left of her mug of soup fell to the floor with a crash along with the remaining bread. Ellen was confused and alarmed; what were they doing? She called out to her parents and her mother grabbed her other arm to prevent the guard from taking her daughter. Without warning, two other guards boarded and Ellen felt a growing fear suffocating her. Her beloved father, realising what was happening, swung a punch at the nearest guard catching him on the side of the face but he was immediately clubbed unconscious to the ground. Ellen knew something terrible was about to happen. Three guards forced Tova to release her and as she did she screamed for them to take her; that she would do anything they wanted, anything if only they'd leave her daughter alone. Ellen stared petrified as her mother begged and she became aware of a deathlike silence flooding the carriage. Everyone kept their heads down; no one wanted to be next.

As she was dragged onto the platform the officer shouted to the guards. Immediately Tova was also grabbed and mother and daughter were dragged side by side along the platform. As Ellen looked back towards her unconscious father she saw Noah and knew he could do nothing to help them.

With her mother at her side, Ellen was forced to the rear of the train and pushed into a cattle truck. It was empty apart from straw on the wooden slats. As she was pushed inside, she listened bewildered as her mother continued pleading with the two men who were with them, the officer and the young man with the piercing blue eyes. As the door slammed shut behind them, the officer screamed at her mother to shut up and slapped her viciously across the face. Ellen watched despairingly as blood oozed from her mouth and nose and moved towards her. She had to help, to comfort her mother but the younger man stood in her way. She tried to push past him but he grabbed hold of her arm and with a lurid smile, ran his free hand over her breasts. Ellen pulled away and tried to hit him but he tore at her blouse, exposing her smooth, delicate skin and caressed her bare breasts. She was in shock as she suddenly realised in utter embarrassment that her nipples were erect from the cold and her fear. She tried to cover herself but the man was too strong and held her arms apart. Appalled, Ellen then felt him lean towards her. His breath smelt of beer and food and she started to retch. The young man swore at her and pushed her away before knocking her to ground. Ellen lay on the straw matting rigidly still, listening to her mother; she sounded like a wounded animal until the officer punched her yet again.

Egged on by his young friend, he began to rip away Tova's clothing; first her blouse, then her skirt and finally her underwear. Ellen was horrified and as pure revulsion overwhelmed her, she wanted to kill the men. As she sat up the younger man knocked her back down and put his boot on her stomach to prevent her moving. Exposed and mortified, her mother screamed for Ellen to stop looking and begged the officer to take her, for both men to take her, to do anything they wanted, 'but for the love of God leave her daughter alone!' Both men just laughed.

But Ellen could not look away and watched as the officer unbuttoned his trousers and with tears cascading down her face, she stared in disbelief as he mounted her mother. Tova, in obvious pain, tried to smile reassuringly at her daughter and kept mouthing that it was alright, that everything would be alright. Ellen may have been petrified, but utter disgust shattered her fear; the man was on top of her mother, thrusting inside her, hurting her and she screamed for him to leave her alone. All Tova could do was close her eyes and shut out both her daughter and the man raping her.

When the officer had finally finished he stood, wiped himself and dressed. Tova was left exposed and bloodied. She tried to cover herself and crawl to Ellen but the officer put his boot on her head, sadistically driving her face into the straw. Both men knew what each other wanted and the officer pulled Tova's head brutally upwards by her hair to make sure she was watching as the younger man moved towards her daughter.

Slowly, very slowly, he began unbuttoning his trousers. He was toying with Ellen; a cat with a young bird and she was terrified weeping uncontrollably. The man with such wonderful blue eyes then slowly opened his trousers, exposing himself. He was stiff, swollen, so ready. Watching the mother being raped had excited him and the officer roared with laughter when he saw his friend's arousal. He was seriously impressed. The young man laughed back and moved to his prey. Ellen tried to crawl away but hit the back wall of the cattle truck; she could go no further, there was no escape.

The man grabbed her ankles, pulled her away from the wall and forced her onto her back. She curled up in a ball but he was so much stronger and prised open her legs keeping them apart by kneeling between them. He then lowered his trousers and pants and grabbed Ellen's hand, forcing her to touch him, to feel his anticipation. Ellen had never seen a man so 'ready' and couldn't believe his size. She screamed thinking he would tear her apart.

Ellen was half aware of her mother lashing out at the officer while she felt her skirt slowly being lifted. The younger man was laughing mercilessly as his hands moved up her thighs towards his goal. Ellen moaned,

"Please, no." But he just continued his journey.

She knew what was coming and had to do something. She kicked out with her feet, catching the man in the face with the toe of her shoe. His smile changed to fury as he slapped her viciously and Ellen buckled, all fight gone. She saw her mother staring, face bloodied and swollen, but heard nothing. Spread-eagled and defenceless there was nothing she could do except close her eyes and pray. Ellen felt her pants being ripped away leaving her naked and humiliated and she again called to her mother as she felt the man's considerable weight ease down on her.

The pain was immediate, excruciating and Ellen screamed out. She looked for her mother and could not believe that the officer was once again in her, behind her, taking her whilst making her watch her only daughter being raped. Suddenly Ellen felt a searing pain through her entire body as the man plunged deeper, faster, more violently and she wondered how much further into her he could go. As he moaned she screamed, and as she screamed he laughed. With tears erupting, Ellen again looked for her mother and saw she was still on her hands and knees with the officer raping her and she had to turn away; the heartbreak on her mother's face was intolerable.

The monster with the bluest of eyes was still in her wanting more but Ellen just felt numb together with an unutterable hatred. Then she saw it; a speck on his neck and as the shirt slipped she saw colours on his skin. As the brute shoved and thrust, grinding away, whilst he ripped her apart, Ellen focused on those insignificant blemishes. She was hypnotised by the images imprinted on his body and something deep down told her that those unremarkable imperfections would save her, would drive her on, would stop her giving in. As she descended into nothingness, they became her one defiant reason to live.

Chapter 13

1919

The war to end all wars concluded with the signing of the Treaty of Versailles, five years to the day after the assassination of Archduke Ferdinand and his wife, and for the first time in years Joseph actually felt free. Two weeks later he found a flight from Rome to New York via London and en route stayed for two days in the UK capital. Although he was desperate to see his family, he needed to use the stopover to follow up on one of his investment ideas.

During his first week in Washington, the family spent the days showing their father the city and surrounding areas and Joseph was surprised how little America appeared to have suffered due to the war. Then, on the second weekend, much to his family's surprise, he invited them to the cinema. Howard accepted but the others declined, needing to prepare for that evening in the restaurant.

"Have you seen any of the latest films?" Joseph asked his younger son as they walked to the cinema. Howard explained that because of the restaurant and the long hours they worked, they had only been once, then as an afterthought he added,

"But I actually find the whole thing enthralling. You know whoever thought of entertaining the public with films is a genius." Joseph smiled.

*   *   *

That evening, after the restaurant had closed, the family sat with drinks whilst Howard enthused about the afternoon's matinee. He told them the film had been called The Heart of Wetona, which had opened in New York in January.

"And it starred Norma Talmadge who's really famous," he said knowledgably. "Fred Huntley, Thomas Meighan and Gladden James were also in it." He was disappointed when no one around the table had heard of them.

"So what was it about," Golda asked her brother.

"It was a sort of romantic, Wild West cum Indian film."

"And?" she asked bluntly when Howard appeared to have finished his explanation.

"Okay," he answered with irritation which his siblings found hilarious and Joseph intriguing.

"A half-breed Indian girl was deceived by a promise of marriage by a white boy. When her father, the Chief of the Blackfoot Tribe discovered his daughter had been defiled, and by a white man, he said the man must die." Although Howard would never admit it he seemed to be enjoying the retelling of the tale, speaking with more and more enthusiasm as the plot thickened and Joseph watched with growing satisfaction.

"On hearing this, the chief's daughter Wetona, contacted a friend who was a Government agent called Hardin to ask if he could get a message to her lover to warn him. Now, what she hadn't realised was her father had followed her and when he saw the two of them together, assumed Hardin was the culprit. The Chief confronted the Government agent, Hardin, and demanded he marry his daughter or face death. Of course," Howard said with even more fervour, "Hardin had no choice and married his daughter. Later on the father discovers the truth and tracks down the lover shooting him dead, leaving Hardin and Wetona to live happily ever after." A smiling Joseph joined in as all around the table applauded.

*   *   *

During his second week in the capital, Joseph spent time on his own in the restaurant on the pretext of wanting coffee or a meal and talked to members of staff and customers. At the end of that week he asked his family to join him for coffee in another restaurant. This immediately increased the siblings' curiosity as to what their father was up to.

Joseph began by congratulating them; the restaurant was making a healthy if not spectacular profit, they'd refurbished the upstairs apartment as well as buying a small house next door, and, it was clear they had all the right skills and qualities to make constructive, hardnosed business decisions. He added proudly that he really couldn't fault them and then said thoughtfully,

"Remember our holiday before the war?" The four nodded.

"Well, after years of being told by my closest friends to diversify and break my dependence on Scalfaro's, I set up banking facilities in the cities we visited and looked at business opportunities.

"I didn't discuss my plans with you during the trip because although Europe was on the brink of war, I was desperately hoping it could be avoided. Anyway war came, you left and any potential for starting new projects was lost." Joseph ordered more coffee and was interested that none of his children had spoken.

"Since the end of the war I don't see Italy as a safer or better place, in fact just the opposite. I remain convinced diversifying into North America and Britain is the right thing to do." Joseph looked at each of his children. "I want to explain my ideas for the future and see what you think." Again there were nods from all around the table but not a word spoken.

"My research indicates London, Canada and America have the most potential."

"Why London? I thought it had been destroyed," Howard said and Joseph was delighted to at last have a response from someone.

"You're right, Britain was bombed but I still believe it is the most powerful nation on the planet. In effect, it won the war and I believe it will again prove to be a world leader and very secure for investment." Then the questions came and a delighted Joseph spent the next ten minutes answering them as best he could however, laughing at one stage, he had to admit he simply didn't have all the answers.

"So, I have a number of options for you to consider," he said. "Emil has already learnt the ropes at Scalfaro's and I would like him to eventually take over from me." Joseph turned to his son with a smile." All three of his siblings congratulated him although it was really just a confirmation of the obvious.

"Barbara, I think you should build on the fantastic success you have created here. I know this is a project all four of you have invested time and energy in but in its present form it will not financially sustain the four of you. With the right investment, I see it going from strength to strength but you must all understand it is a one person business so you must hand over complete ownership to Barbara." Joseph sipped on his coffee to give the surprised siblings time to consider his suggestion. When no one spoke he continued,

"Golda, according to many people I have spoken to, you have a real feel for what's needed to run a successful restaurant and I think you could start up your own place with little difficulty." Golda looked shocked, more so when her father added, "In Toronto, Canada." Giving her no time to answer, Joseph explained that he would provide the initial finances.

“It will be your business to develop and grow as you see fit.” All the colour had drained from Golda’s face but she was smiling and reached across to hold her father’s hand mouthing ‘thank you’ to him.

“Finally Howard; I want you to move to London and lead an investment idea I have put together.” They all looked at their brother who was sat motionless staring at his father. “It will be totally different from anything else the family is involved in, extremely demanding but vital because it will allow a measure of independence from all our other investments.”

Howard remained quiet and Joseph saw stunned looks on the faces around him. For some reason their reaction made him feel uncomfortable. Ploughing on he said,

“Finally, I’m desperate for us to be together but I have to be a realist. I’ve spent a long time coming to terms with the fact that although you are my family I really don’t know you. You have shown me that you are more than capable of living your lives independently of me so what I want is to provide each of you with all you need to make successful lives for yourselves. If we get this right, we will still all be working as a team, just living apart. If one needs help to solve problems, the others will be there.” Joseph looked around the table; all four siblings were absorbed in what he was saying.

“Any money I give to help you is yours and if success follows it will be your success from your efforts. Now, I want to leave you to talk through what I have said.” Joseph rose, leaving four dazed but ecstatic young adults to their thoughts.

* * *

With the exception of the two girls who wanted to reverse their projects with Golda remaining in Washington and Barbara moving to Toronto, Joseph was delighted with their positive attitude. He was however, slightly taken aback by Golda's reason for wanting to remain in Washington; she was in love and explained that after working alongside Joshua in the kitchen of the restaurant for a few months, it had dawned on both of them that they had fallen for each other.

Initially Joseph was extremely apprehensive; his daughter marrying and he had no wife to guide him or her. However, after spending an evening with Golda and Joshua he realised not only what a delightful young man he was, but how organised the two were. They had thought of everything and it was obvious that whatever anyone thought, they were totally smitten with each other.

* * *

"I took you to the cinema the other day for a reason." It was two days after his talk with the family and Joseph was sat with Howard over a cup of coffee. "You see, a very good friend of mine in Turin suggested I met up with a contact of his when I travelled to London; a man involved in the British Film Industry."

"Is that what you want me to be involved in?" Howard asked.

"Yes."

"But I know nothing about films or the film industry. It would be a disaster and you would lose all your money."

"I accept that," Joseph said carefully, "and that is why, if you agree, I have arranged for you to work alongside a specialist in London." He sat quietly for a moment giving Howard time to think before adding, "Look you're young, you have no personal commitments and you have money to back you. All I ask is that if you say yes you totally commit to the project. If you do I am certain you will be a success."

"When do you want this to happen?" Howard asked quietly, obviously considering the implications for both himself and his father's money.

"Well, as soon as possible. I see no benefit in you remaining here so why don't we travel to London together, meet up with my contact and see how it goes."

Howard asked his father for a night to consider. Joseph knew he wanted to discuss the idea with his brother and sisters and of course was happy to agree.

* * *

Three days later Joseph and Howard left bound for London. Emil returned directly to Turin and Golda and Barbara remained in Washington to prepare for the first wedding in the Aizenberg family for many years.

During the journey, Joseph gave Howard an overview of the British Film Industry and why he felt it was the right time to invest.

"The first motion picture camera was patented in the UK in 1888 by a man named Le Prince who then produced the first ever film the following year. The birthplace of film is Britain however, over the last few years the business has been in serious decline."

"What went wrong?"

"Well, a number of factors, none good, I'm afraid. I'm told the problems began around 1910 when two American companies, Pathe and Gaumont, started flooding the UK with American films. Then the war came and one of the consequences was that film production in Britain came to a virtual standstill, but not of course in America. My contact has told me that virtually all efforts to resurrect the British film industry have proved nigh on impossible." Not only concerned but confused, Howard asked,

"Why get involved then?" Joseph ignoring his son continued,

"Apparently British films have always been based on live theatre. This means they have mainly filmed a play exactly as it has been performed on stage even down to the same actors and sets. This has resulted in their industry falling behind its competitors. I'm told the public of today only want to see American films and the result has been a serious lack of investment."

"So why are you so interested in getting involved? Surely it's an enormous gamble."

"Exactly," Joseph answered passionately. "Timing is everything." Joseph laughed as he slapped his son on the shoulder adding, "Films are the future. Just look at how popular they already are so it's obvious very soon cinemas will grab a majority share of the worldwide entertainment industry."

"Why aren't others investing in British films if they've got such a great future?" Joseph liked the way Howard was questioning him; his son was obviously thinking things through.

"Well, don't forget virtually the entire planet has been at war and it has ruined many financially. Those looking to invest right now want as much security as possible and this investment is anything but."

"So why do it?" Howard repeated bluntly.

"Think about it. If we get involved now when there are so many difficulties, we get on the inside track. We will be in the right place to grab any future benefits and profits. I accept we might fail but for me it's a gamble worth taking and I want you as my right hand man."

"So who is the man I'm going to be working with?" Howard asked thoughtfully.

"Well, he's certainly an interesting fellow, quite a bit younger than you and rather, um, different. I'm told he has a unique eye when it comes to films. He originally trained as a draughtsman and was an advertising designer for a cable company. When I met him he told me that whilst working there, he became intrigued by the whole subject of photography so resigned and started to work as a title-card designer in film production. He has recently been offered a full-time position at the Islington Studios which is American owned and the interesting bit is he wants to become a film director in his own right."

"Sounds fascinating," Howard answered before adding, "and what's this fellow's name?"

"Alfred Hitchcock," came the reply.

* * *

On Joseph's eventual return to Italy, Emil informed his father that he wanted to marry Marguerita. He explained that being apart for so long during the war had convinced them they were right for each other and Marguerita's father had agreed. It was only left to Joseph to support the decision and although he had not seen a great deal of Marguerita she did seem perfect for his eldest son.

It also became obvious within just a few months of his return that Emil was proving to be an excellent manager at Scalfaro's. He had clear ideas on the future of the company that both Flavio, and a slightly reticent Joseph, felt would ensure the company's future. As a result Joseph and Flavio discussed whether it was time for both of them to take a step back and let Emil have a free hand. Joseph knew they should, but Scalfaro's was his life's work and he was struggling to let go. However, Flavio would have none of it; he was adamant they reduced their involvement and argued emphatically that as the company was returning to full production following the war, the time was perfect for a change of leadership and for Emil to take over. He then added with a chuckle, that it was also wise for Emil to take over whilst both of them were still around to help, and, that neither of them were getting any younger! Of course, Joseph knew he was right and agreed to talk to Emil and then meet with the mangers to explain the changes.

* * *

It was not that Joseph was idle or bored. On the contrary, since reducing his commitment to Scalfaro's he'd tried to wrap up his three wartime projects only to discover that there were still far too many families in desperate need of significant support. Once again, he took his concern for the plight of members of the Turin Jewish community to the business group and with little discussion, they agreed to continue with the financial commitment for as long as was necessary. There were also many ex-employees of Scalfaro's whose families were penniless and it was decided, with Emil's full support, that the system of providing aid through the three managers would continue.

Finally, Joseph continued to work alongside Eric Manoukian and Saul Tahter on their homeland project as post conflict conditions in their native Armenia were appalling. In fact, it was only once Europe had stopped blowing itself apart that the true horror of the slaughter of Armenians began to emerge.

Verified reports coming out of Yerevan clearly exposed the Young Turk government's premeditated genocide. Claims varied, but it was apparent that between six-hundred and fifty thousand and one and a half million Armenians were massacred between 1915 and 1917. The government refuted all claims, stating categorically that there had been no planned or premeditated mass-murder of civilians. The explanation they gave was that the extraordinary death rate amongst the Armenian public over those two years had been the result of civil war, disease and famine.

As harrowing report followed harrowing report the three friends knew their battle to help their countrymen was far from over. Using existing contacts, they established a system of financial support from Jewish and Armenian communities across Europe, supplying food and basic items to as many victims as possible.

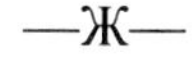

Chapter 14

November 1943

When Ellen eventually regained consciousness, her father was holding her tightly, keeping her close. Her Aunt Marguerita was comforting her mother whose face was bloodied and severely swollen. Ellen was swamped by a bottomless grief at her stolen innocence. Her clothes were ripped but she was covered and her wonderful father, who had a deep cut over his left eye, had wrapped her in his thick, warm coat.

Howard tried to talk to Ellen, to beg forgiveness for not protecting her, but there was nothing to be said, no absolution needed. No words could ever eradicate the revulsion she felt at being so pitilessly abused. In her mind there were two guilty men who should pay for their sins, but with the train heading for Poland, she accepted she would never feel the sheer joy of retribution, never see the destruction of the animals who had dishonoured her.

* * *

Disorientated, Ellen woke with a start. The train had come to a sudden halt and as the door slid open with the proverbial piercing screech, cool air enveloped the carriage. She shivered as she looked out of the open door and prayed they were not at another station. Again she saw a truly majestic landscape with mountains surrounding them, a valley and a wide, elegant river. Even in her traumatised state she could appreciate the wonder of the scene and she longed for the peacefulness it portrayed.

Looking down the length of the train, Ellen spotted groups of guards who seemed extremely relaxed laughing and joking with each other. She then heard an officer call out an order and the nearest guard told her family in broken Italian to get out. They were followed by the rest of the passengers and Ellen jumped as the door was slammed behind them. Looking around she saw the railway track ahead was twisted and mangled and she prayed that it had been a bomb; any device to hurt, kill or maim the enemy. That's how Ellen viewed the monsters who had raped her and the guards who had held her; the enemy. She knew unequivocally that her new found loathing of this enemy was total. She wanted them dead, every one of them.

The guards began to push the prisoners into pairs, shouting that they wanted each child with an adult. Ellen was placed with her father, Noah with her mother and Leon with Auntie Marguerita. They were then told to stand completely still whilst each pair was bound by rope to their partner. Ellen's left wrist was tied to her father's right and as she looked around nervously she saw only panic and fear on the faces of the adults; something was dreadfully wrong. Ellen saw a bomb crater and wreckage of the track ahead; the engine was in the middle of a bridge over the river. Obviously they could go no further. Ellen quietly pointed it out to her father and as he followed his daughter's eyes, a look of horror spread across his face. Clearly unconcerned about the guards, he said to his wife,

"Tova what have I done? Children I am so very sorry." Ellen looked around wondering what her father knew that she didn't. As he spoke she saw her mother's comprehension of his words and pulled Ellen towards her. She was scared; she needed to know what was happening. Part of her was convinced that nothing could be as terrifying or barbaric as what had happened to her and her mother at the station, but why were her parents so scared?

One of the officers shouted and the guards began to shove the pairs into a line. Howard and Ellen were at the front followed by Tova and Noah and then Marguerita and Leon. The other pairs were lined up behind. Howard whispered to Ellen and to her mother to move their wrists, to do everything they could to loosen the rope binding them together. Ellen began to grind her hand backwards and forwards against her father's wrist; it hurt so much but she persevered making sure none of the guards could see.

Howard, his free arm gripped tightly by a guard, was led with Ellen in tow, towards the front of the train. The closer they got to the engine the more clearly they could see the problem and Ellen was delighted. The track and bridge were so severely damaged that it would take months to be repaired.

They were pushed onto a path which ran the length of the bridge and as they passed the engine, Ellen couldn't understand where they were being taken. There was nothing ahead, no station or building for them to be held in.

Once they were three-quarters of the way across the bridge, the guard leading Howard and Ellen stopped and dragged both around to face the river and a low metal barrier. Ellen looked to her left and saw each pair had a guard behind them; all were standing in identical positions facing the river. On a call from the officer the bound pairs were shoved towards the edge of the bridge, right up against the low barrier. She thought they were going to be pushed into the water below but realised it was a silly idea as anyone who could swim would escape. Peering over the edge Ellen saw slow moving water but the currents looked perilous.

"I love you, forgive me," her father whispered to her and then turned towards his wife and son and smiled. Ellen saw tears in his eyes.

As she was about to speak there was the sudden eruption of gunshots and as she looked towards her father, he was already toppling towards the water. She screamed his name as the rope around her wrist tightened and dragged her against the barrier. As she tried to resist, her father's momentum catapulted Ellen over the edge.

Chapter 15

1920 - 25th February 1927.

Following their wedding, Marguerita moved into Hayastan with Emil. Wanting to give them time to settle down with each other, Joseph travelled to see his rapidly changing family as often as they could put up with him.

Barbara quickly fell pregnant following her wedding to Joshua and Joseph was elated at the thought of becoming a grandfather. Howard had fallen for a local Jewish girl called Tova Harazi who lived close by his newly purchased house in London. His youngest daughter, Golda, had been dating Aldo Biton in Toronto for nearly a year and they wanted to marry. Joseph was thrilled, although once again his elation was tinged with sorrow that Elizabeth wouldn't share in his happiness.

There was however, one area of Joseph's life which had begun to cause him considerable disquiet and that was the business meetings as he witnessed his friends becoming more and more embittered with the direction of Italian politics.

The previous year the socialists had easily won the general election and their victory was seen as a direct result of the overriding dissatisfaction with the politicians. Quite incredibly, once in power the new government immediately withdrew from parliament which triggered the first of a series of nationwide general strikes.

To make matters worse, it appeared that initial strikes in the Turin Fiat Lingetto Factory were instrumental in the Italian people finding a means of expressing their discontent and led to nationwide copycat strikes.

Whilst Italy moved towards industrial meltdown and internal turmoil, Emil succeeded in keeping Scalfaro's profitable, to the surprise of many. For a non-essential business, the company was not only maintaining its operating levels but actually increasing demand, especially from abroad. Emil explained that there was no magic formula; Scalfaro's success was built on the excellent workforce and even though many had faced the threat of violence from outside agitators, the norm in other factories, his workers remained loyal and committed to the company. Joseph and Flavio were immensely proud when Emil told them that the lack of industrial disruption was a direct result of their decision to support those made redundant during the war.

Joseph's friends even begrudgingly admitted that the policies adopted by Scalfaro's, which many had initially criticised, were proving fundamental to its ability to survive the ever-deepening industrial storms. They were also so impressed with Emil that they asked Joseph to invite him to one of their lunches and it was only a matter of time before he was welcomed as a full member. Joseph couldn't have been prouder; father and son together, both significant players in the Turin business fraternity.

* * *

By mid 1920 the problems facing the country were escalating and Joseph recognised that it was only a matter of time before Emil would have to make some difficult decisions. As a result he asked his old friend Riccardo Levin to join him for lunch. When Joseph began throwing questions at him, Riccardo joked,

"How long have you got?"

“As long as it takes,” Joseph answered more brusquely than he had meant to. Hearing his friend’s genuine concern, Riccardo said,

“Okay, let’s order first.”

After the waiter had left them, Riccardo asked Joseph what he was worried about.

“That’s simple; Emil and Scalfaro’s.”

“Okay. You do realise that anything to do with Italian politics has to include Mussolini.”

“Why?” Joseph asked genuinely confused.

“Well, last year’s general strike reflects serious public dissatisfaction and politicians like Mussolini are smart enough to know that by supporting increased power for the workers he’s more likely to gain their support.” The wine arrived and Riccardo continued. “You see, in his case public backing is even more important because even though he’s become a major political player he’s never been voted into any of the positions he’s secured.

“So how does he do it?”

“It’s obvious; he’s playing on the anger of just about every Italian over the peace treaty from the war. We were promised certain lands and conditions as a reward for supporting the Allies and then they reneged on part of the agreement.”

The food arrived and Joseph realised he wasn’t that hungry.

“Okay, I understand; but how does it tie in with what you were saying?”

“Following the war, like most other countries, we experienced ever higher prices but because of centuries of chronic poverty most Italians couldn’t cope. Here in the north we have little understanding of what was happening in the rest of the country.”

“So where does Mussolini fit in?” he asked.

"Just consider; the Italian general public are incensed. Take the General Strike, it is only one example of how people are fed up with government ineptitude and this has led to the extreme left and right becoming more powerful. Now, while all this is going on what do you think Mussolini was doing?" Joseph looked blankly as his friend answered cynically, "He was founding a new political group, The Fascio di Combattimento or the Italian Fascist Party." Joseph could see Riccardo's anger rising.

"Mussolini is quite incredible. Whilst strongly promoting Italy's entry into the war, and don't forget he was one of the main advocates for attacking Austria, he was also signing up former officers and soldiers as founding members of this new party. He also recruited disillusioned members of the national Socialist Party such as the ultra nationalists and extreme left wing and, last but not least, he targeted Italian youth." Riccardo paused before adding darkly,

"Most alarming of all is that he has created a military division called the 'Blackshirts'. They are part of his Fascist action squads and worryingly, they appear central to his plans." Riccardo called the waiter for coffee and Joseph could sense his friend was deeply troubled. Of course he'd heard rumours of the Blackshirts but had never taken much notice; however, as he listened, he became seriously concerned.

"What makes you so certain he's not just some one minute wonder?" He asked.

"Evidence," came the reply. When Joseph asked what he meant, Riccardo explained,

"Read the news. Endless reports of Blackshirts using physical intimidation against the public as well as attacking other political groups at parades and demonstrations. It's obvious they will do whatever is necessary to silence anyone who disagrees with them and the government doesn't care. Communists, Catholics, Socialists, Anarchists, Republicans and most of all, the likes of us Jews, have all been threatened, even attacked." Joseph remained silent; he could never remember Riccardo being so incensed.

"So what exactly does Mussolini want?" Riccardo thought before answering.

"It's only my opinion but I'm sure he wants the general public to believe the country is dangerously destabilised and out of control. He will claim to be the one man capable of restoring law and order and will then promote himself as our leader." Selecting his words guardedly Riccardo finally said, "No one should be under any illusions that when this eventually happens it will be too late to reverse his authority."

* * *

The business group continued to meet in the post-war years; several of the 'old guard' having left Italy or retired but Joseph remained deeply aware that membership could be as invaluable to Emil in the future as it had been to him in the past. This would be more so if anything should happen to Flavio or himself. However, Emil showed little sign of wanting to be a regular member, frequently sending his apologies to meetings claiming he had other commitments. When Joseph tried to speak to him about his reluctance to be part of the group, his son invariably steered the conversation away from the subject, usually towards Scalfaro's. Joseph had little choice but to accept his son's reluctance.

More for Emil than himself, he therefore continued to attend and noticed two distinct camps emerging. The first included most of the long-standing members, who wished to meet regularly and discuss business, commercial and banking issues, whilst enjoying each others' company. The second were mostly the newer members (although surprisingly Riccardo Levin seemed to have aligned himself with them) who sought to play a greater part in influencing government policies, especially those concerning Turin and the industrial north.

As the gulf between the two groups widened Joseph felt himself being pulled and pushed between the factions and decided that under no circumstance would he take sides. Meeting after meeting, he listened as the more vocal members of the radical group including Henry Marks and Alon Shum, argued that although they were a small group they carried influence. They insisted members should not back down and watch the country spiral out of control.

To Joseph these ambitions were troubling and he believed, if not held in check, they could lead to the members being exposed to the police.

At his next lunch with Riccardo Joseph made a conscious effort not to be narrow-minded but challenged his friend to explain the benefits of a more confrontational approach.

"Joseph, I warned you and now it is happening; Mussolini is going to take over." When Joseph looked shocked, Riccardo added, "Believe me, it's just a matter of time before he creates a situation from where he can justify seizing power."

* * *

And Riccardo's prediction came true in October, 1922, when Benito Mussolini warned the King that if the government was not conceded to the Fascist Party, they would seize it by marching on Rome. Few in authority took the threat seriously until thousands of Fascists moved towards the capital on the 28th. Prime Minister Luigi Facta decided to confront Mussolini with force but when he asked King Victor Emmanuel III to declare martial law, he refused and Luigi Facta was left with no alternative but to resign.

A grim situation was made significantly more explosive by the King's extraordinary decision to not only cede to the Fascist threat but appoint Benito Mussolini as Prime Minister. Much to the disbelief of millions, he justified the decision by claiming that any other course of action would have led to civil war. All knew the King had committed political suicide on behalf of his nation and that democracy for all Italians was dead.

Within days, Mussolini appointed himself Minister of Foreign Affairs and Minister of the Interior and along with the title Prime Minister; he had control of the police and local government. He appeared unstoppable and consolidated his position with a combination of violence to silence individuals and the suspension of democratic freedom to silence the press.

Popular control of local government was then abolished; elected officials in all towns and cities were replaced by representatives of central government and the nation watched in horror, as democracy was dismantled.

To add to Joseph's problems, the more radical members of the business group began drawing up plans to counter the government's political 'crimes', stating that under no circumstances would they give in to the strangulation of their democratic rights without a fight. Joseph was shaken by their anger but after all he'd faced in his younger life, he could empathize with their fury.

And Mussolini was far from finished as he continued to restructure government. He decreed that no agenda items could be placed before either houses of parliament without his consent, which in effect freed him from dependence on parliament, making him answerable only to the King. Alongside this he also took control of Italy's armed forces and Italians were aghast as political terrorism became an instrument of government policy. Newspapers were censored or suppressed, education controlled and freedom of speech, of both the press and the individual, outlawed.

Two other developments, one overt but operating covertly, the other just plain insidious, put an end to any doubts Joseph might have. The first was the creation of a secret police force called the "Organizzazione Volontaria per la Repressione dell' Antifascismo", known as OVRA; its primary function was to deal with all dissident elements. The second and more menacing was the Fascist's public recognition of their leader's loathing for Jews. For years there had been rumours but as Mussolini had a Jewish mistress, Margherita Sarfatti, these were considered just that, rumours. However, as his power increased, Mussolini's prejudices became more and more blatant and discrimination against Jews the norm.

* * *

Joseph was concerned about the next business meeting due in mid November, reasoning that it might quickly spiral out of control if the antagonism of the members dominated proceedings. He arrived early and the pre-meal drinks were followed by a pleasant lunch but throughout Joseph sensed an underlying impatience around the table.

Following coffee, Paul Grant, the rotating Chairman, began and after welcoming those in attendance spoke candidly,

“Gentlemen, many around this table have asked me about the recent anti-Jewish actions of central government. I propose today’s only agenda point should be to consider these developments.” There was a nod of approval from those gathered and Teddy Dobkin, across the table from Joseph, stated belligerently,

“If a brutal dictator is allowed to govern this country we are finished.”

“Teddy has a point,” Paul grant said, “one many of us agree with, but it is important we keep any discussions relevant.” A considerable debate followed; some comments were well thought out, others emotionally charged and inflammatory. Once everyone had been given the opportunity to air their views, something Joseph declined to do, Paul Grant again stood.

“So how can a small and some would say extremely influential group of Jewish businessmen, help create a platform for a return to democracy? That is the real challenge we face.”

The discussion had done little to ease Joseph’s concern. He felt that if the more radical opinion prevailed then a dangerous confrontation was inevitable. Even accepting he’d felt similar anger in his days in Armenia he could not forget the cost of irrational, emotionally charged actions. He knew the group was defenceless against the Fascists who would sooner wipe them off the face of the earth than negotiate with them.

* * *

Joseph reluctantly attended an extraordinary meeting arranged for the following week. As there was no lunch Paul Grant, the Chair, waited for drinks and snacks to arrive before welcoming everybody. Without delay he then came straight to the point.

"Gentlemen, we are divided in our opinions and as I cannot remain impartial, must resign." He gathered up his papers and moved around the table, deliberately sitting in an empty seat in the middle of the less radical camp.

Joseph was intrigued, but also extremely disheartened as he watched old friends who'd worked together for so many years, struggling to reach a consensus.

After a few minutes of unhelpful debate Axel Steinman rose.

"Gentlemen, in all my time as friend and colleague, I have never known such hostility amongst us. I'm sure some of you think I am part of the problem and without apology, readily concede to having strong beliefs about our future, but we have always been able to reach an accord. Currently though, some around this table feel they can make decisions without going through the accepted process and this I cannot accept. The issues facing us are far too important to allow a few strong minded individuals to highjack our proceedings." Next to rise was Nathan Zolli.

"Let me be frank. As Jews and successful businessmen, how long do you think it will be before each and every one of us is targeted by the Fascist bigots who now hold power?" Silence enveloped the room as Nathan Zolli retook his seat.

What followed was exactly what Joseph had feared; member after member proposing harebrained schemes for opposing the government, the police and anyone else who backed Mussolini. After an hour it was obvious the meeting was heading nowhere. He had just decided to leave when Axel again stood.

"Gentlemen, we are getting nowhere fast and I have had enough. We do not have an army, we are not soldiers, we do not have weapons, and we are, on the whole, old men. For God's sake let's be realistic." As he sat down most around the table clapped but Joseph saw genuine resentment creep over a few faces.

They broke up agreeing to meet again one week later. All were asked to speak to contacts and collect whatever information they could on Mussolini's long term objectives. Joseph finally slipped out; relieved nothing rash had been approved.

* * *

Turin had always been at the heart of Italy's industrial machine and it was in the city's factories that worker power and the unions were strongest. It was in this environment of industrial upheaval that a young Mussolini sought to establish himself as the leader of the people. At that time he understood the importance of aligning himself with the workers but his support proved only fleeting. As soon as the Fascists gained power he performed a complete U-turn, promoting himself as the one politician with the strength and determination to restore law and order to the industrial chaos in the north and he chose Turin as his battlefield.

During December 1922, the city's Fascists launched a violent offensive against the local labour movement, first burning down one of the trade union buildings, followed by attacks on two clubs of the Italian Socialist Party. They kidnapped the editors of the Communist Party newspaper before rounding up known communists and trade unionists and marching them to the central square. In total eleven were put to death; a further ten critically injured.

Mussolini instantly denied any connection to the killers claiming it was a spontaneous act of violence by undisciplined 'squadristi'. There were many however, who believed the bloodbath was the result of a considerable degree of planning and they claimed Mussolini had personally backed them.

The day after the attacks, Riccardo Levin contacted Joseph to explain that two members of the business group had been beaten up. Joseph was shocked, more so when he heard their names, Henry Marks and Alon Shum. The unthinkable; that of having an informant in the business group suddenly became credible.

Joseph had witnessed firsthand, state sponsored mass murder by secret security services and prayed his former life was not returning to haunt him. He even spoke to Emil about travelling to join his siblings, but his son was adamant that with the company hanging on and actually picking up a few new contracts from abroad, there was no way he would leave.

*   *   *

As anticipated, the group's meeting the following week proved more than difficult. Emotions were running high over the attack on two of their members and action was demanded. As there was no standing chairman, member after member stood without being invited to vent their fury and Joseph sensed the group losing control. He then watched with surprise as his close friend Riccardo Levin slowly got to his feet.

"Gentlemen, this cannot continue. We are squabbling like children but what we face is anything but child's play." There were nods of agreement. "I move that we should appoint a member that we trust to the chair." Avi Ziv then shouted bluntly,

"Okay, but who?" Riccardo looked across the room towards Joseph and pointed.

"Joseph Aizenberg is my nomination." After an initial stunned silence, everyone started talking and it was eventually agreed that Joseph would be the most equable and dependable of chairman. He immediately realised he had been manipulated into a corner with little opportunity for retreat and he proposed a short break whilst he discussed the motion with members. Without exception, everyone backed his chairmanship.

* * *

Events began to unfold just one week later. Joseph was having his evening meal with Emil and Marguerita in the dining room of Hayastan when there was a knock at the front door. Carla answered it and returned to tell Joseph two men wanted to see him. She said she had asked who they were and was simply told that it was none of her business. Surprised, she told them to wait. Joseph and Emil both rose and went to the front door.

"Can I help you?" Joseph asked politely.

"Are you Joseph Aizenberg?" one of the men asked formally. Joseph replied in the affirmative.

"Are you Chairman of the Turin Jewish Business Association?"

"Yes." Joseph answered, beginning to feel extremely nervous.

"Then I have here a decree from the Courts banning the group from meeting. Information has arisen that indicates members of the group have been involved in anti-government rhetoric and subversive activities. As a result you are to warn members they are being watched and any evidence of them undermining the government or the country's leadership will be dealt with ruthlessly." Without another word they left the estate.

Sat with a calming drink in the lounge, Emil began haranguing his father about the Business Group, asking why Joseph had never seen the potential for trouble, especially as they were all Jews. His father had no answer. Joseph did not want to get into an argument with Emil; his priority was how to inform the membership the meetings had been banned. Calling the group together was out of the question and he decided to write to each member explaining what had happened and advising them in no uncertain terms that the group was disbanded with immediate effect. He advised that members should not be seen together as they were being constantly monitored. Although not strictly true, Joseph hoped the 'slight' exaggeration would dissuade the more volatile of them that there was no future in openly opposing Mussolini or the Fascists.

Joseph was no coward, however, he was a pragmatist and all his experience told him to steer clear of anyone with unrestrained anti-government sentiments, whilst ensuring that neither Emil nor Scalfaro's was dragged into his problems.

The following day, after another lengthy discussion with Emil and Marguerita, Joseph made the decision to leave Italy and visit his family. So much had changed in their lives in terms of marriages and births that he was eager to see them. Before departing, Joseph spoke with Flavio who agreed to keep an eye on Emil. He then met briefly with Riccardo informing him he was leaving and wrote to Saul Tahter and Eric Manoukian asking them to keep the Armenian project going until his return.

Joseph left Italy early in 1923 and was away for over a year, loving the time spent with his children and grandchildren. He returned to Turin temporarily in April 1924 for the national elections, convinced the Fascists would lose. Quite implausibly, considering how loathed Mussolini and his government were, they won.

In the aftermath of the improbable result, Mussolini claimed the Fascists gained 65% of the vote. He chose not to mention the violence, intimidation and widespread vote rigging that secured his victory.

Joseph left Turin immediately following the result; his bitter disappointment compounded by the knowledge that whilst Mussolini ruled, as Jews, Emil and any other member of his family, had no future in Italy.

*   *   *

For the next few months, Joseph travelled extensively across the UK and North America looking for further investment opportunities. He celebrated his seventieth birthday in Washington with Barbara and Joshua and was overjoyed when the rest of his family secretly travelled to their sister's house for a surprise birthday party. For the umpteenth time he marvelled at his good fortune in having such a remarkable family.

Following the birth of Ellen, his first granddaughter in London in November 1926, Joseph reluctantly returned to Turin. The following day he visited Scalfaro's where Emil explained that the situation had become desperate; orders were down and Fascist corruption was making business impossible. It was bitter-sweet when Emil stated obdurately that regardless of the problems, under no circumstance would he agree to sell up.

"Father, we must never forget that the considerable success our family has enjoyed came originally from Scalfaro's and our workers." He sat looking at Emil astonished; he sounded just like Gabrielle at that first meeting in Al Bicerin so many years before.

*   *   *

Joseph kept his presence in Turin low key, focusing on the three projects and working mainly from home but on the rare occasion when he ventured out, he always ensured nobody was following him.

Not unexpectedly, in his absence Italy had continued its slow but irrevocable decline. Too many of the problems were ingrained; solutions were absent from government policy and undermining everything was the catastrophic state of the national finances. In its simplest terms the Mussolini government was facing bankruptcy and the result was predictable; crippling tax increases which were the most severe in Europe. Scalfaro's remained afloat but the situation was perilous.

*   *   *

After no word from Riccardo for six weeks, Joseph received a dinner invitation from him via a hand written letter. Strangely, he wrote that a friend would pick Joseph up and drive him to the restaurant

As they left Turin, the driver, a young man called Federico, told Joseph that by travelling after dark, they could spot whether they were being tailed by a car's headlights and then added with a smile that nothing was following them.

An hour's drive out of the city, they stopped at a small restaurant and over their meal, Joseph listened as Riccardo explained that whilst he had been away, some members of the original business group had continued to meet. Joseph was furious and his mood was not helped as Riccardo tried to justify the meetings by explaining that the situation facing Jews in Turin had become intolerable and continuing to meet had become an irreplaceable support for their ever more difficult lives.

He went on to say that many of the members had lost their businesses or simply had them confiscated by the Fascists and Joseph began to understand how difficult it had been for so many and how fortunate they were to have Flavio Lotti on their side. However, he acknowledged that even his influence was becoming less effective as the Fascists became more openly anti-Semitic.

The coffee arrived and the evening was coming to an end when Joseph realised how much he had missed his old friend's company. When Riccardo suggested he join him later that week to meet with a few of the old gang, Joseph was torn. Of course he wanted to see his friends but knew for Emil's sake, he had to refuse.

It was late when Riccardo drove Joseph back to Turin and just as they were approaching the outskirts of the city, they were stopped at a roadblock. The police had not been there on the way to the restaurant so it was just down to bad luck. After a few minutes studying their documents one of the officers said,

"What are you doing out of the city?" Riccardo explained that they were old friends who had not seen each other for some time and were meeting up for dinner. The officer gave his partner a disbelieving look and then shone his torch directly into Joseph's face.

"I know you," he said belligerently and Joseph looked carefully in the gloom, but had absolutely no idea who he was.

"You don't remember me do you," came the response to Joseph's silence. "I was sixteen and after just three weeks, what did you do? Got rid of me. Remember now?" And for the life of him Joseph didn't have a clue what he was talking about.

"I'm sorry but you must be mistaken," he answered quietly praying it would end the accusations.

"No way," the policemen answered, "I'd never to forget you. The bakery, remember, my first job and because of what you did my father threw me out of the house..." Joseph couldn't believe it as the policeman unclipped his gun from its holster. Before he could say anything to calm the man down, Riccardo leapt out of the car, pulling a revolver from under his jacket and he fired at the officers, grounding both instantly.

Joseph sat in disbelief as Riccardo sped away from the bloodbath. Eventually they slowed down and drove unhurriedly through the city before they turned into the narrow back streets of Turin.

Joseph's mind was a complete blank. He'd just witnessed his ultimate nightmare; his close friend dispassionately executing two men and worse, two policemen. In the blink of an eye Riccardo had become someone Joseph barely recognised.

* * *

The next day Joseph remained at home waiting for a knock on the door. He spent the day alone in his study trying to come to terms with what had happened and what he should or could do about it. Early the next morning he decided he must speak to Riccardo and asked Umberto to get the car. Joseph was just about to leave when Carla showed his friend into the lounge.

The two men stood awkwardly; the silence was unnerving. Joseph finally broke the ice when he called Carla and asked for coffee.

"I cannot understand what possessed you. Two policemen are dead."

"Joseph. Stop, please." Before anything else could be said, Carla entered with a tray. Once she had left, Riccardo spoke quietly,

"Let me explain please." Joseph nodded his agreement and waited. "As soon as the man went for his gun, any legal authority he carried disappeared."

"Okay," Joseph answered thoughtfully, "what about the other man and what had he done to warrant being killed?" Riccardo thought for a moment before answering.

"Nothing apart from being a member of the secret police. Joseph, he was in the wrong place at the wrong time. Look, I'm sorry to put you in this situation. You've always been a wonderful friend, but when it comes to trying to survive and raise a family in this godforsaken country, you have no idea."

"Then tell me." Joseph said unpleasantly, regretting his tone immediately.

"Since you dissolved the business group, nine members have been killed or disappeared. That's nine Joseph. It's clear Mussolini and his henchmen do not want Jews in Italy and certainly not in any prominent positions." Joseph had never seen his friend so miserable. "Across the country Jews and their companies are being endlessly targeted although nothing will ever be proved. It's only a matter of time before Mussolini introduces anti-Semitic legislation prohibiting Jews from living in Italy."

"If that's the case," Joseph said frankly, "why hasn't Emil been targeted? He's Jewish and running a successful company."

"Simple," Riccardo answered attempting to keep any acrimony out of his voice. "You have always shared the ownership of Scalfaro's with a prominent and extremely influential Italian, Flavio Lotti. Have you any idea how much he has done for you and the company?" Joseph was shocked but accepted Riccardo was right and guiltily realised he'd been so wrapped up with travelling and his projects that he'd hardly seen Flavio since his return.

*   *   *

Joseph made the decision to confess all to Emil when he returned from work that evening. He knew that as a result of the murder of the policemen he would have to leave Italy permanently. His problem was explaining the events without placing his eldest son in a position where he could be linked to the killings.

As Joseph waited with a book and glass of wine for Emil's return, there was a knock at the door and Carla showed Flavio into the lounge. After accepting a glass of wine, Flavio said,

"I have just come from a very close friend, one with contacts in the secret police and the conversation turned to the attack on the policemen the other night. Are you aware of it?" Joseph's heart sank as he nodded.

"As I know you have close ties with the Jewish community, I thought I should come straight here. Apparently, one of the two policemen is still alive." Joseph felt sick. He tried not to show his discomfort but it was obvious Flavio noticed his reaction.

"It's not known whether he will survive and currently he is incoherent. He's slipping in and out of consciousness but has said they were attacked by Jews." Flavio stared at a ghostly white Joseph.

"Are you alright?" Joseph remained silent.

"How long have we been friends? You're like a brother to me and right now you're behaving very strangely. Is it the killing? Do you know something?" Joseph cringed at the word "killing' but that's what it was. He took a deep breath and then answered honestly,

"I'm aware of what happened. Regrettably I know a good deal more than is safe to know but if I tell you anything, your life would be in extreme danger and I would never do that to you." Flavio remained silent before finally asking,

"Is there anything I can do?" Joseph smiled.

"You know you are such a wonderful friend. Anyone else in your position would try to get out of the house as quickly as they could but not you." Joseph looked at Flavio kindly. "Thank you, but I will not involve you. Maybe one day I'll explain, but right now it's too dangerous for you to know. All I ask is that you trust me."

"Trust you!" Flavio gave an ironic laugh. "That's the one thing you never need worry about. After all the years we have been friends and all the troubles we've been through I trust you more than my own life."

* * *

Emil returned later than expected and after supper Joseph suggested they have a drink in the lounge, just the two of them. A little surprised, Emil agreed and Marguerita left them and joined Carla in the kitchen. For the next half hour Joseph explained as much as he could. He wanted to be honest but knew he had to protect his son and that meant revealing nothing that could in any way incriminate him. Even so, as he listened to his father, Emil was devastated.

Joseph implored his son to believe that he was innocent of any wrongdoing, repeating time and time again that he could never have predicted or avoided what had happened. He steered well away from naming those involved and Emil for his part didn't pursue the matter.

Before retiring, Joseph explained that in all likelihood he would have to leave Italy and probably for good. He said the next twenty-four hours would be critical and only then would he make a decision.

* * *

Joseph found sleep impossible that night. He paced his room for what seemed like hours, went to the kitchen for a drink and read a book; nothing helped.

Next morning, by the time he emerged, Emil had already left for Scalfaro's and Carla had left a note explaining that Umberto was driving her to the town to do the shopping. As Joseph sat in the kitchen reading the paper, there was a knock at the front door. Joseph thought it a strange hour for anyone to be visiting and his heart sank as he opened the door to three uniformed policemen.

He was told he must accompany them to the station for questioning and he accepted he had little choice; all three were huge and armed, and he was over seventy. Joseph asked if he could leave a note and was told he could do nothing but get in the car.

Once in the back seat with two of the men sitting either side of him whilst the third drove, Joseph saw they were headed out of the city and knew he was in serious trouble.

After what seemed like twenty minutes, the car left the main road and they drove for some distance along an overgrown track before arriving at a derelict barn. Joseph had no idea where they were but his alarm was intensifying by the second. The car stopped and he was told to get out. He was pushed into the building, thrown violently against a wall and the questions began. It was at that moment Joseph knew his life was over.

With so much experience of man's capacity for inflicting pain on the innocent and such an intimate understanding of life at its most brutal, Joseph knew where the questioning was heading and what the final outcome would be.

In his younger days, he had often wondered how he would deal with his own mortality. On so many occasions he had been close to death and he'd learnt to accept the end of this life as simply a continuum to the next. With those thoughts, he closed his eyes and prayed. As the blows struck, Joseph was genuinely at peace; he was able to focus with immense pride on his wonderful family, his children and grandchildren and of course Elizabeth and Gabriella.

After one particularly vicious punch to the head, as Joseph slid down the wall, he felt his legs give way and an angry, burning pain across his chest. Breathing had become almost impossible and as he sucked at the air, implausibly, and to the disbelief of the thugs who were pounding his body black and blue, Joseph smiled at his tormentors; he was near the end. His body had taken too much punishment and was shutting down and as he keeled over the smile remained on his lips; he had told them nothing.

Joseph sank to the floor as darkness enveloped him and a bitter cold encased him. He lay rigidly still, eyes staring, mouth open and his thoughts drifted between Armenia and Ahmed Bashier; to Elizabeth and Gabriella, his children and grandchildren, and dear Flavio; he then closed his eyes and was at peace.

—Ж—

PART II

The CONSEQUENCES of BETRAYAL.

Chapter 1

October 1943

As Ellen hit the freezing water the breath was knocked out of her and she felt herself being dragged deeper and deeper towards the riverbed. She started to fight, using her spare hand to tear at the rope binding her to her father. Loosening it earlier had helped and by twisting and pulling at the knot she managed to break free. Although desperate to swim up for air, Ellen grabbed at her father, frantically trying to prevent him from sinking further but as she got closer she could see a red mist enveloping him. Ever more frantic for oxygen, she swam closer and wanted to scream out as she saw blood oozing from the back of his head. Forcing his face towards her, she saw jagged bone and torn flesh. Broken-hearted, Ellen realised his eyes were open and he was staring at her. She sensed a fleeting moment's recognition and a devoted smile, before he died.

Ellen was drowning; she could wait no longer. Up and up she swam, fighting the water and as she broke free, gulped at the fresh air. Immediately she heard gunfire and suddenly the water all around her was exploding. They were shooting at her and instinctively she took a deep breath and thrust back under the water. She could see others, some sinking to the bottom, others floating just below the surface and she prayed her mother and brother had survived like her. As she grabbed at bodies however, she found only unresponsive strangers.

Every time she broke the surface for air, Ellen felt bullets striking the water around her. On one occasion she delayed a fraction and saw soldiers on both sides of the river, shooting indiscriminately at floating bodies. She was terrified, knowing if she didn't get to the surface she would drown but if she did, she would be shot but Ellen's will to survive was immense. She was angry, so very angry at what they had done to her family that there was no way she would give in. Finally, in desperation, Ellen snatched at a body floating on the surface. Grabbing the clothing, she pulled it close and lying with her mouth barely out of the water, she tucked her head between the chest and arm. Floating downstream, there was no let-up in the shooting and Ellen carefully steered her protective shield away from the banks. Twice she looked and twice she saw soldiers shouting and laughing, firing at bodies trying to sink them before they floated away. So many times her saviour was hit, so many times it saved her life and Ellen kept asking God to spare her.

As she drifted past the last of the soldiers, Ellen's feelings were confused. Of course she was overjoyed; how could she not be when she was still alive but the horror of her survival suddenly hit home and she began to shake uncontrollably. She needed her family.

Exhausted and frozen, Ellen wanted to swim to the bank but something made her wait and her heart pounded as again she felt bullets thumping against the body defending her. Holding on as tightly as her aching arms would allow, Ellen closed her eyes, prayed and waited.

As she floated on, it was vital to get out of the water. Her body was numb and had begun to shake violently. Ellen had lost all feeling in her hands and feet. As she kicked for the bank it abruptly hit home that she was seventeen and alone, on the run from an enemy who wanted her dead and as her panic grew, her tears flowed mixing with the water surrounding her. She stopped kicking and asked herself whether it wouldn't be better to just let go of the body and sink to the bottom of the river. There she would be peace with her father, mother and Noah, and for the briefest of moments, Ellen truly wanted to die. Suddenly, with no warning, a violent rage overcame her and even though she accepted there was a certain attraction in death, her craving for revenge was paramount. She knew she had to find those who had murdered her family, who had raped her and her mother, and when she did, God how she'd hurt them. She would cause them such harm before she watched them die slowly and in agony!

Ellen kicked hard, grimly hanging on to the bullet ravaged body; she had to live. Spotting a gap in the steep sides of the river bank where she could climb ashore, Ellen again kicked hard with every last ounce of energy. Then finally, exhausted but elated she felt her feet touch the bottom of the riverbed.

Ellen stood and pushed the body towards the bank and wondered what to do with her shield and wonderful protector. She decided to let it continue its journey downstream as just maybe someone, somewhere would discover it and demand to know what had happened. As she was about to push the body back out into the current she recognised something that made her hesitate; something so familiar; that deep blue coat and the fair hair.

"Oh God no, please God, please, please NO!" Ellen screamed, hoping, praying, but somehow knowing. Slowly, so very slowly, Ellen turned the bloodied, bullet-ridden body over. Her knight in shining armour who had protected her became the body she dared not look at. He was so small, so innocent and so special; eyes wide open staring right at her. It was her beloved Noah, her baby brother was her saviour.

Ellen screamed at the sky, screamed at the world, screamed at her God. How could he let her beautiful, innocent family die? With tears flowing and a broken heart Ellen sank to her knees.

Chapter 2

October 1943

Ellen woke with a start. It was dark and she instantly panicked; where was her mother? She always needed her mother after a nightmare and this one had been the worst ever. For a few moments she lay completely still listening, but all she could hear was an eerie silence. She then moved just slightly and suddenly every part of her body screamed out in pain.

With great care, Ellen pulled back the blanket and as her eyes adjusted to the dark, she moved away from the warmth of the bed to a curtain covering a window. Pushing aside the coarse, heavy material she saw a translucent moon lighting up a clear sky. Surrounded by snow-lined mountains, a small stream flowed next to the house. It was idyllic.

Reality rapidly took control. Dark memories filled her thoughts, suffering and pain ever present. Ellen remembered her world being turned upside down, her unimaginable losses and as she stood rigid with fear, her tears erupted. She wept for her family; for Marguerita and the boys, for those on the train who had paid the ultimate price. She wept for the innocents who had been taken away and for those living in fear as their world had spun out of control. Ellen wept for those persecuted and those who had disappeared, and finally, exhausted, she dragged herself back to the bed and hating her self-pity, she wept for herself.

* * *

Next morning Ellen woke late. The sunlight squeezed through the heavy curtains and as she lay trying to understand what was happening to her, the unbearable images returned. The rape, the train journey and the slaughter at the river flashed through her thoughts before a stabbing fear ignited within her. Ellen struggled to remain in control as Noah's lifeless eyes stared straight through her, dominating every part of her being and she knew categorically that the vision would haunt her for all her days.

Ellen fought the tears but it was in vain and she felt the watery liquid cascading down her cheeks, tasting the salt as it passed her lips. "No!" she screamed. "No more crying!" She crawled angrily out of the warm bed, refusing to endure any more of her weakness.

The room was freezing but Ellen didn't care. She opened the curtains and stood looking at the magnificence of the panorama surrounding her, but she hated it, hated everything in her God forsaken world. Ellen punched the wall, first with her fist then with her forehead. She kicked out before using her fist again and again. She needed to hurt, seriously hurt something, anything and her own pathetic body was nearest.

As her anger built, Ellen kept asking why she had lived when the others had died. She despised herself for surviving. Her self-hate was primeval and she wanted, no, she demanded to be punished. She had to harm herself because that's what she deserved.

Suddenly Ellen felt hands grab her from behind and as they tightened she fought like a demon with all the strength left in her battered body.

"You'll never take me again, you'll never rape me again. I'd rather die!" She finally buckled with exhaustion.

Ellen was conscious of waking on numerous occasions but nothing more. She never spoke or moved, she always fell back into an unrelenting sleep. Then one bright morning she woke with the curtains pulled to one side and the warmth from the sun on her cheeks. She sighed with contentment and slowly looking around noticed her hands were swollen and bruised. Remembering, she ran a finger gently over her battered and inflamed forehead. Abruptly her tears began but she refused to let them flow and climbed painfully out of the bed and limped to the window. The scene was still breathtaking, the panorama magnificent and as Ellen stared at the beauty surrounding her she vowed never to weep again until she'd exacted retribution from the animals who had committed the atrocities against her family. Whatever it took, whatever the sacrifice, she would have her time and when she did she would wreak havoc in the lives of those culpable.

Ellen turned back into the room and saw an old woman standing in the doorway watching her. She moved slowly to Ellen and smiling gently took her hand and led her back to the bed all the time muttering in German.

She tucked Ellen up and left, returning just a few minutes later carrying a tray of hot soup and bread, with a very large cup of something Ellen didn't recognise. As she smelt the food, she realised she was ravenous and without hesitation she began to eat, much to the obvious delight of the old lady.

* * *

It had been just on a fortnight and the family who had taken her in was astonished at Ellen's recovery. From almost the first moment she was lucid, she had driven her benefactor to distraction wanting to learn German. When she could eventually walk and go outside, she had immediately begun to work on her fitness, first walking and then running.

Ellen only spoke to the old woman's husband but not her children. No names were ever used and she understood the enormous risk they were taking by looking after her.

As soon as she was ready to travel, she was told she would be taken to a group who could get her home, wherever home was. She left very early one morning with the husband, having tried to thank the old woman, but knew no words could ever express her gratitude.

* * *

They walked side by side for most of the morning up into the mountains, traversing the snow line and she found the journey exhausting. Whenever they stopped to rest she asked questions in basic German about their location, but only ever received a reply of 'I can't tell you' and in the end she stopped asking.

After another long climb, sometimes through thick snow, they came across a small, ramshackle farmhouse. Ellen could see a man looking out of the window watching them approach. Without knocking her guide entered followed by Ellen and after introductions, which meant nothing to Ellen as no names were used, he left to return home. She tried to thank him but he waved away her appreciation as 'nothing', but she knew 'nothing', was everything in terms of her survival.

After refreshments, she was told by her new guide, in surprisingly eloquent English, that she would be taken to a group who were helping to repatriate either Allied soldiers who'd escaped from prison camps or Jews like herself. When Ellen asked how he knew she was Jewish, the man smiled gently and said she would be told once they were safely in the camp.

The late afternoon hike was extremely tiring especially when Ellen had to scramble through snowdrifts and it was after one particularly difficult climb that she realised her fitness was nowhere near adequate.

As dusk began to fall, they entered a narrow tree covered valley and had another awkward trek through the ever darkening wood. It was just when she felt she had to stop and rest that Ellen saw lights ahead and was overjoyed when they entered a campsite. There were tents positioned around a larger marquee with a cottage set to one side and Ellen was amazed at the number of people who turned out to greet them. Her guide whose name she still didn't know indicated she should follow him and they entered the cottage without knocking. Ellen walked hesitantly into a dark room with low ceilings and a roaring fire in the grate and saw two men and a woman sat round a table in the corner. One of the men stood and took Ellen's hand.

"Names are fictional here but please call me Hans," he said kindly in heavily accented but good English. "You will be 'Delphin', that's Dolphin in English," and then added laughing, "You came from the water. You're obviously intelligent, single-minded and stubborn. The name suits perfectly, no?" The others laughed, shook Ellen's hand and introduced themselves as Max, Anne and her guide, Paul. Hans then said, "Before you ask, we know you're English because when you get angry you scream at yourself in the language." Ellen blushed. The ice had been broken and she laughed with them.

She felt at ease especially after the introductions when Anne, who also spoke excellent English, showed Ellen the cottage including an upstairs room she used as a bedroom which she would share with her. There was a primitive kitchen and washing facilities downstairs and a large room full of old clothing. Anne explained that when people returned to the camp they nearly always brought back any old clothes and other items that could be useful. She then started throwing a selection of clothes at Ellen telling her to try them on as it was likely to get much colder.

Ellen chose some clothing and also two pairs of snowshoes; to her they looked like tennis racquets but Anne explained they would be crucial if she spent time in the mountains.

That evening, Ellen joined the rest of the camp for supper. Everyone sat around one large campfire eating and drinking and she was amazed at how friendly and happy they were.

Following the meal, Hans asked Ellen to return to the cottage and Anne and Max were once again by the fire. Over a hot drink that tasted a little like warmed wine, Hans asked her if she remembered anything that happened. Ellen sat for a few minutes and then said unemotionally,

"They murdered everyone." Anne looked sadly at Ellen and said,

"We know but your train should never have been there in the first place."

"Why?" Ellen asked.

"Well," it was Hans that answered, "Switzerland is supposed to be neutral, but it seems they have agreed to let Germany move trains across the border. Usually the Nazis use the Brenner Pass for freight but we've heard it's been damaged by Allied bombers and hit by early snow so they need another route to support Italy's war effort."

"So our train was travelling through Switzerland even though they're supposed to be neutral?" Ellen asked.

"It seems so, although I can't believe the Swiss would ever agree to it," Anne answered.

"We think the bridge and railway track were destroyed in error by Allied bombers," Hans explained. "The damage was so bad your train could not carry on and it certainly couldn't turn back without the Germans being caught transporting Jews through a neutral country."

"So they just slaughtered everyone instead." Ellen knew she had spoken unpleasantly but at that moment she didn't care. After a thoughtful silence, she added quietly, "I'm sorry." She smiled guiltily. "You have done so much for me and all I do is speak rudely to you." Anne moved closer and put her arm around her saying,

"No one should have to go through what you have and I promise, for the few days you are with us, we will do everything we can to help you."

"Over the last few years we have managed to establish escape routes to get people back to England." It was Hans speaking again. "Most make it safely home and you can travel with the next batch that goes."

"No!" Ellen answered bluntly.

"But you must." It was the first time Ellen could remember Max speaking.

"I won't. Whatever you say, whatever you do, I will not go until I have my revenge.' Then Ellen told her story without emotion, just facts.

When she had finished the others sitting around the fire were speechless. Ellen's story was hard to believe but each one knew it was the truth. Sadly, it was not the first or last time they would hear similar accounts of the betrayal of the innocent.

"How old are?" Anne eventually asked.

"It doesn't matter. What has to be done has no age restriction."

"And what is it you have to do?"
"I have to find those responsible and kill them."

* * *

Early in the morning ten days after arriving at the camp, Ellen sat having breakfast and realised it was her eighteenth birthday but decided to tell no one. Later on she then proved as good as her promise when she refused to join three British servicemen on their journey back to England.

Once those in the camp knew Ellen was staying, most treated her as one of their own. They joked with her and although few had the details, it was known that she had been through a horrifying ordeal and as a result there was never any unpleasantness in the banter. It was also clear Ellen was growing into a striking young woman and the potential for complications was obvious. However, with a shove in the right direction from Anne, all agreed she was to be treated like their little sister.

Ellen had no idea what the future held but intuitively knew that not only building up her fitness but learning self-defence, fighting with a knife, learning to ski and how to survive the freezing temperatures were crucial if she was to succeed in her vow to track down her enemy.

A turning point came as she was about to go for a run and saw three men walking into the camp carrying carcases and crossbows. Ellen suddenly realised it was exactly what she had been praying for; a weapon that she would be allowed to use. Guns were banned because of the noise and also the scarcity of ammunition but a crossbow was perfect; no noise. The same bolts could be used time and again and after a few lessons she would need no one to be with her whilst she practised.

Ellen rushed to find Anne, who was in the main tent with one of the three men she'd seen. Feeling a little awkward, she asked to speak to her outside and once they were alone explained what she needed: a bow, bolts and one of the men to teach her.

"Ellen, you have no idea how difficult a crossbow is to handle, load and fire," but Ellen refused to listen and was unrelenting to the point of distraction. Finally, after considerable badgering, Anne gave in and introduced Ellen to Alfred. Within a few minutes and much to Anne's amusement, Ellen had convinced a bewildered Alfred to teach her how to use a crossbow and that they could begin early the next morning. When he tried to explain that he had returned to the camp for some rest, Ellen laughed and told him that teaching her would be far healthier for him. In the end Alfred simply couldn't say no and for the following few weeks, whatever the weather, Ellen worked all hours with him. She wanted to learn everything there was to know about the crossbow; how it was made, how it was maintained, how you made spare parts if anything should go wrong and of course, how to be an expert shot. Alfred pointed out how the bow was mounted onto a stick called the stock or tiller, how this stock held a mechanism for drawing back the bowstring and he watched amazed as every time Ellen became confused, she pushed herself even harder to understand. He showed her how the drawn string was held in place by a rolling cylindrical pawl, known simply as the nut and how the trigger system operated when releasing the drawn string. He told her it was usually made from iron or steel and how it was this that was used to retain the force of the cocked string in the nut and then demonstrated how it released the nut to spin and the string to fire the bolt or arrow. Ellen frequently struggled with his descriptions and she demanded he show her again and again until she got it right. She would not be beaten by anything.

When Alfred moved on to the most basic of skills; how to hold the bow, how to draw the string and load the bolts, how to aim and fire with any sort of accuracy, Ellen floundering at first, but she would not give in and worked endlessly as Alfred, rather grudgingly, realised she really was extraordinary.

Every day after an early meal they would climb away from the camp to a practice area that Alfred had set up about a mile away. Ellen would then spend the time releasing, firing and reloading the bow. Initially Alfred was impressed as although Ellen had blisters across both hands and on all her fingers she would not stop. When exhaustion overcame her they would sit together talking. Alfred told her about the history of the crossbow and Ellen realised how knowledgeable he was.

It was during these breaks that she prised as much information out of Alfred as she could. She asked him how he survived in the mountains, especially travelling within German held territory, and again he readily told Ellen about his experiences. She then asked about guns, explaining that she knew there was no chance of practising but was desperate to understand how they worked, and Alfred taught her all he could about firearms.

Three days before Alfred was due to leave camp, he suggested he took Ellen out to hunt. Hans immediately agreed hoping that once Ellen faced the reality of killing, she would realise it wasn't for her and agree to travel home.

Before they left, Anne asked Alfred where the best kill would be and when he answered, "The other side of the ridge," she stated bluntly,

"Be careful, you know what's over there."

*   *   *

They started out extremely early the next morning, keeping under the cover of the trees to avoid the heavy snow that had fallen overnight and Ellen decided, although she would never admit it to anyone else, that she liked Alfred a great deal. He was nice looking and most importantly seemed quite genuine.

Ellen had been given false papers for the trip just in case they were stopped and throughout the morning, Alfred explained how he lived off the land. He pointed out wild berries, fruits and vegetables. Twice he picked up the tracks of red deer and wild boar, possible targets for Ellen to kill, but on both occasions they led to nothing.

Lunch was taken in glorious sunshine in a pasture surrounded by snow-topped mountains and they talked endlessly. Ellen felt completely at ease with Alfred, something that had been missing from her life since the death of her family, and she wanted to know about him.

"I never dwell on the past, never try to resurrect what's gone before and I don't need memories." When Ellen showed her surprise, Alfred continued,

"There can be no distractions, no hesitations and absolutely no regrets for me to do effectively what I'm supposed to do." Ellen looked confused so Alfred explained, "It is only a question of time before I am caught and when that happens, well…" Alfred ran his finger across his throat. "I live only for today." He then stood and suggested they continue to hunt but suddenly stopped, dropped to his knees and placed a hand over Ellen's mouth. As she was about to hit out angrily, she saw him put a finger to his lips indicating she should be quiet. She lay completely still and heard voices. Alfred pushed her down into a ditch and crouched beside her.

Ellen could make out German words. In a whisper, Alfred told her to remain where she was and he slid out of the ditch. He returned a few minutes later and again placed a finger over his lips. Ellen heard the voices moving away and when it was silent, she looked out and saw three German soldiers disappearing around a hedge. Shocked, a furious Ellen asked Alfred why he hadn't killed them. Alfred sat waiting for Ellen to finish venting her anger at him and in a quiet but uncompromising tone he said,

"Have you any idea what would happen if those three did not return home?" Ellen was puzzled but the fury remained and she truculently shrugged her shoulders. "The Germans would make reprisals. Firstly they would execute at least a dozen locals including women and children, all innocent of any wrongdoing. Next they would destroy a number of nearby farms or businesses and would torture any number of prominent villagers forcing them to reveal who had committed the executions. Finally, they would more than likely flood the area with the military. We are currently only a few miles from our camp which means, what has proved to be the almost perfect base for our resistance group, would probably be discovered and God knows how many of my friends and fellow fighters slaughtered." Without another word Alfred stood up, picked up his belongings and began walking away. Ellen remained rooted to the spot; what an absolute fool she'd been and it dawned on her that if she was seen as a liability, she would have no future in the camp. She might think her resolve to avenge her family was morally right but she understood it could never be at the expense of others.

Ellen felt terrible and tried to catch up, but Alfred was headed straight back to the camp. Her first ever hunt was obviously over.

*   *   *

Alfred and his two companions left camp the next morning, a day early so Ellen missed their departure. She was devastated. After their disagreement, Alfred had not spoken to her, just marched ahead leaving her struggling to keep up. A number of times she had called out an apology to him but Alfred wasn't interested until they entered the camp when he stopped and said plainly,

"You are not a child and although I am sorry for the awful things you've suffered, that does not give you the right to go on some sort of personal crusade and put other people's lives at risk. If you carry on the way you did today, you will not survive more than five minutes outside the protection of the camp." With that he turned his back and walked away. Ellen called out another apology but he ignored her.

She went straight to her room and remained there missing the evening meal. She was mortified as she imagined those around the campfire laughing about her as Alfred explained what had happened.

*   *   *

Early the next morning Ellen was still asleep when Anne came in with a hot drink and sat down on the edge of her bed.

"Tough time hunting?" Ellen opened her eyes and said,

"Not really. I was stupid and deserve to have the whole camp laugh at me."

"What are you talking about?" Anne asked gently.

"I'm sure everyone thought it highly amusing when Alfred told them what happened." Ellen felt like bursting into tears but under no circumstances would she; that would only make the situation far worse.

"Ellen, Alfred said nothing to anyone at supper, just that you were unable to find a kill but still had a good day tracking." Ellen realised, not for the first time, that she'd been too quick to judge. She should have known Alfred would never make fun of her in public.

She then explained what had happened, not expecting any sympathy or understanding and once she'd finished Anne was quiet for a few minutes before saying,

"Now I understand why you've locked yourself away." She moved over and put her arms around Ellen. "I've spent years fighting the Germans and have witnessed some pretty appalling scenes, but I have never experienced the personal heartbreak you have and that's why I want to get you home."

"But I…." Before Ellen could continue, Anne interrupted candidly.

"Let me finish... please." She smiled as Ellen nodded her agreement.

"We have another group leaving for England tomorrow. Why don't you go with them?" Ellen said nothing. In so many ways she was desperate to escape; she was exhausted and drained and the business with Alfred had caused her to question everything she was trying to do. She despised the fact she hadn't thanked him but at the root of everything was Ellen's own self-respect. She knew she could never look at herself in the mirror again if she did not try everything possible to find a small measure of justice for her family.

"Please believe," Ellen eventually said so sadly that Anne squeezed her tightly, "a very large part of me wants to go, to escape, break free...” Quite unexpectedly, it all poured out; her pain, the fear of being alone and her inexhaustible anger but as she talked a clear rationale for what she had to do calmed her cluttered mind.

“You see, I am not a child and I have the responsibility of ensuring there is justice for my family. I am the only one left so it is down to me to find the people who are guilty. Look, I’m no fool, I realise that in war things happen, terrible things that often drag innocent people into actions that are alien to them, but what happened to us was not an accident; it was not misfortune, bad luck or a mistake. The men who raped my mother and me, who slaughtered my father, mother, brother, aunt and cousins, those men enjoyed it, they really enjoyed the game. I heard laughing as I watched my mother being raped and soldiers joking as they fired bullets into the bodies floating down the river. Tell me, where was their guilt, their compassion; where in God’s name was their remorse?” Ellen broke away from Anne. “So that is why I can never walk away from my responsibilities.”

Ellen’s body was taut, coiled tightly, ready to explode and she walked to the window and looked out. Anne sat rigid, tears welling up in her eyes. She was stunned at what she had just witnessed. How could anyone so vulnerable speak with such conviction and clarity but also with such helplessness?

Anne told Ellen to wait and left the room returning a few minutes later with another hot drink for them both. She again sat down on the edge of the bed and said,

“Okay, you cannot kill effectively if you do it only for revenge. Your emotions will destroy your ability to do what needs to be done especially under extreme pressure.”

“But I will have my revenge.” Ellen said coldly.

"Is it only revenge you want?" As Ellen considered the question, memories came into focus; the years being held in the cottage like criminals when they were innocent, the laws introduced against her religion, the camps where the innocent were held and the trains which took them to their deaths.

"No, what I truly want is impossible so revenge will have to do."

"I don't understand."

"I'm a Jew. I should be able to live my life freely, be treated the same, have the same opportunities as everyone else, not be persecuted or killed for my beliefs. The German and Italian leaders have decided Jews are worthless, that we are vermin and the human race is better off without us. Please tell me how that can be right? No sane person should accept what is happening to the Jews." Yet again Anne was astonished at the power of Ellen's argument and simply had no reply.

*   *   *

Christmas 1943 approached and Ellen had been in the camp for nearly two months dedicating every minute of every day to practising her skills and working on her strength and speed. She had quickly become known as Little Delphin; not only the fittest member of the camp but also one of the most proficient with a knife. She was a competent skier and all reluctantly acknowledged she was an outstanding shot with a crossbow.

Every single day she went alone into the woods with a bow and bolts to fire endlessly at targets. She always set herself challenges and refused to return to the camp until she had achieved them, twice staying out all night in the freezing cold, determined not to fail. On both occasions Hans and Anne had been livid and when

Ellen eventually returned told her exactly what they thought, however, their admiration for their young charge was immeasurable.

Week after week, Ellen watched groups of fighters leave the camp and noticed that most returned without a full complement. However, as the established members of the group were killed or captured, others joined and there seemed no shortage of volunteers. Although Ellen always found it difficult to accept the death of friends, she constantly asked Hans to let her be part of a raid and he kept promising that he would, saying he was just waiting for the right target. Ellen never believed him.

Early in the morning three days before Christmas, Ellen set out for her daily practice. She had already completed her morning fitness routine and was feeling optimistic about her life. That afternoon she made Christmas decorations with Anne from local holly and just about anything they could lay their hands on. They tried their best to brighten up the cottage and the area around the main camp fire and considering the lack of resources, the area looked truly festive. Although Jewish, Ellen had spent many happy times with her friends in London, rejoicing in their Christian celebrations and that evening, after the meal, she loved being with everyone as they sat around the fire with the snow falling, singing mostly hymns and carols.

Next morning she woke early and lazily lay waiting for sleep to return. When she knew it wasn't coming, she dressed, went to the kitchen, ate some bread with a drink of goat's milk and grabbed her bow and extra clothes. As she walked past the ashes of the previous night's fire, the camp was deathly silent and Ellen saw that heavy snow had fallen. She began her climb towards her practice area and made good progress, protected from the worst of the snow by the canopy of trees. After fifteen minutes she noticed a strange object lying in the snow and cautiously moved towards it remembering she had always been told that under no circumstances should she touch anything she was not familiar with.

Very slowly Ellen approached the odd shaped bundle and when she was approximately ten feet away saw that it was some sort of material being held down by a rock. Confused but considerably more relaxed, she looked around to check she was still alone and then moved towards the rock. When she gently pulled at a loose rope, the material moved and she saw it was a parachute. After checking to see if there was anything else of interest, Ellen decided to refold it and replace the rock. After her target practice she would carry it back to the camp and see what Anne thought of her find.

Still puzzled by the parachute, Ellen continued to climb to the practice area as more heavy snow began to fall. Fifty yards further on, she spotted another bundle and knew it was another parachute being held down by a rock and then two more adjacent to where she was climbing and her whole body started to shudder. It was so obvious; why hadn't she understood straight away. Ellen suddenly turned and sprinted back towards the camp. She had to get back to warn them. They were all asleep and she knew something terrible was about to happen. Before she'd covered twenty yards there was the most unbearable cacophony of sound; loud explosions followed by a fire fight. The camp was being attacked. Why hadn't she realised earlier?

Continuing to run as fast as her legs would take her towards the sounds of slaughter, Ellen quickly reached the ridge overlooking the camp and stopped quite still dropping to her knees. German soldiers were everywhere setting fire to the tents. Not even the cottage was safe. Not one of her friends, not one of the wonderful people who had saved her and brought her back to sanity, was still alive.

Ellen wanted to kill someone, just as long as it was one of the evil bastards prowling around the camp looking for any sign of life and then extinguishing it. She spotted a German to one side of the cottage, away from the others, about to relieve himself. It was her chance. No matter how unimportant the man was, it was a chance to get one back, one killer less. She loaded the bolt and watched. The man was about thirty yards to her right, a shot she had made flawlessly hundreds of times in practice.

Holding the bow steady, with thumping heart and trembling fingers, Ellen aimed and slowly released the bolt. She watched unemotionally as the soldier's hands grabbed at his neck. The bolt had hit its target exactly where Ellen had aimed. The dying man opened his mouth to cry out but no sound came and she continued to watch impassively as he slid to his knees before collapsing to the ground. She remained still. Her tears were flowing; payback time had begun. At last she could cry.

Ellen reloaded the bow ready to take down another soldier. She had no fear of being caught, no anxiety about dying. She heard shouts throughout the camp. The dead soldier had been found, the alarm raised. Suddenly there were Germans everywhere, fanning out searching. Some were moving in her direction. Very slowly, in complete control, Ellen withdrew from the ridge, away from the camp. She was no fool and understood that if she was caught she would have achieved nothing. Moving further away deeper into the trees, she heard something behind her. Turning with bow raised she was suddenly grabbed from behind. Ellen knew that if she didn't break free she would die and she fought frantically but her attacker was strong and his grip vice-like. She felt a face close and heard a whisper,"Quiet." Ellen stopped struggling and the tension of the grip eased. She turned to confront her attacker; Alfred. He put a finger to his lips. Ellen nodded that she understood and he took her arm and pulled her further away from the camp and the searching soldiers.

As they retreated, the snow continued to fall muffling the sound of soldiers circling them. After a few minutes climbing, Alfred stopped and again put his finger to his mouth. Ellen nodded and watched as he began to clear snow from a small dip in the earth on the edge of the trees. He worked quickly and then whispered for Ellen to lie down on the bare soil and covered her with newly fallen snow. Leaving her mouth and eyes clear he threw old leaves over the area before placing two fallen branches, criss-crossed over the spot where she was lying. As the heavy snow covered any signs of Ellen's burrow, Alfred quietly and calmly told Ellen that the Germans were closing in and she would have to stay hidden whilst the enemy searched. He added forcefully that under no circumstance was she to move until he returned or, for one whole day, if he didn't make it.

Ellen then watched terrified as Alfred moved away; she was alone and could hear German soldiers searching the area immediately below her. Remaining absolutely still, she remembered she'd read that when the body was buried by snow it remained warm and although she felt no discomfort she was shaking.

* * *

Twice soldiers moved within just a few yards of Ellen and both times she held her breath and closed her eyes, willing them to move on. She listened as they called to each other, in no way trying to conceal their positions and she prayed Alfred remained undetected and safe.

In the end the soldiers appeared to give up and called to each other to move back to the camp. Ellen was elated and although her clothes were soaked and she was freezing she accepted Alfred was right and she must remain hidden until he returned.

As the hours passed, her memories flowed: her family, the time she had spent in Turin, her old school and friends. She wondered what they might be doing now and smiled as she imagined their reaction if she told them she was lying in deep snow in some foreign land having just killed a man. Then the hurt of losing so many in the camp overwhelmed her and the fact she had killed began to dawn on her. Her emotions switched from deep guilt to absolute joy and back to heavy remorse but overriding everything was the fact that at long last retribution had begun, justice was on the move.

As dusk fell, Ellen heard a rustle and again closed her eyes thinking the Germans had returned but she heard Alfred whisper that it was safe and it took him just seconds to dig Ellen free. She stretched her stiff body to warm up but was shaking with cold and he told her to get out of her wet things. He threw a bundle of dry, thick winter clothes towards her and turned away. Ellen, not caring whether he saw her naked or not, just wanted to be warm and stripped off.

Once dressed, she began to walk down towards the camp but Alfred held her back.

"I've already checked; there's nothing left, nothing to see and I've hidden anything that might be useful." With that he began to climb. Without argument Ellen fell in behind him but she felt completely lost. Alfred had taken all the risks to ensure she would not get caught and then, before digging her out of her hiding place, he had been back to the horror of the camp to see what remained so she would not have to witness it. Following behind the man, Ellen realised Alfred owed her nothing yet he had done everything to protect her.

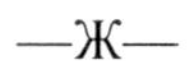

Chapter 3

January 1944

Alfred led Ellen to a stack of essentials he'd recovered from the camp, including their snowshoes, and obviously wanting to get as far away from there as possible, they trekked well into the night, eventually arriving at a shepherd's hut in the early hours.

The one roomed building was empty except for a pile of wood by a small fireplace and Alfred immediately lit the fire. Once it was going, he pulled some cheese and bread from one of his bags and offered it to Ellen. It was simple and cold but she was starving. After they'd eaten Alfred spread a groundsheet onto the floor, threw more wood on the fire and told Ellen to sleep. Hardly a word had passed between them and she lay awake wondering what she had done wrong.

Next morning when she woke Alfred had already made up the fire and was balancing a small pan of water over the flames to make a hot drink. There was also food laid out for breakfast.

Once again, as they ate Alfred said little. Ellen tried on a number of occasions to talk, even apologising again for her behaviour on their day out hunting but his replies were mumbled one-word answers.

After clearing up Alfred finally spoke.

"I must get you to the group who can take you home."

Ellen was stunned. It was the last thing she wanted. After a few seconds she replied, trying to stay calm and measured.

"Look, I'm indebted to you. If you hadn't done what you did, God only knows what would have happened to me but I'm not going home." There was a slight smile as he answered.

"Anne always said you were stubborn." Ellen sensed a change in Alfred as he mentioned Anne's name. "I'm sorry but I cannot take you with me; it would cause problems and with the camp gone my work is even more important, so you can't come."

"Why?"

"I've just said it would cause problems. What I do is difficult and dangerous and although you have tried to learn the skills to fight, there is no way you could keep up with me." He looked at Ellen and said kindly, "You know, every time I returned to the camp Anne spoke about you. You really impressed her but you have to realise I'm constantly on the move travelling huge distances and I don't think you could handle it." Ellen again waited a few seconds, determined not to blurt out some emotional reply that would merely confirm everything Alfred was saying.

"Then go but I'm staying. I am not a child and I want to fight the Germans."

"No you don't," Alfred said brusquely and Ellen stared at him. "What you want is revenge; blind, uncompromising retribution, and because of that your judgement and actions will always cause havoc and extreme risk for anyone with you. As I said I am sorry but I will not take that chance." Ellen was mortified and more than a little embarrassed but deep down she had to admit he was right, but as usual she would not concede.

"As I said," Ellen spoke bluntly, "you must go. You have vital work to do but I also have responsibilities to my family, my friends and myself and I will not run away. Can you understand that?" Alfred didn't reply. He simply gathered a few of his belongings, walked to the door, turned and said,

"Good luck."

*   *   *

Ellen moved to a small opening used as a window and pushed aside the thick hemp sheet. She watched horrified as Alfred walked away into the blizzard. She then crept back to the heat of the fire asking herself what she'd done wrong.

Alone in a small, isolated hut high up in mountains with a blizzard outside, Ellen began to panic. She looked around the room realising that with only a little food and not much wood left, she couldn't remain there for long and then where would she go? She had warm clothes, false papers, a crossbow, bolts and a knife, but no map and absolutely no idea where she was. As she sat close to the warmth of the flames, her anger grew and as it did, she vowed never to give in. She would show Alfred and everyone else she really could make a difference and at the same time fulfil her promise to her family.

After all the difficulties she had faced over the previous few days, Ellen was exhausted and knew her body needed rest. She decided to sleep for the rest of the morning before moving out.

*   *   *

Ellen slept like the dead for the next four hours and when she eventually woke, she ate and felt much more positive about what lay ahead. As she sat by the fire finishing a hot drink she reasoned that she was in the Alps, probably in Switzerland. Although if the camp had been in Switzerland it would not have been attacked. She also deduced that, because of the German soldiers she had come across on her day out with

Alfred, if the camp was in fact in Switzerland, then it had to be close to Germany or a country controlled by the Germans. Also, if those in the camp were attempting to cause maximum disruption to the German war effort, then she had to be in Germany, France, Italy or Austria. Ellen dismissed Italy and France because everyone she had heard was speaking German, which left Austria or Germany. Going through all this she decided she was probably close to the Austrian border.

After packing her meagre belongings, Ellen felt refreshed and ready to move on. The blizzard had subsided and she was about to collect some snow to douse the fire when the door flew open and Alfred burst in. He stamped on the flames and said urgently,

"Let's go!" Ellen didn't wait. She grabbed her bag and followed Alfred out. Both strapped on their snowshoes and headed for a wood about a half a mile away. They made good time to the trees but Alfred didn't stop and moved at a speed Ellen found hard to maintain.

After about an hour Alfred slowed and a few minutes later under the cover of a tall pine tree he stopped, unpacked the ground sheet and told Ellen to rest. He pulled more cheese and bread from his rucksack and said she should eat. She wasn't that hungry but didn't refuse; that was the last thing she was going to do.

Once settled Alfred said, "After I left this morning, I came across a number of German patrols who I assume were searching for survivors from the camp and one of them was headed in your direction."

"Thank you again," Ellen said sincerely, "I'm not very good at all this, am I." Alfred didn't reply, he just sat quietly eating.

As he repacked he said gently,

"Sorry about this morning, I was pretty tough on you." Ellen stopped him.

"No, you were right."

"Anne asked me to look after you if anything happened to her. She really cared about you." And again Ellen sensed that Alfred's mood changed when he spoke of Anne.

"Were you and Anne, um…?" And not quite knowing how to put it she added, "You know, err, close?" Alfred smiled at her difficulty and replied softly,

"Yes we were very close." It occurred to Ellen that Alfred must have lost so much when the camp was destroyed.

"All those friends of yours dead and especially Anne. I'm so very sorry."

"That's why I had to go back before digging you out." He carried on clearly oblivious of Ellen's words. "Everyone, every single one, dead, slaughtered where they slept. Friends, people I have fought with and shared the most terrifying moments of my life with and most of all, Anne. I needed to find her…to... well..." Ellen could see Alfred was welling up and took his hand. Again he didn't seem to notice.

"So anyway I went to the cottage. The soldiers had tried to torch the place using the clothing in the spare room as fuel but the fire hadn't really taken hold. Hans, Kurt and Moritz were dead in the lounge. They were shot while they slept and obviously didn't have time to grab their guns. I went up to Anne's room. She was on the bed naked with her throat slit. It was obvious she had been raped. I covered her up, carried her down to Hans and the others and, after removing anything worth keeping, relit the clothes. You know, as I stood and watched the cottage burn, I felt nothing. There was no anger, no hate, just a vacuum, a complete sense of emptiness." Alfred remained quiet for a few minutes before looking directly at her he said,

"Now, is that what you really want? Believe me, the chances are it will turn out the same for us. Our lives will end just as violently, just as painfully." It was Ellen's turn to remain silent with her thoughts. Eventually she said,

"I've been there. I've felt it and suffered it. I am prepared to die for what I believe in. I don't want to but, if I have to, then so be it. Ultimately God will decide not me." Alfred nodded at her words and said,

"Okay then let's get started." He picked up his rucksack and lifted it onto his shoulders as Ellen asked,

"Just out of interest, are we close to the Austrian border?" Alfred was surprised by the question.

"Yes. How did you know?" He assumed someone in the camp had told Ellen and added, "To be exact, we are currently two miles inside Austria."

* * *

They travelled for a further four hours, mostly through the snow of the mountains, non-stop and at a speed Ellen found difficult but she never slowed or asked for a break. She was desperate for Alfred's trust and, more importantly, was determined never again to give him a reason to leave her behind.

As darkness fell, he led Ellen to a ramshackle hut high up in the snow and as they unpacked she noticed he was not lighting the fire. She asked if he wanted her to collect wood and he replied that from that night onwards there would be no fire and no light.

They again ate a cold, simple meal and as darkness enveloped them, Alfred spread the groundsheet on the floor and after putting on a few more layers of clothes, lay down telling Ellen to do the same.

The winter night came early and even though they were shattered after the day's trekking neither felt like sleep. As they lay in the dark, they talked and as they talked Ellen became more confident in asking Alfred about what he did for the camp. He began by explaining that the camp leaders had made the decision to focus on Austria.

"I know from what you've said you have a pretty good understanding of the early years of the war but what do you know about Austria?" he asked.

"Very little," Ellen replied.

"Okay, I'll bore you," and even though she couldn't see him, Ellen knew he was smiling. "Are you aware that the Austrians were embroiled in their own civil war before this one started?" Ellen answered that she wasn't and as he spoke she once again realised how knowledgeable he was.

"What about Hitler being born in Austria?" Again Ellen replied she couldn't remember ever having read that fact but supposed she must have.

"So why are these two things important?" he asked and Ellen decided she had to interrupt.

"Alfred, you weren't a teacher before the war were you?"

"Maybe." he answered guardedly and they both laughed.

"Please carry on. I really am interested."

So Alfred explained that Austria-Hungary as it was then known, suffered a serious defeat during the previous 1914-1918 War. As a result, the Austria-Hungarian Empire was broken up and what was left included the establishment of a new Republic of German Austria. This would encompass all areas inhabited by ethnic Germans. A provisional constitution was drawn up for this new Republic and part of it stated that German Austria would be part of the German Republic.

Ellen lay fascinated as she listened. This was one of the things she had missed most over the months she had been on her own; someone to discuss her love of history with.

"By the way, the break-up of Austria-Hungary was extremely popular with the majority of those living in the newly created Republic because sooner or later, they could then be annexed into Germany as a whole. However, these proposed changes were unacceptable to both France and Italy who refused to accept the constitution of the new Republic. As they were part of the victorious Allies from the 14-18 war, they were in a very strong position to force Austria to sign an alternative accord. It was called the Treaty of Saint Germain which prevented the merger, creating the Republic of Austria instead. Still interested?"

"Fascinated."

Alfred seemed to enjoy giving his 'lecture' and continued by explaining that during the 1920s and early 1930s, politics in the newly formed Austria were extremely volatile with the Social Democratic Party and its left-wing allies opposed to the Christian Socialist Party who were supported by industrialists and the Catholic Church. He went on to describe how the situation deteriorated to such an extent that in May 1933, as a result of a serious mistake in a parliamentary vote, a politician called Engelbert Dollfuss was able to declare a state of emergency and grab legislative powers.

"It was this that triggered the civil war. You see, the Dollfuss government introduced a new constitution which included the abolition of the freedom of the press and established a one party system of government. This of course was unacceptable to the vast majority of the public.

Ellen was flabbergasted. She couldn't believe what Alfred was saying. It was almost an exact replica of what had happened in Italy with Mussolini. However, any similarity disappeared as Alfred described events only two months after the new constitution was introduced when the Austrian Nazi Party assassinated Dollfuss during a failed coup.

"Bored yet?" Alfred asked and although Ellen was beginning to feel sleepy she was desperate for him to carry on.

"After Dollfuss was assassinated, Kurt Schuschnigg took over as leader and immediately made it clear that he supported and would uphold Dollfuss's constitution. The public were enraged and as a result, the Nazi Party was able to establish very strong power bases across the country. Don't forget, this was whilst a one-party state existed." Again Ellen imagined Alfred smiling as he reminded her.

"Now, at the same time in Germany, Hitler had moved from being an irritant to the supreme leader and in February 1938 he met with Schuschnigg, putting extreme pressure on him to allow the Nazi Party in Austria to operate without hindrance. Schuschnigg of course succumbed, even agreeing to two Nazi Party members becoming ministers in his own government. Of course that wasn't the end of it. Hitler relentlessly continued to pressure Schuschnigg until eventually the Austrian leader agreed to hold a referendum on the future of Austria." Ellen still refused to give in to sleep. She was enthralled as he went on to describe how the referendum was a farce. Apparently a British intelligence report, which had become available to people in Austria, estimated that only about 35% of the population supported an annexation with Germany. He added that quite unbelievably, the figure given by the Austrian Nazi Party claimed it was 80%. Once again Ellen was stunned as Alfred went on to explain that anyone proven to be against the annexation was silenced in the most violent of campaigns. She couldn't believe that two countries at almost identical times in history, had become conduits for a brutal minority.

"The final nail in the coffin of Austrian independence was when the Austrian Nazi Party requested German troops to intervene. The pretext was of course, to put an end to the ever-increasing levels of violence which they just happened to instigate. On March 11th 1938 Hitler presented Austria with an ultimatum; surrender or face invasion. Schuschnigg quickly realised neither France or Britain was in a position to help so had no alternative but to resign. The following day, German troops marched into Austria unopposed." Ellen had noticed how quietly Alfred had been speaking. There was extraordinary sadness in his voice.

"Before we sleep," he added, "one month after the invasion a referendum was held across Austria where it was claimed that 98.73% of the population voted for a merger with Germany. And just like that," Ellen heard him click his fingers, "Austria ceased to exist. That, young lady, is the end of the lesson for today."

Ellen had one last question.

"How do you know so much about all this?"

"Because I am Austrian," he replied, turning away from her.

* * *

For the next three days they travelled almost non-stop, Alfred never revealing where they were going and Ellen never asking. Each evening they talked in the dark, attempted to stay warm and Ellen asked Alfred to carry on with his history of Austria. Alfred was always happy to oblige.

He told her how after the German invasion the general population behaved with surprising loyalty towards the Nazi German Empire, even when the German government began introducing anti-Semitic laws. Ellen again noticed a change in Alfred when he explained specifically about the Jewish communities in Austria.

"You see, Austria had many Jews; over 200,000 living in Vienna alone and as early as mid 1938 they began to be targeted. It started out low key; you know, attacks and street beatings, primarily carried out by German Viennese, but things quickly developed into something more sinister." Alfred stopped for what seemed like an age. Ellen could hear him breathing but nothing else and eventually, she asked if he was alright.

"Sorry," he answered quietly, "just remembering and as I told you, that is something I try to avoid." Ellen was surprised by the answer and confused.

"Look, it's a bit late," she suggested, "why don't we sleep?"

"No, I'm fine unless you want me to stop." That was the last thing Ellen wanted and so he carried on.

"There were two nights; I remember them like it was yesterday. It was the 9th and 10th of November 1938. I think they have actually given them a name; the Nights of the Broken Glass. Ninety four synagogues were desecrated. In addition, countless Jewish businesses and homes were attacked and looking back it was these two nights that represent the beginning of the legitimisation of anti-Semitism. Because of the acceptance of these actions by the general public, it was just a matter of time before this hatred of Jews became endemic." Alfred paused. Ellen was speechless. As a

Jew she had never understood the loathing of her religion in Italy but it was the same in Austria; the same hatred, the same bigotry, the same willingness to kill, maim and destroy anyone who practised her faith.

*   *   *

On the fourth day, Alfred began to lead them down from the mountains, always avoiding built up areas, main roads or anywhere else they might encounter Germans and Ellen realised he had an intimate knowledge of the countryside they were passing through. They left their snow shoes hidden next to a derelict cattle shed and Ellen realised that without Alfred, she would never find them again.

Towards evening, he pointed out an isolated farm in the distance and told Ellen it was where they were heading. When they were about half a mile from the main house he told her to remain where she was and she watched as he approached the buildings cautiously, hunched and remaining out of sight. She saw him disappear behind a large barn and wondered for an instant what would happen if she never saw him again. How would she survive and just as quickly she told herself to shut up.

A few minutes later, Alfred reappeared next to the front door. He knocked and Ellen watched as a woman opened the door and ushered him in. She waited for about ten minutes trying not to become concerned when the door finally reopened and Alfred signalled for her to join him.

Ellen thought the house was as close to heaven as you could get; there was a roaring fire and they ate steaming hot casserole and bread with a glass of wine on the side. For the first time in ages she was warm, replete and extremely content.

After the meal, Alfred and the farmer excused themselves and went to another room whilst Ellen helped clear up. Once again, there were no names used, not even pseudonyms. She had no idea where she was or who she had just met and that gave her great comfort. If, God forbid, she was caught there was no way she could betray anyone.

That night she slept in a bed in her own room with a stone hot water bottle. It was bliss but it seemed she had only just fallen asleep when she was woken and told breakfast was ready. Alfred told her that as soon as they had eaten he wanted to get started and that she should make sure she had collected all her things as they were unlikely to return. This surprised her, but thinking about it, she realised how wise it was. If the farmer and his wife were not to put themselves in danger, one night stopovers kept the risks to a minimum.

On the way out, Alfred took Ellen around the back of the barn to a pile of sticks for the fire and showed her how to make a bundle to conceal the wooden sections of her bow. Ellen's heart skipped a beat. It meant for the first time they were going to where they could be stopped, even searched, and as her unease grew so did her excitement.

Once they got started, Alfred led Ellen away from the farm down a track and through a wooded valley. The most beautiful mountains and majestic scenery surrounded them and for the millionth time, she wondered at the contradiction of God's work; nature at its most stunning alongside the everyday vindictiveness and brutality of man.

Twice during the morning they passed through small farming hamlets where Alfred seemed to know so many people, or rather, they seemed to know him. This again seemed incongruous to Ellen. How could they remain safe from the Germans when so many people had seen them?

That evening as darkness fell, Alfred led Ellen to a large, isolated barn in an enormous field. Once inside, he climbed a ladder to the hayloft and then began to unpack the ground sheet and food.

Whilst they ate, Ellen asked Alfred about the villages and he explained they had travelled through one of the few areas of Austria that was predominantly anti-German, adding that the locals had given safe shelter to groups travelling to and from the camp for a couple of years. He also said that, fortunately, the Germans had far greater priorities and too many problems to worry about 'peasants' who lived in a reasonably isolated valley.

"But we all know," he said dispassionately, "it's only a question of time before someone says something and then the valley will be attacked and the people who have helped us will be tortured, slaughtered, raped or whatever else takes the Germans' fancy."

* * *

Later on that evening, once they were settled down for the night, Ellen asked about the men from the camp.

"They had many jobs, some set out to disrupt or wherever possible destroy the Nazis' communication systems, some set out on assassination runs. Their task was simply to kill as many influential officers as possible but as you can imagine, their own death rate was extremely high." He paused for a moment and then asked, "You remember I told you about the Night of the Broken Glass? Well, for me to explain what I do, you need to understand a few things, okay. Within just a few months of the German invasion and occupation of Austria, it is thought that over forty five thousand Jews tried to leave, seeking sanctuary elsewhere, especially in neighbouring countries. It seems not all these countries were as welcoming as might have been expected and some even complained to Germany about the undesirable influx of Jewish refugees. After what you told me about your family's attempts to get out of Italy, it will come as no surprise to hear that up to twenty five thousand Jewish Refugees were refused entry by Switzerland." Ellen had forgotten that she had told Alfred about her family's failure to cross the Swiss border.

"As a result," he continued, "towards the end of 1938, Germany recalled all the passports of Jews which in effect stopped them having any legal means of leaving Austria. The upshot was obvious, tens of thousands were trapped and most became part of the mass deportation to concentration camps, never to be heard of again." Alfred stopped and although it was dark Ellen sensed great sadness in his words.

"There are still however, amazing people all over Austria who are willing to risk their lives by hiding Jews. Unfortunately they cannot keep these families hidden forever; it's just a matter of time before a neighbour betrays them and as you can imagine, the consequences are appalling. My job is to help get these families across the border to Switzerland."

"But that's wonderful" Ellen said looking across at Alfred, and by the faint light of the brightest of moons, saw him looking at her. "You've spent years risking your life helping Jews escape the Nazis. Why?"

"It's simple really. My parents who lived in Vienna were absolutely appalled at what was happening. Neither was important. They were just good, hard working citizens, but they couldn't stomach what was happening to Jews. You see, we had a lovely Jewish family living next door but many in the street were spiteful, waiting for an opportunity to betray them, probably to get in the good books of the Nazis." Although it was dark, Ellen could still see Alfred by the light of the moon. He was lying on his back looking up at the ceiling completely immersed in his memories. She thought him rather boyish and very handsome.

"About six years ago, I was just about to graduate as a history teacher and had a job in a local school waiting for me. I had gone to bed when I heard a commotion outside. I saw my parents had turned all the lights off so I went downstairs to see what was happening. I found them standing in the dark with next door's three children. Suddenly there were gunshots; it sounded like a war and my father quickly told the children to follow him. We had a cellar with a trapdoor which was well hidden behind some shelving in the pantry and he took them underground. When he returned, I helped move some boxes and other junk to clutter up the shelves over the trapdoor. Dad then told my mother and me to go upstairs and get into bed. I remember lying under my blanket, warm but shaking, incredibly proud of my parents." When Ellen looked, Alfred hadn't moved; he seemed to be in a trance.

"Anyway, about an hour later, German soldiers arrived at our house and searched the place. I held my mother's hand tightly and could tell both my parents were terrified. After about twenty minutes, having found nothing, they left but not before warning my father that those who helped Jews would be severely punished which meant prison and eventual execution. My mother poured each of us a large glass of brandy," Ellen noticed a smile on Alfred's face as he remembered, "and we sat around the kitchen table. My dad was a placid man, really gentle and kind and I could never remember him so angry. He told me that the couple next door were both dead, shot trying to delay the soldiers whilst we got the children out. For the first time ever, I saw tears in my father's eyes. My mother moved over to him and they held each other and I can tell you, it was a defining moment in my life.

My father told us that we should go to his brother who lived about fifty miles away whilst he remained to run the house. He would carry on working but we refused.

About a week later, very early one morning, my father took the three children from the cellar and we never saw them again. He told me that he'd discovered a group who were helping Jewish families escape to Switzerland and from that moment onwards, I understood that my parents were involved in clandestine work on behalf of Jews. From then onwards, individuals or families would arrive at the house, stay for a night in the cellar and next day be gone. My parents never said what they were doing, never involved me and whenever I asked, they laughed and simply said they were helping friends and I should stop imagining things. The inevitable happened; I got back from teaching one day to find the house dark and locked. This was unheard of as my mother always had tea ready. All evening I sat and waited. Throughout the night I never moved growing more and more uneasy. Very early next morning there was a knock on the back door; I thought they were home." Alfred said this with a sense of excitement in his voice before it dropped back to a quiet, sad monotone. "But it was a man I had never met who asked to come in. I made him a hot drink and he told me that the previous afternoon there had been a serious problem involving my parents. I asked him what had happened and he said the information was sketchy. However, it seemed that my parents had delivered a family of three to a group who would help them and they were attacked. He said the only explanation was that someone had betrayed them as the Secret police knew exactly where the exchange would be made. He told me no one had survived.

I asked him if he could wait a few moments and went upstairs. I needed to be on my own, just for a few minutes to come to terms with what he had said but for some unfathomable reason the tears didn't come. Instead I was angry. I wanted to kick out, scream, tear something apart, but in the end I returned to the kitchen to be told that I only had a few hours before the identity of my parents would be established and then I'd be arrested. He said he could take me somewhere safe whilst I sorted out what I wanted to do but you know Ellen, I already knew exactly what I wanted; I wanted exactly the same as you.

Ellen was crying and through the darkness turned over towards Alfred and touched him on the cheek. He took her hand and held it tightly then brought it to his lips and kissed it.

After what she had just heard she wanted to hold him but she didn't want to do the wrong thing for him just to reject her. Ellen then lent towards him and told him she understood and before she knew it she was in his arms.

Initially she was shocked; she didn't know how to react to such familiarity but as she felt his warmth and the strength of his arms around her, she suddenly wanted him After all the pain of the rape and her fear of sex, she now wanted this man unconditionally with a desperation she found exhilarating. Ellen moved towards his face and kissed him and as Alfred responded she began to relax. She was fearful; how could she not be after the last time a man had touched her intimately. Slowly Alfred undressed her and she reached for him and he helped her to remove his own clothing. As she unbuttoned his trousers she felt him beneath the coarse material, rigid and ready. It took her breath away but Alfred was gentle and tender as he explored her body. Caressing and stroking, never hurrying, never forcing, only reacting as Ellen succumbed and responded to the pleasure his hands and fingers could bring her. Ellen had never experienced anything remotely as sensual or as electrifying as Alfred's touch. Eventually when they were both naked, Ellen lay back and gently pulled Alfred towards her. It was the moment she had thought about ten thousand times and always dreaded. The memory of the last time she had been in the same position, when an evil monster had pinned her down and ripped into her could never be forgotten but Alfred waited. He did not rush and Ellen relaxed until it was she who could wait no longer. As he rolled on top of her, she closed her eyes anticipating the razor-sharp pain. Again Alfred slowed and gently entered her. Ellen winced but not from pain, just the expectation of pain. There was none, there was no horror, no shock, no revulsion, just an incredible feeling, a beautiful and breathtaking sensation. At last Alfred was in her completely. To Ellen it was heavenly and she heard herself moan as she felt him move very slowly and tenderly at first and she responded, raising her hips, pulling him deeper into her. She wanted so much more. Then quite suddenly, she felt her whole world begin to implode. Alfred responded moving faster and Ellen answered. Rhythmically, together they reached a crescendo of emotions and feelings that Ellen had never come near to experiencing before. As she cried out, her whole body shook and she grasped hold of Alfred's body never wanting to let him go.

* * *

Ellen refused to let Alfred get up. She held onto him tightly as they made love again and Ellen was more relaxed, so much more secure, not only with herself and her desires but with Alfred's body and his touch. As usual, she wanted to know everything there was to know about what he liked and what he wanted and how she made him feel.

Afterwards, as they lay together, Alfred remained quiet. Ellen looked at him with concern.

"What's wrong?" she asked quietly.

"I should never have let this happen."

"You didn't. It takes two and I wanted you. Look, the only other experience I've had with a man was unspeakable but you've shown me a new world, how different and fantastic sex can be. What is wrong with that?"

"I could be killed today, tomorrow or the next day. What then?"

"Me too, and what better reason is there to grab what we can while we can. There is no way I would want to die not knowing or feeling what we've just had. Just think how terrible it would be if my only experience of sex was being raped by an animal who cared about nothing except himself. You said it yourself; live for today. I can accept that."

Chapter 4

January 1944

Alfred and Ellen slowly approached the farmhouse. It was dark, night had fallen and they had travelled the whole day to make the rendezvous.

Alfred held his finger to his lips indicating Ellen should be quiet and moved away from her to the rear of the house. Two minutes later the front door opened and she was invited in. They stayed only a few minutes and then headed out again. She asked no questions; she simply followed Alfred.

The night was overcast and there was little or no moon to light their way and Ellen could not understand how he knew where he was going.

After about half an hour they came across what looked like a derelict farm. Again Alfred approached the buildings slowly. He listened and then circled the whole area telling Ellen to wait then entered the house, returning a few minutes later with five people, all who were clearly terrified.

Alfred whispered they should follow him as he moved quickly to the cover of some trees and they walked for the next hour before he stopped and told them to rest.

Ellen watched as he searched the area surrounding the group to make sure they had not been followed and then joined her on the groundsheet which he had set apart from the others. Whilst they were lying together, he explained that all he knew was that the family was from Vienna and that the father and three sons had been executed trying to prevent the security police finding the woman and children.

Alfred woke Ellen the next morning and whilst they were waiting for the family to get ready, he gave her an old compass and hand drawn map.

"If anything should happen to me, you head up this valley then using the compass, head west. If you have problems, use the map. It gives you places to stay and people who will help; no names but enough detail. Memorise everything on the map as quickly as you can and then destroy it. Oh, and by the way, I've also marked where the snow shoes are, okay?" Ellen was dumbstruck. It had never occurred to her that something could go wrong. Alfred was always so confident. Seeing her sudden look of panic he said reassuringly,

"Don't worry, everything will be fine. It's a precaution, but you never know and I want you to be safe." He touched her gently on the cheek, smiled and then turned and told their fellow travellers it was time to move.

* * *

They started out just before dawn and walked for about three hours. Ellen couldn't believe how still and quiet it was. There was an early morning mist; it was extremely damp and at that level the snow was a wet slush in most places but she soon warmed up as they trekked firstly through trees and then across open fields always protected by hedges and then back into the cover of trees. Alfred seemed to know exactly where he was going and Ellen marvelled at his ability to always find a secure route alongside somewhere safe to rest.

When he called a halt he told them to relax for the rest of the day. Ellen and Alfred again sat apart from the family and when she asked him why, he replied,

"There's no way I want to know anything about them or them about me. If they're arrested they must not be able to tell the secret police anything about the route they took, names of villages or landmarks they passed and they must not be able to pinpoint the area we're travelling through. It is vital we protect the locals from the Gestapo."

Although contact with them was minimal, Ellen sensed that although they were scared, their smiles of appreciation spoke volumes for their gratitude at what Alfred was doing. For the first time, it also gave her a feeling she was making a difference to people's lives.

For the next two days, they followed the same pattern. Walk early mornings and late evening; rest all other times. Their progress was slow. The old man was struggling as was the youngest of the girls, but there was never a complaint, never a request to slow down and Alfred understood their difficulty, keeping to a fairly undemanding pace. During the rest periods, Ellen worked on memorising the map, repeatedly asking Alfred to test her and when she had convinced herself she knew the information off by heart, tore it into pieces and buried it.

On the third day, she could see they were nearing the top end of the valley. They had been climbing ever higher since the outset of the journey and the mountains either side were squeezing in, narrowing the fertile and usable land alongside the river.

As they were reaching the end of their early morning trek, Alfred pointed to a building far in the distance and said to Ellen,

"That's where I want to be tonight. If we can make it, there will be hot food and we can rest in the warmth of the barn. These people desperately need a really good night's sleep before we go over the mountains to the border." Ellen stared and could just about make out an isolated house, built on steep slopes on the west side of the valley. She also looked at the mountains they had to cross and knew it would be a serious challenge.

Alfred then led them back into the trees and found a sheltered spot for them to camp and Ellen made herself comfortable whilst he removed his rucksack, picked up his gun and bow and began a tour of the site to make sure it was safe.

She waited for the usual ten to fifteen minutes before laying out some cold food for them to eat on his return. After half an hour Ellen began to fret; Alfred had never taken so long to check the area. When an hour had passed she became frantic with worry. She spoke to the two women and old man and told them that they should repack and be ready to leave.

With crossbow at the ready and her heart thumping, Ellen moved away from the camp in the direction Alfred had taken. She stayed very low, crouching as she inched slowly through the trees. She assumed Alfred would check the perimeter of the camp by circling it so decided to do the same. When she thought she was about a hundred yards from the group, she began to circle and was tempted to call out but knew how stupid that would be.

When she'd covered what she thought was about three quarters of the area surrounding the camp, she heard voices fifty yards ahead. Crouching as she moved towards the sound, she saw a clearing with bright sunshine pouring through the trees and had to hold back a cry when she saw Alfred, covered in blood, tied to a tree. There were two men in German uniforms standing, over him. Looking around for other soldiers, Ellen saw nothing except two military motorbikes leaning against a post on a bridle path and knew they were alone.

Ellen shivered as one of the soldiers shouted at Alfred. He wanted to know what Alfred knew about Jews being taken to Switzerland. He answered that he knew nothing and Ellen heard the pain in his voice as he spat blood to speak. The soldier struck him violently across the face.

"Your papers say you are from Vienna; why are you here, eh? Tell me." Alfred's eyes were shut. Ellen could tell he was badly hurt and she knew he could take no more punishment.

"Are you helping Jews escape? Tell me or you will die," the soldier shouted as he raised his pistol and pointed it at Alfred's forehead. Ellen loaded the bow and waited as Alfred spoke.

"There's nothing to tell." The soldier raised his fist to hit him again and Alfred said with resignation,

"Wait." Ellen's heart sank. Was he about to betray them, and for a fleeting moment she wondered whether she would have to shoot Alfred to silence him.

"Okay, I admit I have been involved in moving Jews in the past." Ellen couldn't believe what she was hearing and moving the crossbow away from the soldier she aimed at Alfred. Her hands were shaking but Ellen steadied herself and began to tighten the trigger. Why was Alfred admitting his guilt when he knew he would be executed?

"But there is nothing happening at the moment," he continued. "We are waiting for our next batch and then I will take them over the mountains. Look, I promise you, currently there are no Jews on the move." Ellen's shoulders sagged as she realised her mistake. Alfred would never betray them and she watched as his head slumped forward. His eyes were closed and he was breathing rapidly. The soldier swore and hit Alfred on the side of the head with the butt of his pistol and Ellen heard the crack as blood oozed from the gash. She had to move or Alfred would die and she aimed the bow and fired, shooting the soldier through the heart. Before he'd hit the ground Ellen had sprinted through the undergrowth, knife in hand and leapt onto the back of the second soldier. With absolutely no hesitation, she pulled the knife across the man's throat and heard a hiss of air as his windpipe burst open. Blood gushed out of the cut, covering Ellen's hand, but still she held on and as he collapsed, she released her grip and checked both soldiers were dead. She then grabbed a water bottle and ran to Alfred.

Cutting away the bindings around his wrists, Ellen poured water over his face and into his mouth. Slowly he stirred, opened his eyes and with incredible difficulty looked at the two dead soldiers. He tried to move but it was impossible; his injuries were too severe.

"You must get away now, before soldiers come," he stuttered.

"No," she replied. "You have to get up!" Unbelievably Alfred became angry.

"Listen. You must get that family away. If they are safe then I have done my job. Everything will have been worthwhile."

"'Not without you. I can't! I don't know what to do."

"You do, now go. There's nothing you can do to help; it's too late."

"Stop it. You must get up, please. Get up, I need you. Please my love, don't leave me." Alfred's head dropped forward and Ellen's lover was dead.

—Ж—

Chapter 5

January 1944

Stay busy. Keep moving. Ellen grabbed a pistol and ammunition belt and ran back to the family, all the time asking herself what Alfred would have done.

"Cover the bodies and hide them." When she arrived at the camp, Ellen explained she needed help and led the two women back to the clearing. Both were horrified at what confronted them but they helped Ellen place the three bodies and the two motorbikes in an overgrown clump of bushes, covering everything with leaves.

Although she knew Alfred would have disapproved, Ellen said a short prayer to her lost love. They might only have known each other for the shortest of time but the impact Alfred had made on her life was immeasurable. He had become Ellen's soul mate, her first true love.

Without speaking, the three women then returned to the camp and Ellen told them to collect their bags leaving no trace.

* * *

"Head up to the end of the valley then move west." That's what Alfred had told her but he had also stressed that the family needed rest and hot food before attempting to cross the mountains. This left Ellen with a dilemma; which way should they go. Eventually she decided she had to get them moving before any other Germans arrived even though travelling through the day could be dangerous. She led them away with a confidence she hardly felt. Remaining under the cover of the trees Ellen headed towards the top of the valley and after about an hour, she stopped and told them to rest.

Grabbing her bow and Alfred's gun she made a circuit of the camp just as Alfred would have done. Only then did Ellen return and set up her own private space some distance from the others.

As she lay on the groundsheet she'd shared with Alfred, Ellen accepted that the next few days would be lonely and difficult but she had no choice; she was trapped by circumstances. She tried to sleep but her brain wouldn't slow down and memories kept invading her mind. She smiled and cried at the bittersweet images bursting through her thoughts; the moment she first saw Alfred, the way he put up with her obsessive unreasonableness, his patience whilst she learned the bow, and how he taught her to survive and of course, that magical night; those hours of love when Alfred showed her she need not be afraid of sex or intimacy.

* * *

Late in the afternoon, as freezing sleet was falling, Ellen led the group out and headed for the farm Alfred had pointed out to her. They walked for a couple of hours and as the late afternoon light faded, she began to worry that they would not make it before darkness fell. Their pace was slow and getting slower but fortunately as night fell, the storm had passed, the moon was bright and the sky clear and Ellen managed to coax the last few miles out of the family.

As they approached the farmhouse, Ellen told the family to wait. She had no idea what Alfred would have done or what she would do if there was no one at home. With the gun tucked into the back of her belt and feeling extremely vulnerable, she moved slowly towards the buildings wondering whether there was a secret code to identify herself to let those inside know she was not the enemy.

Ellen tapped lightly on the door and waited and after just a few seconds, a woman's face appeared at the window to her left. She heard a bolt slide back and an old man with a pistol opened the door and asked bluntly what she wanted. Ellen didn't really know what to say so answered disconsolately,

"Alfred is dead." The door opened a little wider and the woman's face from the window appeared alongside the man. She too was holding a shotgun.

"Who are you?" she asked harshly. There was no emotion or welcome in her voice.

"A friend of Alfred. We were travelling together. I'm sorry but I have a family with me. Before he died Alfred told me to take them to the border." The door closed slightly, which gave Ellen some hope and she could hear voices arguing from the other side. Finally it reopened, the couple reappeared and the man said,

"You have a name?" Ellen was just about to tell them when she stopped, realising it could prove fatal so used her pseudonym from the camp.

"I am known as Dolphin," she answered with a smile, trying to sound a good deal more self-assured than she felt. After a pause, the woman finally said,

"Take them to the barn over there." She pointed as she spoke. "Make sure they climb to the high loft. You stay on the ground floor. I will bring food." With that the door closed.

Ellen returned to the family overjoyed. She led them to the barn, found the ladder and told them to follow her. She climbed to the very top and found a small hay filled attic. It was the perfect place and she told them to make themselves as comfortable as possible and to rest.

Fifteen minutes later the woman reappeared with a saucepan full of steaming soup, cups and fresh bread. She laid out the food on a sheet quite close to the door and told Ellen she would be back later. Ellen called the family down and together they ate. The food was simple but steaming hot and delicious.

When they had finished, she told them to return to the loft and waited for the woman from the farmhouse to return. Ellen tried desperately to stay awake to thank her, but she was shattered both physically and emotionally and fell into a deep sleep.

* * *

It wasn't until the early hours when she awoke on a mattress of straw covered with a warm woollen blanket that Ellen realised the woman must have put her to bed. As she lay quietly thinking, she decided she must complete Alfred's work. Slowly rising from the warmth of her bed, she was about to climb the ladder to wake the family when she heard the wind howling against the side of the barn. She looked through a gap in the wooden door and was confronted with heavy snow and blizzard conditions. There was simply no way anyone could venture outside let alone attempt to cross mountains.

Ellen climbed the ladder and told the family they could not leave and that they should take advantage of the delay and get as much rest as possible. She then returned to the ground floor and rejected the idea of walking to the farm house. She lay on her bed and fell asleep but was almost immediately jolted awake. Grabbing her gun she could not believe what stood over her. It was from a nightmare, a dark shape with only the eyes visible. It was when the woman from the farmhouse burst into shrieks of laughter and apologised that Ellen saw the funny side of the situation. She was told to call her Ruth, yet another pseudonym, and as she began to lay out more food on the sheet, Ruth stated bluntly that there was no way anyone would be going anywhere until the storm had passed. When Ellen asked how long blizzards usually lasted she replied,

"Sometimes a day, sometimes a week." After Ruth had left, Ellen called the family down to eat and repeated what she'd been told.

* * *

For three days the storm raged. Ruth brought food regularly and Ellen enjoyed the chance to talk whilst she was laying it out or picking up the dirty dishes. Early on the fourth day the wind eased, the snow stopped and Ellen was able to go outside. The winter scene was stunning but she realised it would be virtually impossible, especially for the old man and children, to walk through the deep, fresh snow. That evening she asked Ruth if they could get to the border.

"You want my opinion? I think you're mad."

"Why?" Ellen asked feeling foolish but also slightly irked, then she remembered Alfred's claim that she was dangerous to all close to her.

"Firstly you have no idea where to go," Ruth stated critically. "Secondly, you have no idea how to move in the extreme conditions that are higher up following the blizzard. Thirdly, you have no equipment especially when crossing deep snow. Fourthly, as you have told me, you have an old man and two children with you, none of whom have any chance of surviving the demands of such a journey. Fifth…" Before Ruth could continue Ellen said, "Stop please." She was mortified by her own stupidity. She would never complete Alfred's work. "Okay, so I'm an idiot." Anger had crept into her voice. Ruth smiled and said gently, "Idiot. Never. You are just a young girl who has seen things she should never have seen and lost people you should never have lost. Alfred was special and you can't just take his place. If you try to go through the mountains with that family, it will be death for all of you."

"So what should I do?"

"You wait. There are some men I know who are due here and I am sure they will help."

That evening Ruth brought two men to the barn and Ellen recognised them as Walter and Heinz, Alfred's two companions from the camp. They remembered her and joked that she was the pesky girl who had hassled Alfred. Ruth, laughing with them, invited Ellen to join them for a meal in the farmhouse and she left the family in the barn with their evening meal.

Seated around the large kitchen table, Walter asked about his friend. As she described his death, Ellen realised that although she could not finish Alfred's work, she would not give up on her pledge. When Walter and Heinz offered to take her and the family to the border, Ellen thought hard before replying.

"Thank you but I'm staying." All around the table looked astonished.

"So what will you do?" Ruth asked with obvious concern.

"I have work to do," Ellen replied cagily. There was a thoughtful silence until Heinz said,

"The rumour in the camp was that you were set on revenge and were going to get yourself killed in the process." Ellen stared at him. She didn't know whether to be angry or not but before she could answer Walter asked, "How long do you think you can last fighting Germans on your own?" Ellen felt like a child being reprimanded but she didn't care. She would not give in and she answered irritably, "I know what you think. Alfred, Anne and Hans; they all felt that I am just a naive child who is a liability to anyone around me. Oh, and I will end up dead before I can achieve anything."

"There is some truth in that," Ruth said gently. "We are overrun with German soldiers. Most of the population support them and we have very few resistance groups. And you, you want to start a private war." Again there was an awkward silence.

"My wife is right young lady." It was the first time the farmer had spoken. "You're unlikely to last for more than a few days on your own, but it's up to you. Alfred told us about you," All around the table including Ellen smiled, "and he was clearly right. But he also explained that you were one of the most dedicated and sincere people he'd ever met." Tears began to well in Ellen's eyes. "If you choose not to go to the border that's up to you, however, before you leave in the morning come and see me. Agreed?" Ellen nodded and the farmer stood, signalling the end of the evening.

On the way out much to Ruth's surprise, Ellen asked if she had a pair of scissors she could borrow.

* * *

That night, Ellen found sleep impossible as the arguments raged within her. Logic told her she was being reckless; that if she didn't travel with the family she'd be dead within days. However, whatever the others may have thought, Ellen was no fool, she wanted to live but not at the expense of her pledge. As she drifted off to sleep, she was certain; it was no longer her choice, circumstances were dictating the path she must take.

The following morning, Ellen awoke and immediately dismissed any lingering doubts. She reached for the scissors. It took less than a minute to cut off her long flowing hair leaving a short thatch; a military short back and sides, but in her case it was anything but neat.

Once dressed and after a generous breakfast, Ellen stood by the barn door and waved to Walter, Heinz and the family as they set off in thick snow towards the mountains. Even with her new determination, she was still surprised at how difficult it was to let them go and she shivered as they disappeared into the trees. As she hesitated by the door, Ellen promised never again to wish, never again to hope. She would just remain focused on the day, the hour, the next action.

After gathering her few things together and hiding her bow in amongst a bundle of firewood as Alfred had shown her, she went to the farmhouse to say she was leaving. Ruth laughed when she saw Ellen's hair but said nothing and after giving her a hug, showed her into the kitchen where her husband was sitting.

To Ellen's amazement the farmer passed her a crossbow.

"Alfred told us how skilful you've become. This is a bow that will never let you down. It can kill from further than any other I've had. Just be careful and practise with it before you need to use it for real, okay." Ellen didn't know what to say and mumbled a thank you. As she was about to leave the farmer pushed a small amount of money across the table.

"It's not much but it will keep you going." She was stunned at the generosity of a family she hardly knew. She moved around the table and gave the farmer a hug much to his embarrassment. He did, however, still manage to explain that to find the enemy she so desperately wanted to kill, the safest way out of the valley was to turn right at the main road and to keep travelling east.

"As long," he added with a sad smile, "as that enemy doesn't turn out to be you."

* * *

And for the next twelve months, Ellen disappeared. The few who had known her assumed she was dead or had been arrested, and prayed for the former. If Ellen had been taken, the brutal torture they would inflict on her young body would be crippling and in the end, whatever her resistance, she would succumb. All they could hope for was that she'd revealed nothing of importance.

Chapter 6

1944

As she walked Ellen set out her plan. She would follow the same routine Alfred used; walk early mornings and late afternoons, rest during the day and sleep during the night. Her immediate aim was to locate the rail link between Italy and Germany which passed through Austria and from there, follow the tracks south to the Brenner Pass. She felt that if she travelled east with the mountains predominantly on her right, she would eventually meet the railway. Whilst she was on the move Ellen decided she would avoid people and built up areas and stay nowhere longer than one night. If she did have contact with others, she would never ask for names of places or people, ensuring she would be of no danger to anyone if she were caught by the Gestapo.

* * *

For eight days, Ellen travelled parallel to the main road, each night wrapping herself up in as many clothes as she carried, trying to keep warm but she was always so cold that sleep was impossible. Her food supplies were low and progress slow but she would not countenance giving up; she would find the railway.

On three occasions she came across rivers blocking her path and had to travel upstream to find a crossing point that was deserted. On the ninth morning however, a wide, fast flowing river confronted her. After searching the immediate area Ellen realised the only way to cross was to use the road bridge through the local town.

Ellen studied it from an elevated position and saw that on her side of the river there were a few houses and the main road, whilst on the other side, there was a small built up area and again, the road twisting and winding its way along the valley. There appeared little to worry her; traffic was light and there appeared to be no soldiers or police around.

Ellen woke in the early hours to find a bright moon and clear sky and she moved cautiously towards the bridge. The town was quiet although she thought she could hear laughter and singing in the distance. As she reached her side of the bridge, she waited, checked it was clear and then began to cross. She'd reached the half way point when there was a sudden blast of music and a door straight ahead of her opened lighting up the bridge and surrounding area. Guessing it was a tavern, she ducked down in the shadow of the wall and watched as two woman and three men left the building.

After a few minutes, Ellen was about to move forwards when the door reopened and she watched in horror as at least twenty people poured out of the building. All were laughing and chatting and she watched intently as the group began to disperse. With absolute dismay Ellen noticed two women walking towards her. Just for a second she considered running but knew it would be suicidal; the police would be called and she'd be hunted down. When they were only about ten yards away, Ellen heard one of the women say, "Is he dead?"

"I don't think so," the other answered, remaining behind her friend as they approached.

Unsure what to do, Ellen moved out of the shadows with her arms out showing she had nothing in her hands to hurt them.

"Don't go closer. He might be dangerous," the second women said nervously but the other ignored her and continued to approach Ellen.

“What are you doing here?” she asked. “You must be freezing.”

“I am a bit cold.” Ellen answered, her lips trembling as she spoke.

“You’re a girl,” the woman declared and then whispered, “You poor dear.” After a moment’s hesitation she said, “We live close,” and she pointed to a cottage. “You must come with us.”

“Agatha, what if…,” said the other one who was immediately cut-off mid-sentence.

“I can’t,” Ellen answered after seeing the reaction. She wanted so much to accept the invitation.

“Of course you can,” the first woman replied refusing to take no for an answer, and grabbing Ellen’s arm, she walked her towards the cottage.

* * *

Sat in the lovely, warm kitchen, Ellen sensed the women were about to introduce themselves and said bluntly, “Please don’t tell me your names,” Both looked at Ellen in bewilderment.

“Whatever trouble you’re in we’re not interested. Now, my name is Agatha and my sister here is Maxine.” Agatha looked at Ellen and smiled gently.

“Now what do we call you?” she asked and Agatha was so welcoming and friendly, Ellen was desperate to tell her the truth but knew it would be reckless.

“I am known as Dolphin.” Again there was incomprehension on the faces of the sisters.

Although it was extremely late, Agatha made steaming soup with bread and a hot drink and the three women sat around the kitchen table eating.

With a roaring fire and a full stomach, Ellen began to feel sleepy but knew she should not give in. She thought the sisters were about forty but saw neither wore a wedding ring. When she asked if they were married, Agatha explained they had both been but their husbands had died during the civil war. As she was describing the war Ellen found it impossible to keep her eyes open. Determined not to fall asleep she abruptly stood up, collected her things and explained that she had to be on her way. When a more than curious Maxine asked where she was travelling, Ellen thought carefully before saying, "West. I'm heading for Switzerland." It was a lie but Ellen justified it on the grounds that it was safer for the sisters if they had no idea where she was going.

"You look exhausted. You must stay here," Maxine said, forcing a smile, again in a tone Ellen found disconcerting, but she was so desperately tired that she put up little resistance when she was led to another downstairs room and put to bed.

* * *

Ellen was suddenly awake; she could hear the sisters arguing in the kitchen and although she hated the thought she slowly crawled out of the intoxicatingly warm bed and began to dress. As she was gathering her things together, she heard a door slam and then a knock on her door. Agatha was trembling as she entered the room.

"You must go. My sister has this mad idea you are on the run. I have no idea where she's gone but it might well be to the police. I'm so very sorry." She looked devastated and Ellen hugged her before saying, "I cannot thank you enough. Please don't blame your sister." Ellen followed Agatha to the kitchen where she had made up a bundle of food and some warm clothing.

"Keep the food for later. I've made these sandwiches for now. Please hurry. If the police come I can only stall them for a few minutes." Ellen grabbed her belongings, the bundle and food from Agatha, put on her coat and gave her new found friend another hug before leaving by the back door.

*   *   *

As soon as she'd left the cottage, Ellen realised she had a serious problem. She still hadn't crossed the river and there was no way she could go back to the town and bridge.

After a few moments she made the decision to travel up into the mountains. By following the river she could hopefully find a crossing point.

Staying under the cover of the trees, Ellen climbed. After about twenty minutes, there was an overhang and she spotted two policemen running over the bridge with Maxine in tow. Without knocking they raced through the front door of the cottage with their guns drawn.

Knowing she had to put as much distance between herself and the town as possible, Ellen prayed that Maxine had told the police she was headed west toward the Swiss border. Climbing most of that day, resting only occasionally, she ate little, relying on the snacks Agatha had made for her and by nightfall she was exhausted.

Even though it was a bitterly cold night and sleep was nigh impossible, Ellen's short time at the cottage had reinvigorated her and renewed her determination to find the railway. Next morning she rose early and within just a few minutes she found a small bridge over the fast flowing river. As she moved cautiously forwards she spotted a small hut on the other bank. Smoke was coming from a chimney and a German soldier was sat outside on a barrel.

Ellen looked higher up the river for another crossing point but saw the valley sides quickly narrowed, becoming so sheer that they looked impassable. She was left with little choice and as she approached the bridge, saw that the guard was asleep. Ellen checked the crossbow was loaded and took her first tentative step onto the extremely old, rickety structure. Three-quarters of the way across, as she put her weight down to take another step, the walkway splintered. Still half asleep, the guard picked up his rifle and wandered towards the noise. Ellen knelt, aimed and shot him through the throat, making sure he died silently. As he fell to the ground, she moved quickly. She searched the body, removed his pistol, checked it was loaded with the safety catch off and moved toward the door. She passed four pairs of skis stacked against the side of the hut and knew there would be three Germans inside.

With a gun in each hand, she pushed open the door and saw a soldier eating at a table. Pointing both pistols Ellen shot him and then seeing two other men lying asleep on the floor she fired both guns continuously until they were empty.

After checking all three were dead, she thanked God that she'd had the element of surprise on her side. Looking around at the carnage, she realised she'd missed the targets far more often than she had hit them.

Taking nothing that could be identified, Ellen then packed as much of their food and warm clothing as she could carry before dragging the outside guard and skis into the hut. She then set fire to the building, hoping anyone finding the burnt out shell would think it an accident.

Ellen accepted that the smoke from the fire might be visible but as the hut was isolated, hoped it would take a considerable time for anyone to arrive.

As she made her way through the trees descending back to the main road, Ellen accepted she'd been lucky. With little idea of how the guns would react when fired she was stunned at the recoil. However, Ellen gave little thought to the fact that she'd killed four men in cold blood, none having the chance to defend themselves. When she did eventually think through the killings she was unforgiving. The Germans had destroyed her family along with millions of others so why should she feel regret or remorse.

* * *

Ellen lost track of how many days she walked parallel to the main road and as the miles became marathons, she accepted her suffering was just a by-product of the pledge. Problems were few; the main one being to find food on a regular basis. Travelling through forests she spotted signs of wild deer or boar but she never got close enough to stalk them or any other game. With little food available she would sometimes resort to breaking into shops and she occasionally had to use the money the farmer had given her.

Whenever the opportunity arose, Ellen practised with her new crossbow and the farmer was right; it was extraordinarily accurate over a greater distance. This was crucial as it gave her more time to move away from the kill. It was when she had to move closer to finish off an attack that she left herself in danger of being seen or confronted and this only happened on one occasion. Ellen had been spotted by the driver of a military car as he was relieving himself in the bushes. As he was about to call out she shot him but not fatally. Moving in to finish him off, Ellen hadn't noticed a second soldier nearby who crept up on her with a knife. If she hadn't turned at the last minute, she would be dead. Later, when analysing what had gone wrong, she assumed the second soldier had also been relieving himself and was out of sight when she struck. Fortunately, he was overweight and had no gun and Ellen found disarming and then killing him easy, although she was wounded in her upper arm by the knife.

Ellen never deliberately searched out German soldiers to kill. She knew if she left a trail of dead bodies behind her, it would be easy to plot her path and either hunt her down or set a trap. Most importantly, the Gestapo would more than likely attribute any deaths to locals and retaliate in the most horrific manner.

* * *

As the weeks passed, Ellen became aware of a slow but profound change within her. She was often sick in the mornings and seemed to have less energy. Initially she put this down to a chill, reasoning that she was constantly cold, often wet, not sleeping and eating the minimum. However, when her periods stopped and her breasts began to tingle, she realised she was most likely pregnant with Alfred's child.

Following the rape, she had often wondered why she hadn't fallen pregnant, but with no one to talk to, she'd simply put it out of her mind. This time it was different; this was Alfred's child, a result of her love for him and it changed everything.

Over the next few days, Ellen was at a loss as to what she should do asking herself the same questions over and over again. 'Should she return to Switzerland to have the baby, try to find Ruth and seek her help or simply carry on and see what happened.' Of course, that was the easiest; do nothing, make no decision, just push on as before but she knew it was no longer just about her. There were two lives at stake if she were killed.

As the miles passed and her indecisiveness grew, Ellen always seemed to convince herself that any decision could wait a little longer and she carried on moving east searching for the railway.

Chapter 7

1944

As the weeks passed, the weather began to warm and Ellen's spirits rose. She was surprised her pregnancy showed so little, especially as she was slightly built but her greater problem was the knife wound. Even though she scrubbed the injury in fresh mountain water whenever the opportunity arose, it never seemed to heal. As with so many things Ellen simply put it out of her mind

Days and dates had always been an issue for her and when she tried to work out how many weeks had passed since Alfred had been in her life, she found it impossible. It was obviously months not weeks but there was little sign anything was happening inside her so in the end she guessed she was approximately fifteen weeks pregnant.

* * *

Late one evening, after another long, demanding climb, Ellen heard the sound of multiple explosions and as darkness fell she noticed bright lights directly ahead and prayed it was an Allied bombing raid rather than the Germans inflicting more pain on some innocent community.

She then shrieked with delight as she spotted low flying Allied bombers and it dawned on her that she was close to an important German facility. Refusing to rest, a mile further on she heard the sound of an engine and increased her pace until she was virtually running. Moving quickly towards the noise, she came to the edge of a wood, looked down an embankment and laughed with delight; there was a railway line cut through the trees.

Not wanting to waste a single second of what little light remained Ellen turned right towards Italy and the Brenner Pass. Twice she fell heavily but still would not stop or even slow down until she found it impossible to see and reluctantly she made camp. After months of believing she would never find the railway, she had arrived and it struck her as almost comical that she had absolutely no idea of what she was going to do next.

Early the following morning after a sleepless night, Ellen felt an odd sensation in her stomach followed by a mild ache. Although slightly concerned, she wanted to get on so ignored the feeling. However, as she attempted to stand the ache deepened and she knew something was wrong. It was what she'd feared; getting sick when she was completely alone.

* * *

Ellen gathered all her clothes together and threw them over her freezing body. She then lay back trying to ignore her ever increasing distress. Waves of pain came and went and she could feel her stomach retching; whatever was going on she knew she was in trouble.

Ellen wondered whether there were any farms or villages close by but thought it unlikely so high up the mountains. She thought about dragging herself to the railway line; it wasn't that far but accepted if the Gestapo picked her up she would be in even greater danger.

She felt wave after wave of a deep, intense pain and then, after one particularly severe cramp, Ellen felt wetness between her thighs. When she finally built up the courage to look down, she saw her fingers were covered in blood. She had no idea what was happening so moved the warm clothes to stop them getting covered in blood and dragged herself onto the cold, damp ground.

Without warning, her body began to shake and a series of spasms nullified what little control she had left. Forcing, straining, pleading for an end, all she felt was more pain, more liquid gushing and she suddenly understood her waters had broken. Ellen cursed knowing it was far too early and sobbed with the realisation she was losing the baby. She screamed to her God to let the baby live and forced herself to look down. She was saturated, covered in blood and there on the wet, unwelcoming ground, lying between her legs was their child, their tiny baby. It was so unbelievable; miniature arms, diminutive hands, short little legs and tiny feet, and God forbid a head. The real head of a little person but it didn't move, didn't cry, didn't breathe.

Exhausted, Ellen moved as best she could. She had to bury her beautiful baby. The ground was frozen but she didn't care. Using anything she could make into a tool, Ellen hollowed out the soil. She would create a resting place, a permanent haven for the son she would never kiss, never hug, never be able to laugh with. The absolute joy of carrying Alfred's little son had turned into deep, burning hatred for a God who had deserted her yet again when she needed him the most.

* * *

Ellen was bleeding from deep inside. She couldn't stop it or control it; it had a mind of its own. The flow never relented and she knew if she didn't get help she would die.

But would it really matter? Looking across at the grave of such innocence, Ellen was overcome with wretchedness. How many times had she seen innocence betrayed? How many times had the innocent suffered and paid the ultimate price? Her dead baby had been born pure, made out of true love, but he was no more, gone before his life had begun. As she lay suffering Ellen knew she couldn't leave him alone in such a bleak place. What she wanted was to lie down next to her beautiful boy and be with her loved ones again.

She had never felt such hopelessness. She was the ultimate fighter, but this was different, this was the rawest, most extreme desolation she had ever felt. With blood oozing from her insides and her emotions ripping her to shreds, Ellen lay down next to the grave on the snow covered ground, closed her eyes and prayed for everlasting rest.

"Get up!" she screamed as vivid images exploded before her eyes: the animals who had raped her and her mother, the prejudiced and bigoted, those who had locked up her father and kept her family prisoner, those who had slaughtered so many on the bridge. Ellen would not give in. Eyes wide she screamed at herself to move and find help. She forced herself to walk. She would live, she would have her revenge; she would kill every fucking German that ever walked the earth.

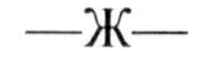

Chapter 8

1944/1945

Ellen woke to the sound of humming. She didn't recognise the song but the warmth she felt under the bedclothes brought both contentment and solace. Slowly opening her eyes she saw she was in a small room with a fire burning. A woman, with her back to Ellen, was placing wet clothes on a rack in front of the flames.

As she turned and saw Ellen was awake she spoke to her in German.

"At last pretty one, you're back with us." She left the room and immediately returned with hot soup and bread.

Although her body was aching all over, Ellen managed to eat a little and drink some water. When she'd finished the woman cleared away the bowl and left the room. Again she returned almost immediately and sat on a stool next to Ellen's bed with some knitting. Feeling so much better after the food, Ellen asked,

"How did I get here?"

"You scared me to death. That early in the morning, there you were at the door covered head to foot in blood, mumbling God knows what. You were such a sight." Ellen looked at her and thought her quite elderly.

"I'm sorry," she said, "I don't remember."

"We were so worried my husband fetched the doctor." Ellen looked concerned.

"It's alright. He's a friend. Now you rest and I'll sit here doing my knitting." She leant over and tucked Ellen in and sat back down on the stool.

The next time Ellen awoke, night had fallen and the room was empty. She heard voices and although she couldn't hear the words she felt safe. As she lay thinking, she became more and more puzzled and asked herself why on every occasion she should have died, something or someone came to her rescue. She had sworn at her God when she'd felt abandoned but couldn't escape the fact she was still alive. Was he watching over her, looking after her and if this was the case, why did he want her to live? Did God want her to make certain there was some measure of justice for those wronged? Did he want her to act as his retaliator against those who had perpetrated acts of such evil to ensure their punishment matched their crimes? Was Ellen still alive to make sure that evil never triumphed?

* * *

Ellen slept well that night, waking early and feeling stronger and refreshed. When the old lady came into the room and saw the improvement, she suggested Ellen should join her for breakfast. After dressing in her own clothes which had been washed and ironed, Ellen went to the kitchen where a man was sat at the table and the old woman introduced him as her husband. Little was said as they ate porridge followed by toast with sweet jam and a hot drink of milk. Once Ellen had helped clear the table, the husband asked,

"Now, what's your name and where are you from?"

As so often in the past Ellen wanted to tell them. She wanted to have someone to confide in and trust and as she sat in the warmth of the cosy kitchen, knew the couple were just that; her harbour in the ever growing tempest of her life. If she told them the truth she would compromise their safety so she hesitated. The man spoke again, this time more candidly,

"If we were not to be trusted, you would already be in German hands. After five days of nursing you I think your secrets are safe with us." Ellen mouthed 'five days', not believing it had been that long. His wife then said gently,

"From the state you were in, some pretty awful things have happened to you and we want to help." Ellen was desperate to tell them everything and share her sorrow, but again delayed answering. It was the woman who spoke again, quietly and kindly,

"We've been married for over thirty years and have never been blessed with our own children. With this war, we now thank God for that. We have watched nephews and nieces forced to fight, some losing their lives, some their minds. The sadness for their families has been overwhelming." Ellen saw tears well up in her eyes. "So when you came to us, and God knows how you found our cottage in your condition, it seemed like it was meant to be. We've talked it through and we really do want to help you." The couple sat looking at Ellen. She took her time and eventually said,

"May I tell you a story?" The man raised an eyebrow and looked at his wife.

"Of course."

"Before I do, I want to explain that I have spent the best part of six years locked up, being hunted, fighting for my life, killing and watching family and friends being killed. All that time it has been drilled into me not to trust anyone nor to reveal who I am and not to ask any questions." Ellen looked across at the couple and smiled sadly before adding,

"It's not that I don't trust you. You see, when I am caught, as I certainly will be, I will be tortured and then it's only a matter of time before I talk; everybody does and with women their methods are particularly brutal, extremely degrading but extraordinarily effective. I will tell them everything I know including details of those who have helped me. That's why I hesitated." The woman reached across the table and took Ellen's hands.

"For one so young, to have been through what you have, well it merely proves that the people you describe have no place in this world, so let us help." Ellen reflected on this and eventually decided that she owed them far more than just an explanation. She described her childhood in London, the trip to Italy and the imprisonment of her family. She quietly and unemotionally described the train journey with the rape and then the murder of her family. She did not omit the killing of the soldiers, her love for Alfred and the resulting pregnancy. It was like purging her soul. She hid nothing, accepting the obvious disapproval. The couple were normal, kind and caring folk and to them her actions must have seemed wicked.

When she had finished, Ellen stood and said,

"Thank you for your help and wonderful kindness. I'll get my things and move on."

"Sit down!" the man said with a force in his voice that stunned Ellen and she sat.

"I have your belongings," he said, "I followed the trail of blood in the snow back to where you had been. I saw the grave and the little wooden sign. I collected your things including those obviously once owned by German soldiers." He stared at Ellen but there was compassion in his eyes and she somehow knew that although he was clearly shaken, he would not criticise her.

"We will never judge you," he continued. "God will be the one for that, but what you have told us is dreadful and the hurt you feel must be unbearable." His wife then said,

"The doctor told me you're not well enough to travel and you won't be for at least ten days." Once

Ellen had agreed to stay on, Jurgen suggested that if anyone was asked about her presence at the cottage, they would say she was their niece from Italy who had been living in Switzerland. Not only was Ellen's Italian excellent but her false papers from the camp showed she had crossed the border into Austria. He stressed that if the police or military became involved, they should keep any explanation simple by saying she was staying at the cottage until her family returned from visiting relations in France.

* * *

Over the next week, Ellen slept, ate and regained her strength. She also talked for hours with Annemarie and Jurgen and she learnt that the house was on the edge of the village of Trins which Annemarie told her proudly, was a historic village dating back to the 11th century.

One evening during their meal Ellen asked Jurgen about the Brenner Pass and he told her it was ten miles from the village.

"The noise you hear at night is Allied bombers targeting the Pass because it is an essential rail and road link between Austria and Italy and is therefore vital to the German war effort." When Ellen asked what effect it would have if the Pass was blocked he said thoughtfully,

"Well, it seems to me that if that happened it would be impossible for Germany to defend the only part of Italy it still holds, the north." He then looked at Ellen sternly. "And don't get any ideas. The Gestapo are not stupid and they are everywhere making sure us locals remain loyal to the Fatherland."

He then quizzed Ellen about her crossbow. It was obvious he was experienced with the weapon and with a smile, asked if she had stolen it. Ellen, laughing at the suggestion, explained she was given it by a wonderful friend.

"I've never been very successful hunting with it," she added, "but it's excellent for killing Germans." Jurgen smiled and obviously impressed, suggested that when Ellen was fit again they could hunt together. She was delighted knowing that might give her the opportunity of travelling towards the Brenner Pass.

*   *   *

The doctor visited Ellen twice and on both occasions seemed satisfied with her progress. He did stress however, that under no circumstances should she go outside or do anything strenuous for at least three weeks.

Ellen being Ellen quickly became bored and began a daily exercise routine. She knew she had to regain her fitness and quickly, so devised a programme beginning with extremely gentle stretches and movements. Each day she extended the programme making it more demanding and as she worked she watched the weather change. Spring had arrived and Annemarie told her that once the weather was warmer their valley, so dead during the bitter winter months, would become a hive of activity as the farmers made the most of it.

Following the final visit from the doctor, Ellen moved outside with her exercise programme and began running in earnest.

Annemarie told her that the following day she'd make her first shopping trip of the summer to Innsbruck and wondered if Ellen would like to go with her. She explained that she loved her days out, although they would have to walk about a mile to the main road to take the local bus, they would spend the whole day in the town and meet up with friends. Ellen couldn't wait.

*   *   *

The walk and the journey on the bus were not too tiring for Ellen and once in the town, she followed Annemarie around the shops. Although many were virtually empty or closed down, they spent the morning browsing and window shopping, loving every minute of it.

As they walked, Ellen was extremely conscious of the number of German soldiers on the streets and when she asked Annemarie why, she was told that Innsbruck was where a lot of the military spent their leave or days off.

For lunch, Annemarie took Ellen to a café where three women were waiting for them and as agreed, Ellen was introduced as Annemarie's niece from Switzerland. After a few inconsequential questions, more out of politeness than interest, the ladies spent the rest of the meal catching up.

Later Ellen excused herself, arranging to meet Annemarie back at the bus station and left as they began to discuss the latest gossip. Wanting to take a look at the railway station and any German supply trains, Ellen made her way through the town and was saddened at the number of destroyed buildings. The Allies must have targeted Innsbruck and she guessed that as usual, most of those injured, killed or left homeless would have been the innocent residents of the city.

As she approached the station Ellen was surprised by how few Germans were around and casually asked one of the railway guards why it was so quiet. He told her that the Germans had built a railway bypass to avoid Innsbruck and only locals were using the station.

Ellen's idea of disrupting the German supply lines had become a good deal more complex.

As she walked back towards the town centre she passed a busy tavern with singing coming from inside. She then saw four German officers crossing the road, heading for the inn door. All four looked at her as she walked towards them and as she passed, one of the men smiled at her. Ellen instantly began to shake and she shut her eyes in disbelief. When she looked again, they had entered the tavern and she walked on, hiding her horror.

Turning at the first corner Ellen dropped onto the chair of a pavement café. After a few moments a waiter asked her what she wanted so she ordered a brandy with the little money Annemarie had given her. When the drink came she downed it in one and felt the burning sensation in her throat, but it had the desired effect and calmed her.

Ellen sat stunned. Could she be wrong? She tried to remember exactly the face, the smile, the look as he had mounted her mother. Ellen would never ever forget those features, the evil in those eyes as he raped her mother, the laugh as he watched the younger man revealing himself. There was no question; it was him and she had to get him alone. She would kill him but before she did, she'd learn where she could find the other monster with the bluest of eyes.

* * *

Ellen walked calmly into the dark of the tavern bar. She accepted it was a crazy thing to do but didn't care. She saw the man laughing and walked to his table as the room fell silent. At that moment Ellen knew there could be no turning back. As she approached, Ellen looked directly at him and he returned the stare. He smiled, stood and offered her a seat and a drink and crazy or not Ellen was exactly where she needed to be.

*   *   *

"Can I take your coat," the officer said as he pushed the door shut. Ellen saw a sparsely furnished room with a bed, chest of drawers, wardrobe and little else.

She removed her coat and casually dropped it on the bed, making sure the serrated knife she'd picked up off the cafe table was close at hand. The officer slipped of his coat, moved towards Ellen and grabbed her but she didn't flinch. Kissing her forcefully, his hands moved to her breasts and he fondled them and as he pushed himself up against her, Ellen felt his arousal.

"You really are gorgeous," he said as his hand went inside her blouse. "We've met before, I know we have; I could never forget such beauty."

"Let's worry about that later," Ellen said with a smile. She pulled away and began to unbutton her blouse and skirt, dropping them to the floor. The man also undressed and when he was down to his underpants and Ellen her knickers, she took his hand and manoeuvred him to the bed, pushing him down and immediately moved on top, straddling him. He stroked her breast and she could feel his excitement growing beneath her. He began to tear at her underwear and as the material gave way he caressed her most sensitive parts. For Ellen it was irrelevant, a means to an end; necessary. She felt nothing because it was nothing. There was no desire, no arousal, just abhorrence and revulsion for the man beneath her.

"Come on, please, he said desperately, trying to turn Ellen onto her back.

"You have to wait," she said teasing him and felt his body relax. Ellen accepted it was a dangerous game to play but she didn't care; this was the moment she'd dreamt of. The animal lying beneath her, begging to let him enter her, was all hers. Ellen felt him lower his pants and could feel his erection. She needed the knife but he mustn't suspect. There was only one way and as Ellen let him enter her, he moaned and she stretched towards the knife. She lent closer to his face and felt his breathing quickening.

"Dear God, that's good," he said and she felt him reaching a climax and smiled. It was time. The man's eyes were closed and he saw nothing as she placed the blade next to his throat. Ellen lifted her hips to remove him from within her and laughed. Immediately he tried to pull her back down so he could re-enter her, finish his delight; he was so close and then Ellen felt him stop. He abruptly opened his eyes as he felt the blade on his throat.

"What are you doing?" He tried to move but Ellen said quietly, leaning to his ear,

"Lie still or I'll cut your throat." She was not surprised to see beads of sweat appear on the man's forehead and again she smiled.

"What do you want? I have money," he said panicking.

"Money," Ellen laughed. "It's not your money I want."

"What then?"

"Shall I remind you of where you saw me?" Fear flooded the man's face. He nodded but said nothing.

"A few months ago," as she spoke Ellen exerted more pressure on the knife and watched a trickle of blood appear on the man's neck, "my family, my Jewish family was travelling on a train." The man's eyes closed; he knew.

"Remember, yes?" Again more pressure on the knife, again more seeping blood, again there was a rapid nod of the man's head.

"You raped my mother, not once but twice. Of course you remember." His eyes were wide open and he was truly terrified and nodded. He was incapable of speaking.

"If you want to live, I want answers. Understand."

"Yes," he choked out.

"What was the name of the other man, the one who raped me and where do I find him?"

"I... I... I..." he stuttered, paralytic with fear, "I... don't know his name; we called him Johan." Ellen pushed the knife harder and saw the blood flowing onto the pillow, crimson and captivating.

"Where do I find him?"

"The train was travelling through Switzerland. I met him there."

"And the name of the station?"

"Zurich."

Ellen had what she wanted and dragged the knife across the man's throat, moving away to avoid the spurting blood. Staring pitilessly as he tried to move and call out she watched as his life drained away. She felt no sympathy or regret.

"Now, you fucking bastard, tell me, how does it feel?" she shouted as his eyes slowly closed.

It was only later that Ellen realised she had no idea of his name and decided it was simply unimportant. All that mattered was the monster was dead.

—Ж—

PART III

The PRICE of BETRAYAL

Chapter 1

1945

Ellen returned home to London three months after the end of the war and found the destruction heartbreaking. Her family home was still standing which was a miracle, and as she approached the house in the early evening, she saw lights behind curtains. She had often wondered what would have happened if the house had been destroyed or occupied by strangers; she had no documents and six years had passed. How on earth could she prove she was the daughter of Howard and Tova Aizenberg.

Seeing the lights on, Ellen walked tentatively to the door and knocked. After what seemed like a lifetime she heard locks being turned and her Aunts Golda and Barbara appeared. She struggled to believe what she was seeing; the aunts on the other hand, had no idea who she was and looked concerned at the exhausted, emaciated young woman who stood before them. Suddenly Golda said,

"Dear God, is it really you?" and the three fell into each other's arms and sobbed.

* * *

Over tea in the kitchen, Ellen listened as they explained that once the war had come to an end and they had still heard nothing from anyone since the funeral of their brother Emil, they had agreed to travel to London to see if they could find any news of their family. There was no mention, of course, of the numerous reports of death camps and the slaughter of Jews throughout Europe, which had left both sisters accepting that there was little chance any of their relations had survived.

After making hot soup the three sat around the kitchen table. It was clear that Ellen had changed dramatically since they had last seen her. She was still only nineteen years old yet there was no spark in her eyes, no joy in her heart. Their niece was like an old woman who'd lived a thousand lifetimes. Ellen said nothing but just sat and listened as Barbara told her that they had been in London for two weeks and had planned to stay about a month before flying to Turin to visit Hayastan. Golda then described their journey to Europe but Ellen remained withdrawn, appearing almost indifferent to what was being said. Barbara, determined not to give up, explained,

"When we still had no news, we were desperate to make sure this house and contents were safe for when any of you returned." It was Golda's turn.

"And when we arrived, you'll never believe it but we found a family living here. They had lost everything during the war and had nowhere to go. They had spotted the house was empty so moved in." Barbara continued, saying that there had been no arguments or unpleasantness. In fact, she told her, they were both deeply saddened as they listened to the dreadful story the father had to tell. In the end though, they agreed to leave.

Ellen stayed silent and Barbara and Golda were becoming extremely concerned, but they persevered. They talked alternately about their own families and what effect the war had had on them and then as Golda stood to clear the table, Ellen placed her hands over her eyes and said angrily, "My father, mother, brother, aunt and cousins were all slaughtered." The sisters were completely heartbroken by the news but Barbara moved across to her niece and held her tenderly. Ellen remained unresponsive to any attempt to comfort her.

Eventually she asked if she could go to bed; all she wanted was to sleep and as she climbed under the blanket, her feet on the hot water bottle, she prayed that when she woke her world would be back to normal.

She slept the whole of the next day with one or other of the aunts by her side. Barbara took the first shift whilst Golda visited Howard's solicitor to ensure that if Ellen's parents were dead, the ownership of the house and all their belongings would pass to their daughter. She was aware that her brother had been extremely successful before the war and, although not common for pre-war London, he owned the house outright. The sisters hoped that proceeds from its sale would give Ellen a chance to begin a new life.

Golda faced endless problems. Not only was Ellen unrecognisable, she possessed no documents and there was no evidence her parents were dead. However, problems were the norm for the chaos of post-war London and ambiguity simply a part of everyday life. Golda refused to give up. She fought bureaucracy, incompetence and indifference and all other obstacles linked to a country recovering from the horrors of war but eventually she was told there would be no problem with Ellen inheriting everything.

* * *

For the next month, Golda and Barbara remained in London. Both had family and business commitments at home but neither was prepared to leave Ellen alone. It wasn't just her physical state; although her body was wrecked and needed time to recover, a far greater worry was her mental and emotional state of mind. She remained withdrawn, rarely speaking and spending most days doing nothing. At mealtimes or in the evenings, the aunts found it impossible to involve Ellen in a conversation. She was always polite but said little and Golda likened her to a broken doll that could not be repaired without expert help and so the aunts searched the city for just that; specialist help. However, the few experts who were left in London were committed to supporting returning soldiers, many of whom had suffered the most awful mental damage and so the aunts asked Ellen if she would like to go to America. There was no mention of doctors, but they knew the medical treatment she needed would be available in the States.

It took a further week for Ellen to agree; her uncertainty heightened by her strong desire to stay in the family home and Barbara used that time to return to Howard's solicitor. With a considerable payment up front, he agreed that if the house was made secure, he would look after the property until Ellen returned.

Golda also spoke to the neighbours and explained, in as much detail as was necessary, the situation and it was agreed that for a small retainer they would check the house daily.

* * *

Ellen slept for most of the first week in Washington and once the aunts were confident she was settled, Barbara returned to her family in Canada.

After the first month, Ellen began jogging every day. Only short distances but it was a start and a week later she asked Golda if she could visit the local library and became a member and avid reader. There was undeniable progress for all to see but Ellen was far from cured and this was most apparent whenever she was in other people's company. She was always reserved, rarely joining in conversations, but Golda's family was wonderful; they simply behaved normally, discussed ordinary subjects and although they were conscious of Ellen's past, they treated her just the same as everyone else.

Ellen understood this and was grateful but she knew that what they really wanted was for her to talk about the war. It wasn't that she didn't want to, she just couldn't trust herself to look back without resurrecting an uncontainable rage in her mind.

* * *

Ellen's first visit to Aunt Barbara's family in Canada was followed by a second, two months later. She loved to travel and spending time with her relations brought her genuine happiness. However, as pleased as everyone was with her progress, few knew that Ellen continued to face violent flashbacks; moments when she cried at dark memories and nights when it was impossible to sleep because of the remorse, guilt and shame she felt.

It was on that second visit to Canada that she decided to talk to her aunt. For a number of weeks she had become uncomfortable at being such a burden on Golda's family. At only twenty years of age, with her whole life in front of her, Ellen felt it was time to move on; to live independently and stop simply being a part of other people's lives.

"I want to study and finish my education," she told Golda. "I want go to college." Her Aunt's reaction was mixed; if Ellen was recognising what she wanted for her future, that was stunning progress, but if it meant cutting herself off from all the support around her, then it became a concern.

For the next three days, whenever possible, aunt and niece looked at the options open to Ellen. They researched colleges across Britain and North America, listing the pros and cons of each location and it was Ellen who decided she would like to stay close to Washington.

After further research, it was decided she should visit Mount Vernon, an all female college on the other side of the city from her Aunt Golda. However, the question of cost then arose and Ellen was incredulous at how expensive it would be; she simply couldn't afford it, but Golda had other ideas. After phoning Barbara in Washington, she told her niece the family would pay. Ellen flatly refused. There was absolutely no way she could accept, however after a number of international phone calls to Barbara, she agreed that when any money from her parent's estate came to her, she would repay whatever she could afford.

* * *

Ellen signed up for a one year course in history and as the college was some distance from Golda's house, it was also agreed she would live on campus.

The time passed quickly and whilst she achieved everything she could have hoped for academically, and she became more independent and self sufficient in her everyday life, Ellen continued to struggle with relationships. Other students quickly realised she was different and this manifested itself in her appearing distant and uncommunicative and eventually they stopped trying to gain her friendship, leaving her isolated and lonely.

As the year drew to a close, Ellen told her aunts that she didn't want to continue at Mount Vernon but wanted to return to London and apply for a History

Degree at London University. She explained she also wanted to live in her family home and, when she'd qualified, she hoped to teach. Both Aunts again had mixed feelings. Ellen was clearly ready for more independence but they worried about her being so far away and living alone. Ultimately though, both could see their niece was developing into a beautiful, intelligent woman with boundless potential.

As the journey to London was being finalised, Ellen asked her Aunts if she could travel home via Italy. When she said she wanted to find the people who had helped her during her time in Turin, especially Carla, both asked if they could go with her. They had cancelled their original trip due to the seriousness of Ellen's condition and it would be the ideal opportunity for them to visit Hayastan.

Ellen was delighted; having her Aunts as company would be wonderful.

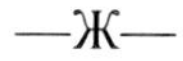

Chapter 2

1947

As Ellen sat on the train, travelling towards Turin, her thoughts drifted back to the war but she immediately scolded herself. These were memories she had buried and she was determined not to give in just because she was returning to Italy. As hard as she tried, as they moved through the outskirts of Turin and she saw the bombed buildings and dejected faces of the people, the thought of loved ones created an overwhelming sadness in her. Closing her eyes, determined not to submit to her emotions, Ellen argued with herself that it was bound to happen. Returning was never going to be easy.

*   *   *

It was during their first evening meal at the hotel in Turin that Ellen began to speak of the war. Neither aunt knew what had triggered her need to talk but both understood that it was part of the healing process and wanted her to confide in them. She was initially hesitant, often reflecting on small but significant moments that had impacted on her and the more she spoke, the more self-assured she became.

"Following the funeral of Uncle Emil our problems began," she said, remembering. "Of course, as children much of it was kept from us, but I knew my parents were extremely worried. My father needed time in Turin to sort out family business but mummy wasn't happy and I heard them arguing. She wanted us to leave there and then along with Aunt Marguerita and the boys but my father said we would have to wait until the following day." Ellen stopped thoughtfully before saying, "But it never happened." She continued, "During that day, whilst my father was at Scalfaro's, the police arrived. We weren't told what they wanted but they returned later and arrested him. When I asked my mother why he'd been taken, she said there had been a terrible mistake and it would be sorted out." Golda interrupted Ellen to insist she eat some food but she said she was not hungry, although she did pick at a few mouthfuls before carrying on.

"But it wasn't sorted. I didn't see my father for four years." Golda and Barbara both were astonished, each asking themselves why Tova or Marguerita hadn't let them know what was happening.

"Mummy did write to you; I saw the letters," Ellen stated bluntly and then a moment later added, "although I remember hearing that foreign mail was being censored or confiscated by the police, so maybe they never arrived." It was Golda who then said,

"We did hear about you once. The British Embassy contacted us to say they had information concerning our family from their contacts in Turin. They explained that although the details were vague, you wouldn't be allowed to leave until certain discrepancies in Emil's business records had been sorted out."

Barbara then spoke for almost the first time.

"Ellen, we tried to find out what was happening. The Embassies in Washington and Quebec were always sympathetic but could never help. You know," she said taking hold of her niece's hand, "we even looked at travelling to Italy, but what with the war, it was impossible."

"Anyway," Ellen continued, not responding to Barbara's attempt to explain, "the day after my father was arrested, my mother told Noah and me that we were leaving with Aunt Marguerita and our cousins.

When I asked her if she was coming, she said no and I got so angry. My father had been arrested and I was being sent away from my mother; I just couldn't understand why. She said she had to stay and help get my father released but that really didn't help."

Ellen took a small amount food, then pushed the plate away so Barbara called the waiter and ordered coffee. Both Aunts waited patiently for Ellen to continue.

"That night we left with Umberto driving. Do you remember Carla and Umberto?" The Aunts nodded. "Well, we hid on the floor of the car so the police watching the estate would not see us, and headed for Switzerland. Aunt Marguerita told us we were going there because it was a neutral country." Again Ellen paused and remembered.

"It was so difficult saying goodbye to Mummy, especially for Noah but we had to do as we were told. So we drove to the border and joined the queue to cross and I remember being quite excited. Then, just as we were about to walk into Switzerland, we were stopped by these dreadful men. We were told later they were the Gestapo who were looking for Jews trying to leave Italy. As they were talking to Aunt Marguerita, I saw Umberto running towards us shouting and then suddenly..." Ellen stopped with tears in her eyes as she said softly, "I heard gunfire and Umberto fell. They shot him right in front of us without caring how much we loved him." The aunts sat speechless; they were struggling to believe what they were hearing.

"We were arrested and for the next few days we were moved from one place to another. We were hungry, always cold and then quite unbelievably, we ended up back at Hayastan. They placed us under house arrest but it didn't matter; we were home. Carla was still there but then my delight changed to heartbreak when she told us that not only was there no news of my father but my mother had also been taken away by the police. I was still a child and couldn't understand what was happening. My life had gone from an almost idyllic childhood to a frighteningly cruel nightmare. And, well... I began to hate." Ellen stopped suddenly. With misery and aggression in her watery eyes, she stated, "For the first time in my life I hated. I truly hated those people who were treating us so horribly." Once again she paused and the aunts noticed her shiver. "It's easy looking back to see that many Germans were not bad and that there were many other nationalities; Italians, Swiss, French, who were just as determined to get rid of Jews but it was the Germans I really hated." She looked at both her aunts and nervously took their hands, holding them tightly as if she was desperate for their support. "And you know, it was that hatred that kept me going. It was the driving force behind my survival. I was determined to see justice done, to seek retribution for what had happened to us. It's only now that I understand what I really sought was absolute revenge." Ellen then again looked at her aunts and said miserably, "And I know that in God's eyes it will lead to my eternal damnation."

* * *

After lunch on the following day, a Sunday, the three women found a taxi to visit Hayastan. Nothing was said about the previous evening or the abrupt end to Ellen's story. The aunts were only just beginning to grasp the horrors their niece had endured and accepted she may never open up like that again.

As they travelled across the city, Ellen recognised little; just the occasional silhouette of a building or junction that awakened some distant memory. So much had been destroyed by Allied bombing, that she felt as if she were visiting Turin for the first time.

When they finally arrived at the estate, Golda asked the driver to stop and they walked along the glorious tree lined drive. Little had changed; the gardens were beautifully manicured and the magnificence of Hayastan then came into view. Ellen shivered; facing her was the house where her childhood had been stolen. However, as they approached the front steps it was clear the building was terminally damaged. Apart from the front façade, it was a complete ruin. What had once been one of the most breathtaking houses in Turin was just rubble. Ellen stared towards the cottage; her home for so many years and again it was derelict apart from a small extension where the kitchen used to be.

Ellen then saw a man walking up the drive and although she had spoken little Italian over the previous two years, she acted as a translator for her aunts. She told him their family had originally built the house and it had been their home before the war. When the man clearly didn't believe her, Ellen asked him who he was.

"I live in the gate-house and keep an eye on the estate. I'm expected to inform my boss if anyone shows any interest in the house."

"And who is your boss?" Ellen asked.

"Flavio Lotti."

When Ellen suddenly squealed both aunts assumed something dreadful had happened but she explained that Flavio Lotti was still alive. When the aunts looked confused she said, "Mr Lotti was one of Grandfather Joseph's closest friends and he worked with him and Uncle Emil at Scalfaro's. Don't you remember? He was at the funeral."

Ellen explained to them that Flavio Lotti had always been there for the family and when they lived in the cottage, he'd visited all the time, bringing food, wine and even books for her. Then she remembered the last night she'd seen him because he was in danger and had to leave.

Ellen began walking around the side of Hayastan. She had suddenly recalled the boxes her father had placed under the floorboards of the lounge of the cottage. She had completely forgotten about them and even her precious journal. However, the man called her back and when she ignored him said he would call the police. Barbara told Ellen they should leave as the last thing they needed was problems with the law.

*   *   *

Although the caretaker at Hayastan had been irritated by Ellen, before they left he gave them Flavio Lotti's office address. The following morning, as it was a Monday, Ellen insisted they made an early start and they walked across the city, arriving at the office block at ten o'clock. As they entered the impressive building, a nervous Ellen was surprised to see it was law firm; she hadn't been aware that Mr Lotti was a lawyer.

A rather unhelpful receptionist told them that Mr Lotti was extremely busy and tied up for the entire day, however, when Ellen insisted they would wait she left them in an extremely comfortable reception area. A few minutes later she heard a loud voice, then an adjacent door burst open and an old man in a wheelchair rolled in. He nodded to the two aunts and moved quickly toward Ellen.

"Dear God," he said breathlessly in near perfect English, "it is you, it really is. I can't believe it!" With tears in her eyes Ellen leant over and gave him the most enormous hug. Flavio, who was also crying, squeezed Ellen so tightly she wondered whether he would ever let her go. Her aunts stood mesmerised as the affection between Flavio and Ellen was so genuine. It was so incredibly moving that once again they were acutely aware of how little they understood of the immense heartache and trauma suffered by so many during the war.

After moving into his impressive office, Ellen and Flavio, as he insisted on them calling him, didn't seem to stop talking for what seemed like hours and Barbara and Golda watched, listened and laughed and even cried with Ellen and Flavio on many occasions. Mid-morning they had coffee and eventually his rather frustrated secretary entered the office to inform him he had a meeting immediately after lunch. Much to her frustration, Flavio cancelled everything for the rest of the day and told her to book a table for four at his favourite restaurant.

The meal proved to be a mix of reminiscing, catching up and establishing where things stood for the Aizenberg family. Over coffee, Flavio said, "After the war I returned to Turin but was so saddened by what I found. Not only had the city been heavily bombed by the Allies, including thc industrial centre and Scalfaro factories, but they'd also targeted key German military buildings, one being Hayastan."

When Ellen asked him about the future of her old home, Flavio told her that the estate was situated in just about the most desirable area of Turin, adding with a chuckle, that as usual, Joseph had picked the perfect location for his home.

"Right now though, because the authorities have been unable to locate any members of your family, the estate is in a sort of limbo. All I've been trying to do is make sure the land doesn't fall into the wrong hands until one of you turned up. You see, unfortunately, there are wealthy people as well as large companies who view the Aizenberg estate as the perfect city location for post-war development." Flavio turned to the aunts.

"Although we met at Emil's funeral, once the house, cottage and everything inside had been destroyed, there was no way of finding you and believe me, I have tried. To see Hayastan and its land auctioned off with profits going to the government, well, I couldn't accept that so, with help from some very influential friends, I've been delaying any compulsory sell-off. However, that is about to change. Originally, we managed to get a moratorium placed on the estate to give my lawyers time to prepare; that time runs out shortly." Again Flavio looked around the table at his guests.

"If we still had the ownership documents, would that help?" Ellen asked and Flavio laughed.

"Absolutely but I've always assumed your father took them when you left and well..., I'm sorry because I believed no one on that terrifying journey could have survived and how wrong I was, because you, my dear sweet child, are here." He took Ellen's hands and smiled.

"Do you remember Carla?" Ellen then asked.

"Of course I do." For some reason Flavio laughed again much to Ellen's confusion.

"Well, the day we were taken away," she continued, "my father and Carla collected our most precious items and hid two metal containers under the floorboards in the lounge of her cottage." She looked at Flavio intently as she added, "Do you think they could still be there?" Flavio replied, "Ladies I insist you check out of your hotel and move in with me. My home is at your disposal for as long as you are in Turin. It really would be an honour." When all three women began to protest, Flavio stopped them abruptly explaining that having their company in his very simple house would be wonderful and that brought to an end any dissent.

* * *

Following lunch, on the way to his house, the car stopped at the hotel and much to the surprise of the receptionist, Ellen and the Aunts packed and checked out. They then drove for only a few minutes before entering a beautiful square near the town centre and as the car slowed, Flavio pointed out an old four storey building with a series of pillars and arches and said, "Home."

They drove to the rear of the house and as they stopped an old woman appeared. Ellen took little notice; she was astounded by the beauty of the ancient Italian building and it was only as the woman helped the driver move Flavio into his wheelchair, that they faced each other.

"Carla!" she shouted as her old housekeeper recognised her and the two hugged, both speaking and laughing together. Ellen tried to use her rusty Italian and Carla, her out of practice English; it just didn't matter as they held each other and sobbed in utter disbelief.

* * *

Once Carla had shown Ellen and her aunts their bedrooms and given them a tour of the rest of the stunning dwelling, they returned to the kitchen and sat around the large table drinking wine.

All afternoon they sat and talked and eventually Ellen asked Flavio about the wheelchair. He explained that he'd been paralysed after an accidental explosion.

"I was in a small village in the mountains with some Resistance friends and we were making bombs to use against the Germans. Well... in truth we were a bit like excited children playing at war games and had no idea what we were doing. Not unexpectedly, the thing exploded and you may not believe it, but I was incredibly lucky. Four of my dearest friends were killed, another blinded and another will never live a normal life again so, well…" he tapped his legs under the blanket, "I was fortunate. The local doctor was superb and without him I would have died.

"A few months later after the German defeat, I returned to Turin to build a new life and, as you can see, I have but not without this wonderful woman," and Flavio took Carla's hand as she blushed and in broken English said,

"Stop it. These lovely people aren't interested in us."

"But we are," Ellen immediately answered and the aunts nodded and smiled.

"Okay," Flavio continued, "well, I saw Carla when I first visited Hayastan after my return." He laughed at her embarrassment. "I was being pushed around what was left of the main house, horrified by the damage and of course, far worse, finding it completely empty of people. Anyway, I was just about to leave when Carla appeared. Now you tell them dear." Carla again reddened but said quietly to Ellen, Speaking timidly, often hesitating whilst she tried to find the right words, Carla explained, "After you all left the Germans took over the main house and told me I had to leave but I had promised Madam Marguerita I would look after the house." Carla had tears in her eyes.

"I had a little money and even though I knew your father had put money and jewels under the floor boards I couldn't use that." Flavio reached across the table and again took Carla's hand so gently that she smiled at him and Ellen felt tears welling up in her own eyes.

"So I moved out and found work. I lived with a distant relative on the edge of the city but every Sunday I walked back to check on Hayastan and every week the guards would shout at me and threatened me, but I didn't care.

When I first heard the estate had been bombed, I was happy. It meant that the Germans would be gone but then I saw the damage and I was dismayed. I looked through the destruction and only my old kitchen in the cottage was still standing and I went to live there. There was no running water. I used candles for light but the fire worked and I could cook on the stove so I had more than most people. Then Flavio arrived and when he saw where I was living he insisted I move into this house. I asked if he needed a housekeeper, to which of course he said no, but he admitted that as he was invalided, he could do with some help around the house. From then onwards we've been together." Carla again looked at Flavio and smiled lovingly.

"Once back in Turin," Flavio again took up the story, "I decided I had to make myself useful. Scalfaro's was beyond help so to stop myself becoming completely idle, I opened the law practice. Mind you, I do very little. I just hire an enormous number of young, energetic lawyers who are so much more competent than I am and let them do all the work." Again he smiled towards Carla as she tried without success to disagree with him.

"I had plenty of time on my hands so I tried to find out what had happened to you all but it was all in vain. I employed the guard to live in the gatehouse to keep an eye on Hayastan and, as I said, I am doing my best to keep the estate out of the hands of the authorities."

"Do you think there is any point going back to look for the boxes my father left under the floorboards?"

Ellen asked Carla but before she could answer, Flavio replied laughing,

"When we first met up again Carla explained all about the boxes so I had them dug up. She told me in no uncertain terms that they were not to be touched until you returned." Flavio looked towards the sideboard and Carla stood up.

"So," Flavio said slowly, again laughing with Carla, "living in fear of the consequences of touching them, they have been up there ever since," and he pointed to the top of the sideboard as Carla climbed onto the chair and passed two boxes down to Ellen.

"Everything inside may have been destroyed when the cottage was hit," Flavio said as Ellen placed both boxes in the middle of the table. When no one moved, Flavio asked, "Is anybody going to open them?"

"But there're locked," Ellen replied.

"There were keys but I'm afraid they've gone missing."

Flavio wheeled himself to a drawer in the sideboard and returned with a screwdriver and hammer. After a few minutes of banging and swearing, one of the locks shattered and Flavio moved on to the second box. When both were finally unlocked, Carla pushed them towards Ellen whilst the others waited expectantly. Holding her breath she slowly lifted the first lid as Carla suggested they all retire to the lounge and leave Ellen. Although she protested, once on her own her excitement mounted. Slowly she began to remove items one by one, piece by piece, and for the next half hour Ellen laughed, cried, got angry and swore. Finally with all the contents laid out on the table and sorted into groups, she called for the others and Carla gave her another hug as they retook their seats.

Ellen then went through her family's belongings; all that remained from three generations of the

Aizenberg's in Turin, and the aunts sat speechless as they understood their family history had vanished. Grandfather Joseph, brothers Emil and Howard and their sons Simon, Leon and Noah, Tova, Marguerita and not forgetting Umberto; all so innocent but in the wrong place at the wrong time and all sacrificed in the name of an Aryan master race and Fascist omnipotence.

*   *   *

With the agreement of the others, Ellen distributed her family mementoes. Documents relating to the Hayastan estate and the original Scalfaro's contracts, she passed to Flavio. The jewellery left by her Aunt Marguerita and mother was divided amongst the four women even though Carla was adamant she should receive none of it and then Ellen laughed for the first time as she revealed her journal.

Finally, she gave an opened envelope with the name of her aunt on the front to Flavio who began to read the enclosed letter.

"My Dearest Marguerita..." but he stopped and looked around the table asking,

"Is it our place to read this?" It was Ellen who answered.

"I remember Aunt Marguerita giving it to my father for safe keeping. She said something about it being important for the future of the family so I think we should." There were nods of agreement from her aunts.

"Okay," Flavio said.

"My Dearest Marguerita,

I asked Riccardo to make sure this was delivered to you but only if something terrible happened to me.

My love, I have never been able to accept Grandfather Joseph's death was an accident. I don't know whether Riccardo or Eric have spoken to you but

I want to say that at no time did my father or myself have anything to do with illegal activities, especially against Mussolini or the state.

I am certain my father's death was not an accident and with Eric and Riccardo, we wanted to discover the truth. However, we were immediately warned off asking questions and understandably the other two were frightened for their families so stopped searching for answers, but my love I couldn't and I am so sorry.

My father was not a criminal or a danger to the state. Yes, some of the people he associated with may have been, but not him. He was in the wrong place at the wrong time and because of this, the police believed he posed a threat to the government and the country's leaders and as a result, I'm certain he was executed by the secret police.

I also believe, because I attended the business group on a few occasions and my name is Aizenberg, the secret police see me in the same light as my father. As a result, I have been receiving terrifying threats from them.

As with my father, it is likely that my death is being explained away by the police and 'official' doctors but as you know, I am healthy and fit so there is no reason why I should depart this life apart from the fact that I've upset powerful people by asking questions about my father's death.

My love, if the ultimate has happened to me then..."

And Flavio stopped, saying that the remainder of the letter was too private.

*　　*　　*

Following a late afternoon walk, Ellen and her Aunts joined Carla and Flavio for dinner and the evening proved to be one of the most enjoyable and moving she could remember. As they sat around the long kitchen table telling stories and laughing, she understood that as long as she had those she loved in her life, there would always be magical moments.

Sitting drinking coffee after a delicious meal cooked by Carla and a liberal amount of Italian wine, Golda asked Flavio about Scalfaro's.

"That's another dreadful regret," he replied. "As soon as I returned to Turin, I visited the factories and café. Although two of the three cafés had survived the bombing, the third and both factories had been destroyed. As with Hayastan, I've managed to ensure that all the land, buildings and other assets owned by Scalfaro's have been protected from speculators. Apart from the two surviving café, none of the property is on prime land, however, I see the city developing appreciably over the next decade so its value may well increase significantly." Flavio sipped at his coffee waiting for questions. When none came he said,

"The three of you are more than likely the only remaining members of Joseph's family. Of course I will go through all the documents to confirm ownership, but assuming you are, then before leaving Turin, decisions will need to be made as to what you want to do with the assets." Again there was a measured silence until Ellen said,

"What about you? I recall once overhearing your ownership of Scalfaro's being discussed."

"You're right," Flavio answered with a smile. "When the company was originally passed on to Joseph, I received 20% of the business. However, I made a decision when I returned to Turin after the war that if any of Joseph's family returned, I would include my share of the company in any compensation that may come from its sale."

"But that's not fair," Ellen said crossly.

"Ellen, look at us. We have everything we need and much more. I am extremely wealthy in my own right and I want to honour Joseph's name and all he did for Scalfaro's." Flavio stopped and stared at Carla, who nodded and smiled tenderly at him. "You see, your grandfather was the most amazing man I ever had the privilege to call a friend. Singlehandedly he rescued the company from bankruptcy and turned it into one of the most profitable and successful businesses in Italy. As his only surviving family, you three deserve to benefit from his labours." Again there was silence around the table until Barbara spoke.

"I am also incredibly fortunate. My father set me up in my own business in America and my family have everything we could hope for. Anything due to me I want transferred to Ellen."

"Same goes for me," Golda stated emphatically. Ellen looked at both of her Aunts with her mouth wide open.

"Well Ellen," Flavio said lightly, "it looks like you are now the proud owner of what's left of Scalfaro's." Then he added more seriously, "Assuming you wish me to carry on representing you, before you leave Turin I will need instructions on how to proceed. Also, I'll require a contract from both you Barbara, and Golda, confirming your gift to Ellen."

In unison Ellen and the aunts asked Flavio to carry on advising them.

* * *

The next day Flavio went to his office early. Over breakfast Ellen talked to the Aunts about their decision to leave everything to her and both were adamant that it would give her the sort of start they'd been given by their father. Later, whilst they went for a walk, Ellen talked things over with Carla and decided she should visit the two remaining Scalfaro cafés. She wanted to see them without anyone knowing who she was and visited the first immediately after lunch. She then travelled to the second café and was just leaving when Flavio arrived. He told her he was going to discuss the ownership of Scalfaro's with the two managers before suggesting she visited them with him. As they sat drinking some of the last remaining Scalfaro's chocolate in stock, Flavio asked Ellen what she wanted to do with the land and cafés.

"Initially nothing," she told him and asked about the operation and maintenance costs of the land and businesses, compared to the profits being made. Flavio was impressed and explained that apart from operational costs there was no further expenditure.

"But what about the security man at Hayastan?" she asked.

"That's covered by my firm."

"But surely, his salary should come from any profit made by the cafés?"

Flavio explained that any profit made was going mainly on staff including the manager in each café. He also told Ellen that he had worked closely with them on staffing levels and other areas such as purchasing, menus and prices and with a wicked smile told her that if she was to remain in Turin, he could hand control over to her.

*   *   *

That evening, with everyone again sat around the kitchen table enjoying yet another wonderful meal prepared by Carla, Ellen thanked her aunts for their generosity, Flavio for working so hard on behalf of the family and finally Carla for being the perfect hostess.

She then told them she had visited the cafés and by chance met Flavio but didn't mention his proposal, although she had thought of little else since they spoke.

After the meal, Flavio again told stories of the war years until Carla asked innocently, "Ellen dear, what happened to you all after you were taken from the cottage?" The table fell silent; everyone understanding that the question was a turning point for Ellen. Was she able to describe her past or was she still so emotionally scarred she would find it just too heartbreaking?

Quickly realising the position she had placed Ellen in, Carla apologised saying she had been thoughtless and had no right to ask.

"Don't be silly." Ellen moved around the table to a tearful Carla and gave her a hug. "You have every right; you all do." Ellen smiled before adding to Carla, "You have been part of our family for so many years; firstly with Grandpa Joseph and then Aunt Marguerita and Uncle Emil. You've all been so kind to me and so I'll try."

Flavio wheeled himself around the table pouring more wine as they waited for Ellen's story.

"The night before last, I began to describe what had happened to us whilst we were in Turin during the war but got no further than when we were told to leave the cottage, so I'll carry on from there." Flavio nodded and the more Ellen recounted, the more the reaction of Flavio and Carla mirrored the disbelief of Barbara and Golda two nights earlier. Neither could believe the violence she'd endured nor the extreme personal heartache she'd suffered.

Ellen told her story up to the train's arrival at the station in Switzerland. When Flavio asked how she knew it was Switzerland she told him bluntly that she just knew. Flavio, apologetically, said he thought the Swiss had declared neutrality during the war. After a moment's silence, Ellen said, reddening, "I'm sorry I spoke rudely," and looking at Flavio, she smiled remorsefully adding, "It will become clearer I promise." She then hesitated, unsure as to how much detail to go into and after some consideration said," The next two years of my life, well, they are in many ways a blur and the memories I've got are painful. You see, I'm afraid I do not come out of that period of my life particularly proud of myself." Again she stopped. Again it was as if she was unsure what to say and then Barbara reached across the table and took her hand.

"You don't have to give us details." Ellen nodded, looked around the table at those who had done so much to help her and with tears in her eyes said,

"I'm afraid I do. You see, if I am to accept your wonderful offer of owning Scalfaro's and maybe starting a new life or trying to run the cafés rather than selling them," she stopped and wiped her eyes aggressively, "then I must conquer my past, cleanse my soul and have closure." Ellen stood and walked around the kitchen, trying to ignore her friends and family, trying to gain the strength needed to speak. Finally, continuing to prowl, she said,

"At that station in Switzerland, my mother and I were raped." There was a gasp from around the table and Carla crossed herself, a mannerism Ellen remembered so well. "My mother by a German officer;" she carried on resolutely, "myself by a young civilian. We were together, side by side in a cattle truck."

"Ellen stop!" Golda moved towards her niece, wanting to hold her but Ellen turned away.

"Please leave me. I must do this." Golda hesitated and returned to her seat.

"I was forced to watch my mother being defiled and she was forced to watch me, her daughter, lose her virginity to a callous, vicious animal."

"My poor child," Carla whispered again crossing herself.

"After being raped," Ellen carried on steadfastly, her narrative quickening as she tried to ignore the reactions, "we were taken back to the carriage where my father, brother and other Jewish families were being held. We continued on our journey as if nothing had happened until the train stopped again. We were then herded out, because that was what we were to the Germans, just animals, Jewish vermin." Ellen's voice was growing animated, becoming ever more hostile as she spoke.

"I saw the train had stopped because the track had been bombed; we could go no further. The guards tied us by one wrist to a parent. I was roped to my father, Noah to Mummy and Leon to Auntie Marguerita. They then marched us in pairs to a bridge over a river and once there we were told to turn and face the water."

"Ellen, no, please," Flavio begged as he wheeled his chair over to her and took both her hands. "Stop, please; you don't have to do this." Tears were cascading down Ellen's cheeks but they were tears of fury not hurt and she pulled her hands away screaming, "I do! God damn you. I do!" And she fell into Flavio's arms saying softly, "Can't you see, it's driving me mad! I have to get the poison out of my head and the evil out of my heart. I have to cleanse my soul."

* * *

Sat around the table, Flavio, Carla and the aunts found it virtually impossible to come to terms with what was unfolding. Ellen quietly retook her seat and apologised.

No one answered, no one knew how to, they just waited for Ellen to take the next tentative step in easing her troubled mind.

"Deep in my head," Ellen said, so quietly it was difficult to hear her words, "there are memories destroying me, images crippling me and dreams sucking the life out of me. I try to hide them and ignore them but…" She then laughed so forlornly that those witnessing the scene were under no illusion that she was failing in her attempt to do so.

"I cannot excuse my behaviour and I understand you do not deserve to suffer the misery of my confusion. It's just I have nowhere else to go and no one else to tell."

The room sat in complete silence; how could any of them know how to deal with such an ingrained, deep-rooted crisis.

"Should I go on? I would like to." Ellen looked around and saw four shaken faces nod. So she did, calmly and with a self-discipline that was quite extraordinary.

"Once my wrist had been tied to my father, he whispered that I should try to loosen the rope. I didn't know why, but as we were being marched to the bridge I heard him tell my mother and aunt the same, so I tried and it saved my life." Ellen shut her eyes.

"I so often wish I hadn't succeeded because then I would still be with my family... Anyway," Ellen took a deep breath preparing for another reaction, "as I watched the fast flowing water below us, my father turned to me and whispered, 'I love you, forgive me'. I wondered what he meant and then I heard a deafening series of gunshots. Before I could grab hold of the small barrier in front of us, my father was falling towards the river dragging me with him." Ellen spoke faster, more animatedly; she was reliving the terror of that moment.

"As I hit the water it was freezing and we went under, my father kept dragging me deeper. I fought against the rope and eventually it slipped off my wrist and I swam to Daddy. All I could see was a bright crimson colour and... I saw the top of his head was missing." Ellen was shaking, completely oblivious of where she was or who was listening.

"His eyes were open... I could do nothing to help... but he knew it was me; somehow he knew it was me and, you know what, he smiled... so gently and lovingly... then he was gone." Ellen brushed away her tears with a rage that alarmed those watching. "I was drowning. I had to get to the surface. I tried to drag my Daddy up with me but it was impossible... so God forgive me, I left him behind. Can you believe that? I left my own Daddy, my beloved father to the river. As I hit the surface and gulped in fresh air, bullets began to hit the water all around me... there were soldiers on the bank shooting at anyone who made it to the surface... I found a dead body floating by and grabbed it for protection from the bullets and let it carry me downstream. And do you know who saved me, whose bullet ridden body I had grabbed and hidden behind? No, of course you don't" Again that haunting laugh as Ellen stopped and looked defiantly at each of them.

"Noah! Yes, that's who! My brother... my wonderful, innocent brother who I loved so much." There was utter disbelief and fury from those listening but Ellen hardly noticed. She then stood and with strained self-control said,

"Will you excuse me, I need some air." And with that she left, walked to the square and sat on one of the empty seats. Night had arrived but Ellen had so much more to tell and she prayed she had the strength and willpower to get it finished.

*   *   *

When she returned to the kitchen, it was as if no one had moved, spoken or even breathed. Ellen smiled and simply said, "The evening is so beautiful."

She retook her seat, asked Flavio for some more wine and Carla for coffee and then for the next hour told the story of her life as a killer.

She described being found on the river bank and being taken to the resistance camp in Switzerland. She added to Flavio that it was at the camp she was told her train was travelling through Switzerland. He, of course, immediately acknowledged he'd been wrong.

She detailed her ever growing hatred for all things German and the way it had led to her learning to fight and ultimately to kill. She then struggled to describe the attack on the camp and the massacre of so many of her friends, but then she came to her relationship with Alfred. Ellen was completely honest in her description of their time together and smiled as she told of his gentleness in the way he understood her problems.

"Alfred was my first true love," she admitted gently, "but as with all the others, he was taken away from me when he was killed by German soldiers." She went on to describe how she had found him, how he had died in her arms and how as she walked away from his resting place, she'd never felt more isolated or lonely.

"That was probably the lowest point of my life; I just wanted to die."

As late as it was, no one moved, no one stirred and no one asked Ellen to stop or suggested a break. They understood she was beyond the point of no return and prayed that all the pain and heartache she was enduring would result in her finding the peace she so desperately craved.

When Ellen described her first 'kill', she didn't try to justify it or to persuade the others that it was necessary or unavoidable. Instead she spoke so candidly and with an honesty that left those listening acutely troubled.

"I longed to kill Germans. I needed retribution for my family, my friends and all the innocents so cruelly butchered. I never for a moment considered the people I killed and never ever thought it was wrong.

After Alfred's death, I travelled and killed Germans. I understood that the more I killed the more likely it was I'd be caught, but I didn't care... I really didn't."

With her eyes closed and head down, Ellen continued, ignoring the disbelief and sorrow that was enveloping the room. She had to finish and put an end to her living hell.

"From our short time together, I fell pregnant with Alfred's child." She kept her eyes closed not wanting to see the reaction of her aunts, because she felt no guilt about her pregnancy.

"Being pregnant was actually one of the few bright spots in my life from those years but it changed everything and altered my entire perspective on what I was doing. However, no matter how hard I tried, I could not break my obsession to kill Germans, even with a baby growing inside me.

Anyway, I had just discovered the railway line I'd been searching for, when I woke one morning and knew something was wrong. I was about four or five months pregnant and I so longed to have Alfred's child, so longed to have my baby but I lost it, and it is only now that I understand I never gave it a chance. With the way I was treating my body; always hungry, always cold, walking miles and miles every day, I never gave the baby a chance." Ellen was again tearful but carried on doggedly.

"In amongst the trees surrounded by newly fallen snow, I miscarried. I had lost my baby but I'd lost so much more…" Ellen stopped as she wiped away her tears.

"Anyway, after burying my son I realised something was seriously wrong. I couldn't stop the bleeding and if anything it became worse. I was in so much pain and felt so utterly distraught by the loss of my baby that I wanted to just lie down next to the grave and go to sleep forever." Ellen appeared to be in a trance and those listening looked at each other with concern.

"But, and I remember this so very clearly even all these years later, just as I was ready to give up extraordinarily vivid images flashed before my eyes. I saw the faces of the rapists and heard their laughter as they defiled us and I screamed at myself to get up. I may have been dying but I would not give in, I would not stop killing Germans."

Ellen stood and began to prowl around, walking and thinking before saying, "Looking back now I realise that I had become everything I hated so much about the Germans. I was killing without so much as a thought and those people I murdered were probably just as innocent as my family." As she sipped her coffee, her hands were shaking.

"So many times in so many places I survived when others didn't. Why? It's a question I keep asking myself and my guilt from living when my family died is intolerable. I feel such… oh, God... I don't know how to describe it, but it's like I feel I've dishonoured all my friends who died when the Germans attacked the camp. Why was I out practising when the attack came? Why was Alfred on his own when he was tortured and killed, why wasn't he with me?

And, do you know, at the end of all my soul searching, I've never found a single answer so I assumed that for some reason God decided I was meant to live. And can you believe this; from that assumption I figured God's sole purpose in keeping me alive was to kill Germans. Now how stupid is that."

Ellen continued pacing the kitchen. The room remained silent. Still no one had a word to say.

"I was absolutely convinced, absolutely certain that I only survived to kill and so that is what I did." She stopped, waited thoughtfully, but immediately continued. "Anyway, I remember bleeding heavily and shouting at myself to move and I then woke up in a warm bed being looked after by the most wonderful couple. I have no idea how I knew where to go or how I got to the farmhouse but it merely confirmed my crazy belief that God wanted me alive; he needed me to do his work." Ellen hesitated knowing the next chapter of her story would cause those around the table even more pain.

"Once I was fit again, I went shopping to the local town with the woman who had cared for me and after we'd had lunch, I left her with friends and went for a walk. I noticed three Germans coming towards me and recognised one of them immediately; it was the German who'd raped my mother. I couldn't believe it was him. So you tell me," Ellen turned to those around the table and challenged them. "Why was I in that place at that time and why was he also there? Was it fate?" Ellen knew there'd be no answer.

"So stupidly I followed them into a tavern." Ellen smiled as she remembered her foolishness. "Somehow, as always, I got away with it and ended up in the officer's room and he died. He had no chance, but I only killed him after he had convinced me he knew nothing of my own attacker. And do you know what, as I watched him die I was ecstatic. The man who had raped my mother whilst making me watch, was dead and believe me, it had not been an easy death. I felt no remorse even though the man had suffered terribly but after what he'd done to Mummy and God knows how many other women, he deserved it. I was judge, jury and executioner and felt a warm, glowing contentment." Ellen avoided eye-contact with her aunts.

"I returned to the farm and the next day heard rumours of the murder of a German officer and a girl who'd been with him. That evening the farmer asked me if I knew anything about the death. I told him quite honestly that it was me and that the officer had raped my mother. I added that I would move on and he laughed and told me he thought I was wonderful. He couldn't get over the fact that with a few friends he had spent the war trying to disrupt the German War Machine and I arrived and managed to kill a German Officer. From that moment onwards, whenever he went out to fight the enemy, I went with him. The Germans were losing the war and retreating which left them vulnerable to surprise attacks. This was the most effective weapon we had as a small group. Every night we went out hunting Germans and killing them. I don't know how many deaths I am responsible for. It was never about numbers; my sole purpose was to kill the enemy and I was very good at it." Ellen looked up at those around the table and smiled sadly.

"My story ends in March 1945 when American troops entered Austria, quickly followed by Soviet troops. The family I was with was adamant I should not be found by the Red Army so the farmer and his wife drove me to the Americans to keep me safe."

Flavio looked at the clock; it was one-forty three and all were emotionally shattered. As he was about to speak, he realised Ellen was fast asleep, utterly exhausted and Golda and Barbara slowly lifted her out of her seat and carried her up to bed.

—Ж—

PART IV

CLOSURE

Chapter 1

1957

As Ellen travelled by train on her way to the Rath Museum in Geneva, she looked out of the window at the stunning scenery and was reminded of that fateful journey with her family. She could visualise the crack she had discovered in the wall of the cattle truck and the spectacular peaks of the Alps as they passed by; such a contrast to the dark of the carriage and bleak mood of those sat around her.

Ellen was at last happy in her life; she had turned thirty the previous year and had learnt to accept that on occasion, especially when she travelled by train, disturbing images of her past would try to overwhelm her. As always, she steered her mind away from the shadows that lurked in the depths of her mind and instead recalled the night at Flavio's with Carla and the aunts and how, even though she must have caused them so much heartache, it had quite literally been the dawn of her new life.

She remembered her mixture of sadness and excitement when, three days later, her Aunts had returned home. Ellen felt she was at last becoming truly independent. Flavio and Carla as usual were just wonderful; encouraging her to remain with them and then within weeks converting the top two floors of the house into an apartment for her. Ellen could come and go as she pleased but always knew that if she felt like company, they were always there for her.

Ellen also followed Flavio's advice about Scalfaro's. She didn't sell but focused her efforts on the two cafés and it quickly became apparent that she possessed perceptiveness for business rarely found in post war Italian women. Ellen had that rare combination of a hardnosed exterior together with a caring nature and all who worked with her completely trusted her. The result was the two cafés became extremely popular and turnover and profits increased significantly.

By the start of the nineteen fifties, the land value of Hayastan had grown appreciably just as Flavio had predicted and with his approval, Ellen decided to sell. The final bid at the auction stunned those in attendance and Ellen became extremely wealthy overnight. Even after paying back her college fees to her family, she was able to reduce her commitment to the cafés and concentrate on other interests. Firstly she began supporting organisations that protected children, especially those orphaned, handicapped or victims of conflict and secondly, she began to rekindle her love of history. She visited museums and art galleries and her childhood dream of visiting Rome and Venice became a reality. Journeys further afield followed and on her return from a two week visit to Athens, she was asked to write an article by her local paper. Her submission was published and interest from a national newspaper followed. Ellen's career as a travel writer had taken off. The combination of travelling and writing was perfect and she appointed managers to run the cafés whilst she travelled Europe.

As the train entered Geneva, Ellen was looking forward to visiting the city's oldest museum, The Rath. She'd been invited to the opening of a new exhibition and had been asked to write a review of the event. Never in her wildest dreams could she have envisaged the terrifying consequences of accepting that invitation.

—Ж—

Chapter 2

Ellen watched impassively as the attractive, immaculately dressed gentleman stepped out of the chauffeur driven Silver Cloud, briefcase in hand and entered the impressive house.

Darkness was falling and as the temperature plummeted she wrapped herself in her newly purchased winter coat and glanced dispassionately at lights going on and off and shadows moving behind expensive curtains.

She had not for a single moment entertained the thought of abandoning her vigil. She accepted that a few hours of discomfort was the price she was happy to pay for the reward that would be waiting in the morning and she caressed the silent killer lying in her arms. Making herself as comfortable as the frozen ground would permit, Ellen leant back against the trunk of a large fir tree and hoped sleep would come.

* * *

She woke with a start and looked at her watch; five-fifty; there was still a long wait ahead. She stood up and stretched her arms and then moved about trying to get her blood circulating and some warmth into her body. She was incredibly stiff and accepted it was hardly surprising considering the temperature and the fact it had been years since she'd slept outside.

She took a drink of water and settled herself back down. This was not a man who would rise early and he would only go to work when he was ready.

As she rested her head back against the tree and closed her eyes, Ellen's thoughts returned to the moment she'd first seen him; she had thought he was lost to her forever. She then smiled as she remembered her immediate disbelief. Part of her wanted to ignore his face and disregard the similarity. She tried to shut away the obvious but she couldn't.

As she considered the chances of their meeting, Ellen laughed at yet another of those coincidences and her discarded belief that it was obviously God's will. She was in Geneva by invitation, the Rath having invited her to the opening of their new exhibition and 'He' was there, the guest speaker, the guest of honour. How incredible was that!

*   *   *

He was introduced as the ex-Minister of Finance and as he stood to speak, Ellen saw those eyes. They were piercing, penetrating, the purist blue eyes she had ever seen and her body began to tremble. As she heard him speak he looked up, scanned the room and focused on her; those eyes were on her. He smiled imperceptibly at her and Ellen felt sick. She told herself it could not be him but again he looked up from his notes and again his eyes fell on her and she knew; Ellen was as certain as she'd been about anything in her life.

As his speech came to a close and the opening ceremony began, Ellen excused herself and made her way to the bar. Desperate to sit down and gather herself to get a grip on her exploding emotions, she readily accepted a glass of champagne from a waiter and much to his astonishment, drank the ice cold liquid straight down.

A few minutes later, as she was slowly sipping a second glass, people began to drift in from the ceremony and she watched as the men headed for the bar and the women waited by the door. When the man with the blue eyes entered, he was immediately surrounded by women which to Ellen bordered on the surreal. The animal who had raped her with such callous ease appeared to be much-loved.

Ellen stood and feeling calmer, she moved towards a group of national art specialists she knew and joined in the discussion on the merits of the new exhibition. As they talked she scanned the room. It was not that she wanted to meet him; on the contrary, she was troubled as to how she would react if she did. She just wanted to know where he was.

The lady standing next to Ellen noticed her looking around and said,

"Gorgeous isn't he!" Ellen immediately blushed but said nothing.

"Don't be embarrassed; we all think the same." The woman laughed and then without warning she took her by the arm and dragged her across the room. Ellen was mortified.

"Johan!" she called out and the man with the bluest of eyes turned, looked at Ellen and with an engaging smile took her hand and kissed it. He was introduced as Johan Schanner.

"How truly delightful," he said oozing charm. "I gather we are all under your critical eye tonight." Three women stood around him laughing but Ellen just smiled and decided he really was the consummate charmer and, although she struggled to admit it, extremely attractive with it. Ignoring all other admirers, Johan Schanner then took Ellen's arm and moved her towards the bar.

"Champagne?" he asked.

"Thank you," Ellen answered intrigued. How on earth was it possible that the brute who had so viciously robbed her of her innocence was so... endearing? The contradiction was bizarre.

As she stood sipping her drink, a number of people approached and spoke to ex-Minister Schanner. He was always gracious, attentive and humorous in equal measure and without warning, the most disconcerting thought struck Ellen; could she have made a mistake? The more she watched him and the longer she listened to his words, the more preposterous the notion became. The man next to her was genuine, and understanding. He was everything the man who had raped her was not. The two could not be the same person.

As her confusion grew, so did Ellen's ability to rationalise what was happening and as the guests began to leave, the wife of the art critic who had originally dragged Ellen to meet Johan Schanner, asked whether she would like to join them for supper. Before she could reply, she was being led out.

The party was shown to a side room in a restaurant next to the museum where wine, coffee and hot snacks were being served.

Ellen stayed deliberately close to Johan. She had to find out one way or the other whether it really was him. If she had got it wrong the consequences would be unimaginable.

As the evening wore on, Ellen sensed Johan was becoming quite flirtatious with her; a situation she was happy to go along with.

She listened to and joined in with much of the conversation and was teased mercilessly about the article she would write on the exhibition, the museum and of course, the guest speaker. It was all in good humour and Ellen actually enjoyed the company.

There was, however, a moment as she was listening to a conversation on Swiss politics that her thoughts drifted and she was suddenly confronted with the vivid image of the naked German officer dying before her eyes. She saw the depths of her depravity in killing him and in celebrating his agonising and brutal death. As disturbing as the images were she couldn't help but wonder if she would feel the same as she watched the charming man stood next to her die in the most brutal of circumstances.

Just after midnight the majority of the guests had departed and Ellen remained behind with what seemed like an intimate group of twelve friends. As they all found chairs around a large oval table and waited for more drinks to arrive, Johan asked her to sit next to him and she sensed that the evening had only just begun.

The drinks flowed but Ellen made sure she remained clear-headed; she was determined to establish whether Johan Schanner was who she thought he was even if it meant spending the whole night with him. Almost immediately they were seated, one of the men suggested that as only friends remained they should remove their jackets and ties and all agreed. It was at that moment, that exact moment that Ellen had her answer. As Johan Schanner removed his jacket and tie and pulled open the neck of his shirt, Ellen stared mesmerized at the birthmark on his neck; those distinctive colours that could never be removed.

Breathing deeply and feeling weak at the knee, Ellen excused herself and walked hesitantly to the restroom; she had finally found her nemesis.

Slipping away from the restaurant without anyone noticing, she spent that night in her hotel room planning her next move. Early the following morning she drove a hire car across the border into Austria and returned to the home of Jurgen and Annemarie, spending a wonderful evening and night with them. When she left the next day, it was with her crossbow, the weapon that had been so important to her. Ellen was ready to kill once again.

*   *   *

Seven forty-three and Ellen heard a car moving towards the house. She calmly checked the bow, the sights and the bolt knowing it would take only one shot. She wanted Johan Schanner to suffer, to know he was slowly bleeding to death and there was nothing anyone could do about it. She decided on the neck; a target she had used so often in the past and there was no doubt in her mind that it would be the most horrific, slow and unbearable way to die.

Ellen watched a car approach and the front door opened. She could hear talking and laughing from inside the house and raised the bow, fixing the sights on the door. She was completely calm and focused, ready to execute and it was that calm which convinced Ellen she still had the skills that were needed. She smiled as there was no question of her failing.

In her peripheral vision, Ellen saw the chauffeur driven car stop under the front porch. The pillars reminded her of a Roman temple; they were such an extravagance but she grinned dismissively and whispered coldly, "You can't take it with you."

The crossbow sights remained fixed on the door waiting for her target to emerge and finally she saw movement. There he was, smiling and happy and unaware of his imminent death.

Ellen moved the sights to his face. 'God those eyes, those beautiful eyes,' and she lowered the bow to his neck. It was time.

Tightening her grip on the trigger, she hesitated as a child's voice came from inside the house and she watched as Johan Schanner turned. A young girl ran out laughing and pushed her arms up demanding to be held. Ellen slowly lowered the bow and released the pressure on the trigger as Johan placed his briefcase on the ground and lifted his daughter. She giggled and put her arms around his neck and kissed him.

Ellen watched stunned as father lifted daughter into the air. He started to tickle her and she squealed excitedly. She smiled sadly as the laughter turned to hugs and the small girl said goodbye to an adored father. Ellen remembered so profoundly her own father and the overwhelming love she'd had for him and she continued to stare, captivated, feeling the intense love between father and daughter.

A woman then emerged from the house. She was beautiful and elegant and she moved to Johan, who was still hugging his daughter, and kissed him. It was the most perfect of scenes and Ellen's tears flowed. This was how she remembered her family, the wonder of being loved and cherished. It was everything she'd ever wanted and so desperately missed.

As she watched such incredible affection, Ellen was bewildered.

"Where's the evil monster from my nightmares, the animal who destroyed everything I ever had?"

She lowered the bow and removed the bolt. She could not kill him. As much as she detested, reviled and hated the man who stood before her, she could not inflict the same unbearable heartache on the little girl hugging her father.

—Ж—

Chapter 3

Ellen returned to Turin the following morning determined to forget what had happened, but Flavio and Carla immediately sensed something was wrong.

After a few days of watching a moody and unhappy Ellen, Carla was so worried she told Flavio to talk to her. They invited her to supper that night and after they'd finished eating and were drinking coffee, Ellen was not overly surprised when the question came. She loved Flavio and knew he was one of the most perceptive men she had ever met. She also knew she was struggling to hide her feelings and realised she needed to talk through what had happened. Her difficulty was however, that she didn't want to open up simply to be congratulated. She needed to know whether leaving Johan Schanner alive would finally draw a line under her past, whether she could look forward with confidence, or whether there would always be that part of her which would never be content.

Ellen realised Flavio and Carla were concerned and decided to tell them everything. She futilely tried to explain the explosion of emotions at finding her rapist after so long and described her need to inflict intolerable pain before finally killing him. She told them about returning to Austria to pick up the crossbow; how she had found his home and then that final moment when she had him in her sights and the child had appeared. Ellen tried and failed yet again to explain that as she had watched his family, all together, her absolute confusion led her to simply walk away.

Carla and Flavio sat quite still, both knowing that if a solution could not be found, Ellen would be haunted by her past for the rest of her life. Wherever she went, whatever and whoever she met, there would always be some reminder. Because of her, the rapist still lived and although she could still kill him if she chose to, that was no longer an option.

"You did the right thing," Flavio said. "I admire you so much for walking away."

"But that's not what I want. It's not what I need," Ellen replied emotionally. "I'm sorry but whether it was right or wrong is unimportant. I need to know whether leaving him alive has atoned for the wrongs I've committed. Will it release me from my past?"

"Ellen dear," Carla answered gently, "You've always done what you thought was right; you made decisions and lived with the consequences. Why is it so different now?"

"Do you know why? I cannot get the thought out of my head that by allowing someone so evil and immoral to live that I have risked the future of other innocent, young girls. I feel I have let people down by not removing him from this world."

"You once said war makes people change," Flavio said. "It makes them commit evil acts which under normal circumstances they would never have contemplated. I agree; war brings out the worst in people and yes, sadly, it is the innocent who are so often the victims. Ellen, I would never try to condone what happened to you or your family, but it is possible the man who raped you has changed."

"Okay, I accept the majority of people are not evil," Ellen answered harshly, "but to suggest a man like Johan Schanner..." Ellen stopped; she had not meant to reveal his name.

"You mean… Johan Schanner, the Swiss minister?" When Ellen slowly nodded, Flavio said,

"Come on Ellen, are you sure. I mean absolutely certain?" Again Ellen nodded and Flavio sat in deep thought.

"That's crazy; a man like that with his international reputation and influence, how could it be that such a man was your rapist?" Eventually Ellen answered,

"I have no idea but I can assure you it is him and I chose to let him live."

Chapter 4

Ellen tried everything to return to the relatively contented life she had had before Geneva. She had talked things through with Flavio and Carla and readily acknowledged it was her decision not to kill Johan Schanner and she had to accept the consequences of that decision. It was never going be as straightforward. No matter how hard she tried, Ellen couldn't move on. His piercing blue eyes constantly preyed on her mind and those moments of pure happiness she had witnessed at his house, were incessant images. Every night he was in her dreams.

Ellen was at a complete loss and couldn't break the vicious circle of thoughts and emotions. Ultimately she could never forgive herself for leaving Geneva. She tried to justify the fact that Johan Schanner was still alive. Had it been the right thing to do? She accepted not killing him in front of his daughter but she should have returned to the city and waited for a more opportune moment.

And Ellen being Ellen, she wouldn't let it go. It gnawed at her, drained her feelings and it was only a matter of time before she returned to Geneva to finish the job.

She knew she had to solve her problem and eventually made the decision to return to Switzerland towards the end of February. She would not hurry. She would wait until the perfect moment to kill Johan Schanner. She had also decided not to tell Flavio.

*   *   *

Three days before she was due to leave, Ellen was sitting in the kitchen with Carla having breakfast when Flavio called them to his study. He was sat at his desk holding a copy of the newspaper with an incredulous look on his face.

"Come quickly and look at this," he said.

"What is it?" Carla asked with concern.

"It's beyond belief?" Flavio pointed to an article on the third page.

Although it was written in French, because her Italian was near perfect, Ellen understood most of the article.

'Ex-Minister feared dead!'

'Confirmation has reached us from local police that Johan Schanner, ex-minister of finance has disappeared whilst skiing.

Ellen quickly read on. The article said that Johan Schanner, an experienced skier, was on a weekend trip to his family chalet with a group of friends, when the party was caught in a whiteout. All other members of the group returned to the chalet safely but there was no sign of the ex-minister.

Ellen quickly turned to the front of the newspaper; it was a copy of Le Journal De Genève dated six days previously. Flavio, seeing Ellen's surprise at the Swiss newspaper, explained,

"One of the lawyers in the office receives the paper every month for financial news. I was in his office when I saw the headline."

Ellen turned back to the article and read out loudly,

'Once the weather eased, search parties failed to find any sign of Mr Schanner."

Looking at Carla and Flavio in turn, Ellen said quietly, "It cannot be true." She closed the paper and looked at Flavio feeling utter disbelief.

“Do you want me to make a few calls?” He asked, and when Ellen nodded, he left her with Carla. Nothing was said until Flavio returned ten minutes later.

“It’s now twelve days since he disappeared and officially, as of today, he is missing presumed dead.”

—Ж—

Chapter 5

1961

Flavio's health had been deteriorating for well over six months, when he died in 1961 at the age of eighty-three. Ellen was heartbroken but Carla, in her usual stoic manner, told everyone that Flavio had on many occasions expressed how fortunate he'd been in his life, so asked that his death not be mourned but his life celebrated.

Although the end was inevitable, Ellen was still inconsolable. Flavio and Carla were her family and although she was grateful to her Aunts, Barbara and Golda, for being there when she so desperately needed them, it was Flavio and Carla who had given her back her life. They were always there making sure she wanted for nothing, especially love.

Flavio's funeral was held in the church across the square from the house and the size of the congregation was a tribute to a much loved and greatly respected friend. It was only later that night when Carla and Ellen held each other and cried together that Carla eventually gave in to her grief; they were the first tears she'd shed and they would be the last.

* * *

Two weeks later, Carla learnt that she was the only benefactor in Flavio's will. Although she had expected to be cared for, there was so much more and this reflected Flavio's love for her.

One month after the funeral, as Carla and Ellen were sitting in the kitchen with a glass of wine, Carla said,

"You do know how much Flavio loved you, don't you?" Ellen was surprised.

"Of course, as I adored him."

"You were the daughter he never had. Actually, you were the daughter I never had." She reached across the table and took Ellen's hand.

"Well, Flavio had a secret; one that he didn't even tell me about and it concerned you." Ellen was mystified as Carla went to Flavio's study and returned with an envelope.

"He told me, and I must say, reminded me on many occasions," and she smiled as she obviously remembered Flavio's insistence, "that four weeks after his death, I should give you this." She passed the envelope across the table. "Four weeks he said. He was adamant and I could never persuade him to tell me why."

Ellen took the envelope and carefully opened it. Inside there was a letter in Flavio's distinctive handwriting.

"Come join me," Ellen said and together they read.

'My dearest Ellen,

Both women smiled and both had tears in their eyes as they read on.

'I got the idea of writing this letter from the one Emil left for Marguerita. Unfortunately, in my case it was more through cowardice than anything else.

Ellen, I was heartbroken to see how unhappy you were after your visit to Geneva all those years ago. The decision to let Johan Schanner live was one of the bravest and most courageous I have known. Under those circumstances, I would not have been so charitable and I was immensely proud of you.

However, none of us could have predicted the difficulties it created for you and I guessed that one day you would return to Geneva to put an end to things. Not the date or the time, but I knew. How could I not when I witnessed the conflict going on inside your head. Day after day, you were battling your demons and we couldn't do anything to help.'

Carla moved towards Ellen and gave her a hug.

'I then did something which I am not proud of and ask your forgiveness. You see, I told your travel agent, who is a friend of mine, to let me know if you booked any trips and he told me you were travelling back to Geneva which I knew meant you were going to kill Johan Schanner.'

Ellen took Carla's hand; she was obviously shocked by Flavio's words.

'Knowing this, I had to act quickly and I am fortunate to have some very loyal and trustworthy friends. Two of those friends travelled to Geneva and were responsible for Johan Schanner's disappearance.

He died knowing why he had to die and I can assure you it was a painful end. His death was, to say the least, extremely slow. They placed the body where it would be immediately covered by the heavy snow and it will probably remain lost for many years.

My Dear Ellen, I want no thanks for what I did. Do any of us have the right to take a life? I really don't know but I can assure you he was every bit as evil as you said and he absolutely deserved to die.

So why am I telling you this?

With this letter I pray your journey to Hell and back can finally be over. You see, even after the confirmation of Schanner's death, you were still not the same beautiful young woman, not the same wonderful girl Carla and myself loved so dearly. You never regained your pleasure for life. It was as if allowing Schanner to live meant you had to give up your right to happiness and that I couldn't accept.

I remember after his death was reported, you said part of you was angry because if God had decided Johan Schanner should die, it should have been by your hand and your hand only. I remember those words so well.

You may not have pulled the trigger but believe me you played the most significant role, and therefore have part ownership of the killing. Between us we carried out the vow you made to your parents, Noah and all the others. In the end, justice was done and you had your revenge.

My dear, so often I wanted to tell you and my beloved Carla but of course it was impossible. Those who brought an end to Johan Schanner on our behalf are still alive and only with my death will their names be completely protected.

Ellen, now is the time to forget the horrors of your past and remember those special moments, those unforgettable times that brought you such joy, and please, please live the rest of your life to the full. With my passing and this confession, you are free of guilt. You are forever forgiven.

Now promise me my dearest young lady, you will be at ease with yourself and the world for the rest of your days.

My everlasting love.

Flavio.'

THE END

Author's Note

Swiss government claims of neutrality during the 2nd World War have proved a contentious subject, more so since information has emerged of Nazi trains carrying human cargo through Switzerland, linking Italy with the concentration camps in Poland and the north.

For those sufficiently interested, reading the transcript of the BBC/FRONTLINE interview by David Marks with 'Elizabeth' will prove not only moving but also extremely disturbing. Readers can draw their own conclusions as to her claim that she accompanied her mother to Zurich station in 1943 to give soup and bread to families tightly packed in cattle trucks. It is significant that 'Elizabeth' is not her real name as she wished to remain anonymous for fear of reprisals against her.

To quote from the BBC/Frontline report:

'After months of investigation we found three witnesses who told approximately the same story. They were extremely nervous; one aggressively terminated all contact with us on the grounds we were reviving the ghosts of a dark and shameful era. But the essence of all three stories - plus our interview with 'Elizabeth' - was the same, long trains with sealed cattle wagons rolling into Zurich Hauptbahnhof in the middle of the night, carrying Italian Jews and other prisoners north.

We were not able to locate anyone who may have been on forced transports through Switzerland during the war. There is additional investigative work that can be done with the co-operation of the Swiss, German and Italian governments. But this investigation raises new disturbing questions about Swiss neutrality. And, along with other elements of our documentary "Nazi Gold," the accounts of these transports may dramatically change the previously accepted history of wartime Switzerland.'

The Hamidian Massacres of Armenians during the latter part of the 19th Century are well documented as is the systematic murder of Armenians by the Young Turks Government during the early part of the 20th Century. Millions were slaughtered in premeditated acts of brutality designed to eradicate all Armenian nationals (as well as their homeland) and although the evidence of genocide committed against Armenians is irrefutable, accusations of these atrocities continue to be denied and/or excused by the relevant authorities and governments.
APC

Acknowledgements

As with my first novel, No Turning Back, self-publishing The Betrayal of Innocence has only been possible with the support and hard work of many friends and I would like pay tribute to them all. However, a special mention must go to Daniel Cook and Sam Rennie of New Generation Publishing, Alan Smith and Ben Roach from Kolor Schemes, Janet Watt, Ellis Davis, Marion Woodward, Anne Poole and as always, my wife Gail.